# BROKEN PROMISES

DIANA MUÑOZ STEWART

*Broken Promises*, copyright 2021, Diana Muñoz Stewart
Published by Diana Muñoz Stewart
Cover by Kris Keller
Layout: www.formatting4U.com

All rights reserved. Thank you for respecting the hard work of this author. No part of this book may be reproduced in any form or by any electronic or mechanical means, including information storage and retrieval systems—except in the case of brief quotations embodied in critical articles or reviews—without permission in writing from the author. This book is a work of fiction. The characters, events, and places portrayed in this book are products of the author's imagination and are either fictitious or are used fictitiously. Any similarity to real persons, living or dead, is purely coincidental and not intended by the author.

For my dad, who passed while I wrote this.
And for all the wonderful men in my life.
You've proved good men aren't hard to find.

## THE AUTHOR: DIANA MUÑOZ STEWART

Diana Muñoz Stewart is an award-winning author who writes diverse characters with a focus on justice, family, and love. Her stories reflect the optimism of a growing and inclusive society. As *Booklist* noted about her unflinching look at today's relevant issues in her Black Ops Confidential series, the author "gives these topics hope."

Diana Muñoz Stewart's work has been a BookPage Top 15 Romance of 2018, a Night Owl Top Pick, an Amazon Book of the Month, an Amazon Editor's pick, a Pages From The Heart Winner, a BookPage Top Pick, Golden Heart® Finalist, Daphne du Maurier Finalist, A Gateway to the Best Winner, and has reached #1 category bestseller on Amazon multiple times.

Diana lives in an often chaotic and always welcoming home that—depending on the day—can hold her husband, kids, extended family, friends, and a canine or two. A believer in the power of words to heal and connect, Diana has written multiple spotlight pieces on the strong, diverse women changing the world. Find out more about the causes Diana supports at her website, https://DianaMunozStewart.com/activists/

## Praise for Diana Muñoz Stewart

"Muñoz Stewart skillfully questions the difference between loyalty and subservience, enculturation and indoctrination as she weaves a tender romance around a thrill ride of a plot that will keep readers guessing until the final pages."
—***Kirkus Reviews***

"Sizzling with sensuality."
—***Washington Independent Review of Books***

"*The Price of Grace* is Diana Muñoz Stewart at her best."
—***Fresh Fiction***

"[Diana Muñoz Stewart's] talent shines in this suspenseful story."
—***Publishers Weekly***

"Thrilling, sizzling, and full of adventure."
—***American Library Association-Booklist***

"Tantalizing intrigue, effective red herrings, and red-hot romance combine into a powerful tale. Readers will be sad to see this heart-pounding series end."
—***Publishers Weekly***

"Hang on tight! This story features passion, betrayal, redemption and plenty of kick-butt action, so enjoy!"
—***RT Book Reviews***

"Muñoz Stewart gives us a high-octane adventure with her new series."
—***Booklist***

"Stewart's badass Band of Sisters romantic suspense series adds a high-octane installment with this satisfying roller-coaster ride."
—***Publishers Weekly***

"Layered personalities, shifting motivations, and a smart, twisty plot push this thrilling romantic suspense series into high gear."
—***Kirkus Reviews***

"Fast-paced and edgy, high-octane and sexy, *I Am Justice* is a must-read!"
—**Julie Ann Walker**
***New York Times* and *USA Today* bestselling author of the Black Knights Inc. series**

# CHAPTER ONE

Pedal to the floor, heart in her throat, Felicity Shields raced along a dry desert road lined with sharp shrubs and twisted trees. Red dust ballooned over the hood of her VW Golf.

Her eyes focused on a distant, lavish, two-story adobe house. Backdropped by New Mexico's Sangre de Cristos mountains, the McMansion appeared inconsequential, isolated, and abandoned. Its colorful inlaid tiles shimmered through the hazy air. Fee gripped the steering wheel. *Why wasn't Mom answering?*

A series of chimes blared through her car speakers. Startled, she glanced at the touchscreen, and accepted the call. "Hey, Mae."

"Oh, good. I caught you. Tell your mom I'll be watching her speech online from my bed. This pregnancy is a killer. When do you take off?"

She wiped sweat from her forehead. "We missed our flight."

There was an ominous pause on Mae's end. "What happened?"

*What happened?* Fee swallowed. "Mom was supposed to pick me up. She never showed. I called; she didn't answer. I'm on my way to her place now."

Another pause, this one punctuated by heavy

breaths that reflected Fee's own budding panic. "Your mom always answers when you—" The connection cut out and back again. "She once picked up your call during a CNN interview."

True. So many people thought that call had been staged to show Mom as likeable and motherly during her trial. The truth was, she'd called Mom in a blind panic after having destroyed things with the love of her life, Brooks. In her desperation, she'd forgotten Mom had had the interview. "Look—"

"You're cutting out."

Of course she was; the service out here sucked. "I'm almost there."

"Maybe you should call Liam? He does work for the Santa Fe PD."

Ugh. She'd intended to tell Mae all about Detective McCheater at the conference, but with Mae on bed rest, she wouldn't make the conference. A turn of the wheel and she bumped onto the brick-lined driveway. "I'm here. I'll call you back in ten minutes."

"I'll—" Static. "—five minutes—." Silence. "I call the police."

She wanted to tell Mae not to worry, but, first, she'd have to convince herself. Mom was in great shape but older now. What if she'd fallen? Should she have called an ambulance? "Give me at least ten minutes"

Mae didn't answer.

Fee fished her cell from the cup holder and glanced at the screen. Lost connection. Great.

She hit the garage remote. Bay one didn't open. She hit the other two buttons.

Nothing.

Relief loosened her tense shoulders. This was

why Mom wasn't answering. Something had happened to the power and, without the cell extender, Mom couldn't make or receive calls. And, of course, the generator hadn't kicked on.

She'd told Mom she needed propane. For such a brilliant woman, Dorothy "Never Surrender" Shields was often absent-minded. Time to pressure Mom to get over Claire retiring and pick a new personal assistant.

Slipping her phone into her yoga pants pocket, she flung open the car door and climbed out. A hundred-degree dry wind gusted her hair into her face. The direction changed when she turned to the house and her blonde hair flared behind her.

She jogged up the slate stairs. Her flip-flops swept against the slabs. The backs thwacked against her heels, the loudest sound out here.

Crossing the portcullis, she inserted her key into the lock. Huh. One of Mom's planters was upended.

Squatting down, she righted the cracked pot then cupped the dirt and deposited it back inside.

Dusting the soil from her hands, she stood, turned the key, then pushed the bronzed handle.

It didn't budge.

Had she'd locked it?

Fear hijacked her nervous system, spiking her blood pressure, sending cortisol and adrenalin to work.

*Stop*. She breathed deeply. No reason to be afraid. This was so like Mom. The woman had once been protected by Secret Service, but, now, she couldn't be bothered to lock her front door.

Annoyed, Fee unlocked the door and readied herself to give Mom a piece of her mind. Then they'd eat breakfast because she was starving. She'd arrange new flights later. Thankfully, they had some time. Mom wasn't speaking until tomorrow morning, but she'd miss today's afternoon meetings. Maybe she could livestream in.

Backhanding the front door closed, she tossed her keys into the metal bowl atop the foyer table. The *swish* and *clink* echoed down the stairwell, nearly drowning out a muffled grunt from downstairs.

Mom often did morning yoga on the lower deck. Fee let her fingers brush the smooth iron railing as she headed down to the terrace level that Mom refused to call a basement, because she'd spent so much money on the gorgeous space. "Mom? It's—" she worked moisture into a dry throat "—Fee."

Blinking at the change of light, she shivered in the cooler air. She hit the light switch. No lights. *Duh.* No lights without electricity.

Flicking her sunglasses up, she let her eyes adjust. It was dim, though long glass panels opened to a stunning mountain view. Outside those panels, chaise lounges sat on a large deck with a gas fire pit and an infinity pool.

She sniffed at a heavy, metallic smell. Her stomach rolled as her vision adjusted. Muted mustard walls, colorful patterned chairs, tan leather couches... and Mom.

Sitting on one of the couches, Mom had on a red mud mask. Unbelievable. "A facial, really? Today's Friday. We've missed our flight."

She crossed the room. Mom groaned. The facial dripped into her eyes.

Not a facial.

"Mom!" Fee slid to her knees, her hands skirting over her mom's wrists. Wires? Blood. So much blood. What was happening? What had happened? Had to stop the bleeding.

Her mother made a sound—a protest or maybe a plea. Dark red blood gushed down her chin.

*An ambulance! Call an ambulance!*

*Please let her phone work.* She reached for her cell. Mom's eyes rolled up.

"Hold on, Mom." Please, hold on. "I'm calling for help."

Shaking, she dialed 911.

"Ffff," Blood shot from her mom's mouth, landing across Fee's lips.

A swish of sound from behind. A shadow arm.

Terror seized her. Twisting away, she smashed the call button. A whistle of sound and a sharp crack of pain snapped against her head, dragging away consciousness.

## CHAPTER TWO

Fifty feet up a sheer rock face, Brooks Delgado dipped his fingers into the brown chalk pouch that appeared green through his night vision goggles. A flash of light. He cringed. *Coño*. He'd told all his trainees to turn off their phones and smartwatches, but he never did.

Turning off all messages, alerts, and using silence was usually good enough. In fact, the only messages he allowed were related to...

Fee.

His heart jumped into his throat and he tapped his smartwatch. The words that appeared sent a chill through him. *Dorothy Shields found murdered in her Santa Fe home.*

His stomach dropped. Pulse pounding, he dusted off his fingers, clicked, and read. "Former Vice-President Dorothy "Never Surrender" Shields was found brutally murdered in her Santa Fe home Friday afternoon. Reports indicate she was discovered by her daughter, Felicity Shields, who was injured by—

"Brooks?" Carey called up from below the trainees. "You okay?"

"Gotta—" He choked on the pain. "—make a call."

"Now?"

There was grumbling along the line as private security trainees held tight to their positions. They'd survive. They were seasoned climbers, most former soldiers. Even though the skills they learned tonight were new and difficult, they could hold their ground for a couple seconds.

Re-securing his own feet, he hit the speakerphone on his watch and made the call. It rang. *Pick up, Felicity. Please pick up.*

A sharp squeal and announcement broke across the line. He flinched. He'd been in enough hospitals to know the paging of a doctor. Wind whipped his back. He leaned closer to the watch. "Fee, it's Brooks. Are you there?"

There was a long pause filled with deep breathing. Unease double-timed against his ribs.

"Someone... killed Mom."

Grief pummeled his body. Muscles clenched. Fingers dug into stone. "I'm so sorry." She sounded... "You're hurt?"

"I'm fine. Mom... so much blood... I couldn't save her."

"Jesus," one of the men below him said.

"I'm coming, querida." Could he still call her that? She was still dear to him. "I'm there. As soon as I can get to my plane."

Silence fell. He waited for her to tell him not to bother. Waited for her to tell him that he'd deserted her eight years ago and there was no place for him now, but she whispered, "Promise?"

He squeezed his eyes shut tight, hearing the echo of meaning, the undercurrent of emotion in *that* word all the way to his bones. How many times had they used *promise* to reaffirm their love? In how many different ways over the two years they'd been together? A thousand. A promise that had been brutally, irrevocably broken eight years ago when she'd decided to postpone their wedding. And he, hurt and angry, had left.

He swallowed and told her—as he'd done back when it had been their love against the world—"Promise forever."

#

"This is some crazy." The Lyft driver double parked on a side street near Felicity's house.

Brooks grunted his agreement. The block was lined with news vans as large as tactical response vehicles topped by glaring satellite dishes. He knew the media circus would be bad, but he'd had no idea just what would happen when one of the most infamous women in the world—a former vice president who'd narrowly avoided jail—was murdered in a brutal, sick, and dramatic way.

Helicopters? Four circled Felicity's neighborhood. A police cruiser sat by a blockade at the top of her street. The cop okayed cars trying to get home, denied reporters and their cameras.

Grabbing his duffel from the floor, he climbed out. He slipped between two towering news vans to the sidewalk, bypassing reporters, cables, and mysterious black trunks. A reporter blandly narrating details of Dorothy's murder into a camera made his muscles tighten. Damn, he'd forgotten the callousness inside the media cage match.

Rolling his shoulders, he let the tension slide off. He wasn't going to go back to being the angry, confrontational guy he'd been. That was the *last* person Fee needed. When they'd been engaged, he hadn't understood that his agitation fed her anxiety.

A flash of unwelcome memory shot down his spine: Felicity's lowered head. A tear falling, puddling onto her hand.

*"My mom is fighting to stay out of jail."* She'd looked up, begged him to understand. *"Hate is hate. Whether it's ours at them or theirs toward us… I don't want a wedding surrounded by hate. Let the fire burn down, okay?"*

It hadn't been okay with him. He'd told her, "You cancel this wedding, you cancel us."

He hadn't looked back—well… he had. But, by then, it'd been too late. Lesson learned.

Losing the love of your life had a tendency to teach you shit.

He walked up to the barrier blocking off Felicity's street. The officer, a big guy with a beat-up nose and teeth too straight to be real, put up a hand. "Do you live on this street?"

"Brooks Delgado. I'm Felicity's..." *Díos*, he'd almost said *fiancé*. But, last he'd checked, that role was being filled by Liam Forster. "Friend. She's expecting me."

Cop didn't look convinced. "Show me your ID."

He flashed his credentials.

The officer looked at it. "You don't look Canadian."

"Yeah. I left my hockey stick at home."

The cop glowered suspiciously.

Should he tell him he was a dual citizen or pull his American passport from his pocket?

Nah.

The cop reached for his two-way, his eyes sliding over Brooks' wrinkled *Delgado's Land, Sea, and Air* T-shirt, his utility cargo pants, and worn boots. He pointed at Brooks' shirt. "What's that all about?"

"Survivalist training. Northern Vancouver Island."

"Survival?"

*Play nice, Delgado.* This idiot was his gateway to Fee. "Navigation, tactical climbing, evasive maneuvers, survival at sea, living off the land, tracking, shelter, keeping safe from predators. Two- and four-footed."

The cop's eyes widened. "Can anybody get in on that?"

"We train private security forces."

"Hired guns." The cop grunted and spoke into his two-way. "Brooks Delgado's here. Says he's a friend."

Brooks didn't point out that, without private security, this guy's job would be a lot harder. A few photographers snapped Brooks' photo. Must've heard the cop.

Brooks lowered his ball cap. He was going to be on the news. Hadn't thought of that. Nat might see him. She might worry. Maybe he should've called? No. Though they'd been friends-with-benefitting for over a year; they rarely shared anything too personal.

One reporter, a thin guy with thick jet-black hair, called to Brooks, "What do you think of the Puppeteer's manifesto? Is Felicity Shields afraid?"

He cringed. They'd nicknamed Dorothy's killer that because the sick fuck had tried to make her into a puppet—cutting out her tongue, sewing a wig onto her head, and stabbing cables through her wrists.

Word came down that Brooks was cleared. He adjusted his bag as the officer swung the barrier back like a door. He started past, stopped, and lowered his voice. "You know anything about this manifesto?"

The cop averted his gaze and answered out of the corner of his mouth, "Early this morning some guy claiming to be The Puppeteer put a manifesto online. Includes a list of women he says need to be killed because they inherited a bad gene—an *Eve* gene." The cop looked at him. "Your friend is at the top of the list."

Leaden cold seeped into his bones. He fought an urge to sprint down the street. "Why would the guy put out a list? Makes it harder for him."

The cop jutted out his chin. "These guys love to taunt the investigators. Even sickos want fame."

Brooks wasn't so sure. "Thanks."

Checking his fight-or-flight reflex, he loosened his stranglehold on the duffel strap and walked down the street. He rounded the corner and spotted the house he and Felicity had once shared, a traditional Santa Fe one-story with a terracotta shingled roof. He doubted the actual murder scene had had more cops in front of it.

Anxiety getting the better of him, he started to jog. His duffel bumped against his back.

A cop stepped onto the sidewalk in front of him. "Drop the bag. I'm going to need to search you and it."

Damn. Hopefully this wouldn't be a problem. "Sure thing. But, so you know, I've got two weapons, registered, and a tactical knife in my bag."

"Step away from the bag. Spread your legs. Put up your hands."

Brooks did. The cop waved another officer over. "Weapons in the bag."

The officer patting him down asked, "Why didn't you tell the officer who let you down here?"

"Didn't think about it. I flew in from Canada—

The first guy jerked his head up from the duffel. "They let you take weapons on a plane?"

"They do if you have the proper paperwork." *And are flying your own plane*, but he wasn't going to mention that.

The first cop pulled out one of the weapon cases. He opened it and whistled. "What is this? A tricked-out Glock?"

Tricked-out? "It's fitted with a night scope and laser. Sometimes I hunt at night. My other gun is smaller sidearm—a Beretta."

As the second officer finished patting him down, the first took his weapons and moved off a distance. There was a long discussion with more cops. They looked back at him every once in a while.

Good to know Fee had people looking out for her, but, damn. He really hoped they wouldn't take his weapons. Getting replacements would be a pain in the ass.

The first officer came back. He handed Brooks the guns and knife. "You check out."

With a *we're-good-here* nod to the officers, he stowed his weapons and made his way up the walkway. He lifted his hand to knock.

"Get out. Now!" Fee shouted.

Nerves stretched tight, he grabbed the handle and pushed open the door.

A barefoot Felicity stood among multiple vases of

flowers, squaring off against a man he'd seen only in photos.

Liam Forster was white where Brooks' skin was tan, blond where Brooks' hair was black, blue-eyed where Brooks had brown.

Liam towered over Fee. Her fists were balled, hair wet and tied back in a bun, face freshly scrubbed. In simple jeans and her threadbare Arizona State college sweatshirt, she was as beautiful as he remembered.

Hurt and heat spread through him equally. An emptiness in his soul, a hole he'd grown so accustomed to he'd forgotten it was there, refilled with a slow, weighted sigh. Oh, fuck. He'd missed her.

She poked a finger toward the door. "Out now."

Fee was angry at Liam? As angry as he'd ever seen her. Considering she'd been a pacifist who'd thought she'd change the world one happy public relations article at a time, that came was a surprise.

A surge of reciprocal anger washed over him. What had this pendejo done? Felicity's mother had been murdered; this guy was supposed to be there for her. But, judging by the red in her cheeks, the set of her jaw, and the tone of her voice, the last thing she wanted was Liam Forster near her.

And that shouldn't make an irrepressible and alarming parade of hope whisk through his body like thrown confetti, but there it was. Neatly erasing all the lies he'd ever told himself about being over her.

## CHAPTER THREE

Felicity's two worst romantic mistakes—the one she should never have let go, and the one she should never have let in—stood in her foyer on her cracked terracotta tiles, backdropped by mauve walls, wood-framed vacation photos, and the honey-sweet scent of condolence flowers.

*First things first.* She pointed at Liam. The Cheater. "Out. And leave your damn key."

Had it only been a few weeks since she'd discovered he'd been cheating on her? It seemed like a lifetime ago. Without his presence in her life, she mostly felt... relieved.

"This isn't about you and me." Liam tugged on the lapel of his charcoal gray suit. His gaze flicked to the professionally dressed woman beside him. "Special Agent Annie Meeks and I arrived while you were in the shower. We've been waiting for you. There's been a development."

A *fed*?

She dropped her hand, addressing the special agent with the direct brown eyes, short blonde hair, and at least five inches of height on Felicity's 5' 6. "I thought my mom's case was the jurisdiction of local law enforcement."

"Before I explain, I'd like to apologize, Ms.

Shields." The special agent's voice was as sharp as the creases in her pantsuit. Her tone suggested it could curdle even the *hint* of bullshit. "I was unaware of the situation between you and Detective Forster when he let me inside."

Of course. Liam never hesitated to step all over boundaries.

"I'm here," Meeks continued, "because someone claiming to be the man who killed your mother has put out a manifesto, suggesting he intends to come after you. And others."

Sour saliva flooded her mouth. Her vision dimmed.

"Fee?" Liam put a steadying hand on her shoulder.

Reflexively, she flinched away. "Don't touch me."

His jaw tightened and he glared. Heat climbed up his neck.

She refused to feel bad. Years of making excuses for his behavior stopped now.

Mom was right. Actions spoke louder than words. He'd shown her who he was. Not just by cheating, but by not calling after Mom's murder. He'd chosen keeping her mother's case over keeping *her*. "Get out, Liam. You don't need to be here for this."

"Actually, as lead detective and someone with knowledge of prior attempts on your mother's life—"

"It's okay, Detective Forster," Agent Meeks interrupted. "I can handle it from here."

Red spread up Liam's neck like lava from a volcano. His annoyed gaze jumped from her to Brooks to Meeks. His jaw ticked.

"Right, then." As stiffly as if the starch in his collar had hardened into his knees, he made his way to the door and pulled it open. Before stepping out, he turned to her. "I'll be there for you at the funeral."

Like she'd ever fall for his faux sincerity again. Not a chance. It was all about the high-profile case, not her. Not them. "All assholes need an invite. And you're not on the list."

The front door clicked closed. The foyer descended into harsh silence.

Brooks stared at her like she was a demon wearing a Fee suit. The twenty-three-year-old Felicity he'd known, Miss Sunny Optimism, didn't exist anymore. That naïve girl had thought positivity *out* meant positivity *in*. In reality, it'd ended up giving everyone who'd step all over her a free pass. Exhibit One had just left.

Brooks would have to deal with the fact that she'd changed and not just emotionally. Like normal people, she'd aged.

He looked the same. Healthy tan skin. Thick black hair. A jaw line of a model or a god. And those eyes... Honey-brown ringed in black. The effect turned his light-brown eyes gold. Sheesh. The man actually looked hotter than the last time she'd seen him.

His healthy glow was a balm to her regrets. He'd lived a better life without her and her family drama.

Crossing her arms, she gathered her elbows in each of her palms. "Why are you staring at me like I killed your kitten, Brooks?"

His eyebrows rose. "I have two dogs. Sappho and Blanco."

Regret gagged her throat and strangled her words. They'd planned on getting a dog together. Now he had two? Those could've been *her* dogs, *her* tan and toned man, and *her* outdoorsy life if she'd followed that path, if she'd have gone through with their wedding...

She mentally scrambled away from a decade-long list of *what ifs*. It followed her all the way to the present with... *what if* she'd called the police when Mom hadn't shown up? Or when she'd noticed the garage doors hadn't opened. Or what if she'd left her home a half hour sooner or—

"Fee." Brooks moved toward her. "You're shaking." He opened his arms. "Can I hug you?"

An unfathomable well of longing unrolled inside her, and yet, accepting that invite struck her as wrong. As if Liam, the man who'd cheated on her, should be the person she let comfort her.

Forget that.

She slid into Brooks' embrace. His strong arms wrapped around her and the masculine scent of him brushed over her like a forgotten dream. His natural aroma sent memories of long, satisfying nights wrapped in his arms surging through her.

He gathered her closer, encircling her with his strength and caring. Her whole being cried out with a release of tension as deep and warm as a bath. Oh, she'd forgotten his embrace. To be held by Brooks was everything she needed just then.

His breath heated the edge of her ear. "I'm so sorry, Fee. I loved Dorothy. I'm so very sorry."

A tidal wave of grief washed over her. Tears swamped her eyes. His steady strength sent her a direct message: if she gave way to her pain, if she broke, if she cried and wailed her grief, he would catch her.

But that wouldn't be fair to him. She couldn't force him to carry her pain on top of his own. She had to be strong. She had to rely on herself now.

Her windpipe thinned with emotion. She fought the uprising tears. Breaking away, she saw him wipe his eyes. Emotion clutched her.

He was the first person she'd seen since her mother's death who grieved with her—and that wasn't because of the police barrier at the end of her cul-de-sac. It was because of the barrier she'd put up around her life, her heart. When you had a mother as notorious as hers, when the next fight was always in front of you, putting up walls was the only way to survive.

Most definitely couldn't break now.

The next fight was already here.

## CHAPTER FOUR

Standing in the foyer of Fee's house, Brooks watched her become all business. Her shoulders rose, she ground her jaw ground, and her fists tightened at her sides. This Fee was harder than the woman he'd known. Or more injured. Or both.

Keeping his distance, he followed her and Special Agent Meeks into the living room.

It was the same—and different—from when he'd lived here with her. Lots more trophies—their name for trinkets they collected on their travels.

The travel and hiking photos of him and Fee were gone from the familiar sofa table. They'd been replaced by photos of Fee and a bunch of smiling people dressed in work attire.

Didn't recognize a-one.

There was an adorable photo of her and her mother wearing matching wide brim hats in what looked like India. A photo of her and her best friend Mae wearing hiking gear and backpacks, faces shiny with sweat, smiles wide as they stood atop a mountain. No photos with Liam. Again, that irredeemable balloon of hope rose in his chest.

Calling himself a selfish, degenerate bastard, he popped that balloon and stuffed it into his shame box.

And then he saw the couch. The scroll-armed, tan

chenille-and-leather couch brightened by Navajo designed blue and brown pillows.

They'd pooled money to buy it from a Santa Fe designer. How many times had they made love on that couch in a frenzy of ripping clothes and surging lust?

Not enough.

Felicity looked toward the couch and back at him. Pink crept up her cheeks, highlighting her tired eyes.

Her gaze moved to the duffel on his shoulder. "If you haven't arranged for a room," her face flushed pinker, "I have an extra."

He hadn't. Hadn't even thought of staying anywhere else. "Thanks. I'd like to stay here."

Tears swamped her eyes. She blinked them away. "You know where the guest room is. Why don't you get settled? I can handle this."

*"It comes down to this, Brooks. I can handle the media attention; you can't. Now, you've lost your job. It's all too much."*

Her words dropped out of memory, stirred up an old feeling, and then fluttered away. He'd been so angry, so sure her choice of calling off the wedding had been because she feared being judged by the media. He'd thought she'd chosen public opinion over him. He'd been an idiot. He'd learned the hard way. *Don't take everything so personally, wait emotions out, and apologize when you have the chance.*

The pain and regret of eight years wouldn't allow him to make the same mistake again. Shouldn't have left then; damn sure wasn't leaving now.

"I have no doubt you can handle it." This time, he wasn't the easily offended *culo* he'd been. "But I'm here for this. For Dorothy."

*And you.*

Not that he'd say that last. She was under enough emotional stress. And, truly, his relationship with Natalie, even as casual as it was, meant he had no right to even *think* about Fee in those terms. He was here for her as a friend. He wouldn't mess that up. "Unless you'd rather I not be here for this."

She smiled gratefully. "I'm glad you're here. And Mom would've been…" she motioned between them, "…over the moon to see us here together."

He knew that. Wished he could have some time alone to grieve with her.

"Ms. Shields." Agent Meeks tone briskly swept aside his wish and his desperate need to comfort Felicity. "I'm sorry to rush you."

Felicity waved her to continue.

Meeks nodded. "Early this morning, a man claiming to be The Puppeteer posted a manifesto online."

In a flash as sudden and jarring as a blaring car horn, Fee's gaze turned hot and focused on Meeks. "Was it him?"

Meeks opened her mouth but Felicity cut her off. "I deserve the truth. I saw…." She grimaced. "I saw what he did."

Meeks' eyes narrowed. "I don't do bullshit. I do cautious."

Wasn't sure that made a difference right now. "How about you throw caution to the wind?" he suggested.

Meeks looked to him then to Felicity. She relented with a sideways flick of her head. "It's most likely him. The BAU... sorry, Behavioral Analysis Unit. It's the—"

"I know what the BAU is." Felicity massaged three fingers into her temple. "Please continue."

A curt nod. "The BAU anticipated the suspect would want attention for the crime. The manifesto, which named seven women directly, states you and women like you—"

"*Like* me?"

"Women with notorious mothers. He claims you've inherited a bad gene, an *Eve* gene that needs to be eradicated. He went so far as to specify qualities like being outspoken or sexually active as being tied to more violent crimes like murder, robbery, treason."

"Díos," Brooks said. "That's crazy."

Meeks gave him a whole face full of side-eye. "That's a given. But worse than a crazy suspect with an impulse problem is a crazy suspect with an agenda."

Fee pulled her hand from her face. "There was another case. A man threatened Mom. Years ago. Bart Colson. He was inspired by misogynistic writings. He wrote a manifesto, too."

Meeks nodded. "Detective Forster filled me in. We're looking into it."

"And since this man is trying to establish an ideology through killing, he's a terrorist, right? Labeling him as such would benefit the case."

He understood her point instantly. If it was terrorism, it meant more resources, more money to investigate, and more agents.

Meeks' eyebrows rose. "Crimes of this nature aren't deemed terrorism."

Fee squared her shoulders. "That's the kind of bull Mom spent years fighting. Men infected by radical, misogynistic ideologies killing women, but we don't dare call it by a term as ugly as the crime. Femicide is ignored—"

"Ms. Shields, although we're examining all possibilities, the BAU has theorized that the killer hadn't originally intended to write the manifesto or the list. He did so only after you interrupted your mother's murder."

Fee's posture shrank, making him aware of how delicate her tough façade was. Her hands curled and uncurled. "I don't think I understand."

"Your mother likely served as a focal point for his hatred and desire for years. He had anticipated the... outcome. Likely every detail. To him, there could be a sense of incompleteness. He needed to devise a way to expand that focal point, a way to satisfy himself and justify to the world his rage and need for revenge. He, therefore, compiled a list of traits he deemed inappropriate in women. He cross-referenced those against notorious women—women who had daughters around your age. Thus, the list."

"And what of their mothers? Are they in danger too?"

"In all but one case, the mothers are dead, in jail, or otherwise inaccessible."

"He's created this list of women like me *because* of me?"

"It's a working theory. One of a dozen. He could've had this list-plan all along. It might have nothing to do—"

Fee blinked rapidly, brushing away the glossy sheen of unshed tears. "But if he hates me so much, why did he let me live?"

Meeks frowned. "Honestly, there's no immediate

answer. Perhaps the perpetrator was startled, maybe because your call to 911 went through, or it could be he's playing a game. My point in telling you all of this isn't to get caught in *what ifs*, but to ask you to reconsider your plans for a public funeral. The BAU believes it could trigger him to come after you."

Felicity shook her head so adamantly a strand of wet hair escaped her bun. "He doesn't get to take her life and her voice, *and* have the last word on her. I will honor my mother with a funeral."

Meeks' frowned. "And provoke this nutjob?"

*Coño*. The detective was really laying it on Fee. More than anything he wanted to hold her. Or go back in time and not let go. Because this Fee… she was as different as she was distant.

"Special Agent, I know all about acquiescing to the haters. After Mom was acquitted, I convinced her not to be so political, to focus on women's issues, to live a life of service without confrontation. I begged her to stop pouring gasoline on the fire."

Her gaze flicked to Brooks then away. Her cheeks reddened. Fee had often told him the same thing.

"You know what? It didn't work. No strategy works in the face of hate." Her voice broke. She swallowed. "If I'd asked her to demure and try to get along, the haters only drove harder. If I told her to try calm and reason, they screamed louder, accused her of horrible crimes, and spread lies about her. And if she ignored them… Well, silence was proof that their ideology was right and that she was worthy of scorn. I'm done trying to appease the haters. I can't talk; I can't *not* talk. These people want me dead or broken. They will get neither."

*Broken P*

Felicity's face flushed. Her jaw set.

She was furious at the world. She was...

Díos. The way *he'd* been. Memories fell on him like a ton of bricks, hard and fast enough that the ground shifted.

*He leaned over the table as he stood to leave. "One day, Fee, you'll realize what you should've fought for—us— was worth fighting for."*

*Her eyes widened, hurt and accepting. "And one day, Brooks, you'll realize that, by saving you, I'm fighting for the best part of us."*

A scalpel of pain sliced through him, ripping open every stitch and suture he'd made in his heart over the last eight years. She'd been right. She *had* saved him.

These past eight years without her had been hell—but the anger, and the social media and public harassment that had been near constants—the looking around for an enemy and the intensity of that spotlight-existence had all vanished.

But not for her. She'd started doing PR for her mother, throwing herself into the fire.

And had been burned...

Meeks looked his way. "Talk some sense into her. The amount of VIPs at this funeral—the number of people needing to be protected... It will be incredibly difficult to secure the area."

The thought of "talking sense" to Felicity made his palms sweat. He'd been away for eight years. He couldn't imagine what she and her mother had been going through.

"Special Agent," he said, genuinely angry that the fed had put him in this position, "she's made her choice. And just so you know, I'm on her side all the way."

Felicity's mouth dropped open and. Her eyes grew wide.

Heat crawled up his neck. He hadn't meant to march over to Felicity's house and declare himself her ride-or-die buddy, but he'd effectively done just that. Fuck. So much for not putting her under any more emotional stress.

*were raised, to think of themselves as special, precious. Men think of themselves as functional. What ability do I have that can support me and aid society?"*

Must feed and water the hate algorithm. Team_Leader: *"But a woman thinks, 'how can I use adoration or cuteness to get what I want?'"*

As expected, the group jumped all over that comment, agreeing and expanding on it.

Oneproblem: **"Everything revolves around their specialness."**

MarkHer2: **"So special, men can't talk. Christ, whole meeting has to slow down to let some bitch collect her thoughts."**

RedPills: **"Eyes forward, soldier. Them peepers feel threatening. FFS. Just looking. Not shoving my dick up your ass."**

On and on, the hate spun. That's how you did it, friends. The Great One, the author whose brilliant writings this group had been formed to exemplify, would be impressed with that smoothly tossed nugget of red meat.

At least, Ed hoped and prayed, he'd be impressed. The man was a mystery to most people. The Great One's writings on how to save the U.S.—and, indeed, the world—were on the Deep Dark Web, but a limited few had knowledge of who'd written them.

The feds had tried and failed to identify him for years. When they'd first started, Dorothy Shields had been VP. Apparently, the feds had worried enough about the writings—which had mentioned the VP in the worst of ways—that they'd warned her about them.

Years later, when running for president, Dorothy had thought she was being clever, calling The Great

One out by using her presidential campaign to explain her version of the country in stark and open contrast to his writings. And the response? No rockets were launched. No threats were spoken. The Great One had simply revealed the truth about Dorothy Shields' crimes. Her campaign had gone under. She'd been put on trial. She should've gone to prison. She'd gotten off. *That* final injustice had been irrevocably corrected.

"*I want to live. I want to live.*"

This, the killing and the group perpetrating the killing, stood as testament—a resume of sorts—to earn The Great One's good graces, to take part fully in his grand plan to silence the voices of those who would label themselves victims and put them back where they'd be safest: in the home. First, there were a few problems to take care of. All of them bitches

Marker362: **"Can't believe how she bled."**

Let them talk. This was their reward. And the evidence that would mark them each as fully participating in the crimes. The evidence that would get each of them sent to jail while this Team_Leader went on to bigger and better.

After thirty minutes of debate and rehashing, one of the members asked the question everyone had been waiting on.

MetooFU: **"When do we take out her daughter?"**

This brought every man in the place to attention and sent negative comments and threats flying.

This was why it was so hard to be Team_Leader. **"Settle. The next assignment will soon be given to one of you. So, let's sit back and wait for our brother to deliver unto us a world in which another of Eve's sins is finally, joyfully, removed."**

## CHAPTER SIX

The morning after he'd arrived at Fee's home in Santa Fe, Brooks rolled out of bed and made his way to the kitchen. He rubbed his face and eyes. Jetlag, déjà vu, fuzzy head... whatever this feeling of walking back through time into his old life was, it was unsettling.

The familiarity of being back home... in *Fee's* house. The bright walls, the cool tiles against his feet, the familiar smells—her lilac shampoo, the little pouches she called sachets in his room, even the cleaner she used for the house. He inhaled frankincense and myrrh. So familiar. The memory bombardment was excruciating.

Every inch of this place brought forth something. A glance in the living room and he saw them laughing, talking, and watching television. He saw them on the couch, their twisted bodies, moving together, sighing together. He walked down the hall and another image appeared.

This wall. He put his hand against the ochre paint. That day... the two of them wet from the rain, stripping off their clothes in the mudroom, darting through the kitchen and into this hall. Making it two steps before he grabbed her, pushed her up against this wall.

He'd made love to her right here. And when they were done, she laid a hand along his jaw, looked into his eyes, and told him for the first time, "I love you."

He hadn't been able to breathe for the joy of it, the wonder of her loving him. Like a disbelieving idiota, he'd blurted, "Promise?"

She'd offered him her pinky. "Pinky swear."

He'd shaken his head. "What I feel for you is too big for a pinky swear."

Her eyes had misted. "Promise?"

"Promise forever," he'd said. And that had become the way they'd said "I love you" for the rest of their relationship.

Damn it. The ache of loss thickened his throat. He pushed off the wall and strolled into a sunny, yellow kitchen with bright red cactus flower tiles.

Fee sat at a wood table, on one of the mismatched red-and-teal chairs, her laptop open.

She was so beautiful. Sunlight reflected off her blonde hair, stroked her pale skin, and highlighted dark circles under her eyes.

He moved across the kitchen. Hard not to gawk at the perfection of her in that light blue camisole and matching boxer shorts. Those legs. Still had great legs.

Lust flared, flashed, and popped inside like a firecracker as heat propelled through his blood. *Easy, there.* The length of time he'd been friends-with-benefitting Natalie put him firmly in the no-right-to-indulge-these-feelings category. That, along with the emotional anvil Fee struggled under, meant he had to button his shit up. Not easy when every part of this house made him long for what had been. But this wasn't about his feelings; it was about hers. "Buenos días, Fee."

She looked up. "I left a cup out for you."

The dart of her briskly tossed words burst his fond-memories bubble, jarring him into the present.

*Broken P*

She looked back down, bit her lip, and typed furiously. He poured coffee into the cup she'd left for him. It had a Canadian maple leaf on it. She'd always done thoughtful things like that.

He took a sip and cringed. Ice cold. How long had she been awake?

Still typing, Fee cursed under her breath.

Re-familiarizing himself with the kitchen, he made a new pot of coffee, adding the cinnamon he remembered she liked. While it brewed, he microwaved the cold cup. Same old retro red-and-silver microwave they'd purchased on Amazon. He took the heated cup out and sat across from her.

His seat rocked a little. He tested it. Easy fix. He set it on his list of things to repair. He'd noticed a couple things needed his attention around here.

Felicity still hadn't looked fully in his direction. He placed his cup on the table. "¿Cómo estas?"

"Have you seen the hashtags trending on social media?"

Was she kidding? "It's 8:30 in the morning. I've seen toilet water, you, and this coffee. In that exact order."

She snorted, stopped typing, and looked up at him. An unexpected smile lit and died on her face. Her eyebrows pinched together. "When do you normally get up?"

"I wake up when I wake up. I rarely set an alarm. Even when I'm leading deep woods training, I don't need to set one."

She went back to her computer but spoke to him over the silver rectangle. "I get up at four a.m. every day."

His soul recoiled. "That's not humanly possible."

"It is if you want to exercise before work and you work an hour away in Albuquerque."

She worked in Albuquerque? A long drive every day. He'd flown into a small, private airport there. "But you're not working now. You're up out of habit, right?"

She met his eyes. "I read the manifesto last night and woke up determined to learn more about my list-sisters."

List-sisters? His heart broke a little for her. She lost her mother, the only close family she had, so she'd taken on a new family overnight. "What did you learn?"

"Meeks was right. Like me, each woman has a mother who has committed, or been accused of, an infamous crime."

He'd have to play catch up today, learn more. "Give me some examples."

"One of the women's mothers actually tried to murder her *and* her father. Another woman, Weaver Jukes is the daughter of the famous singer Skye who made that yearlong video-journal of her sex life. Supposedly, without permission from her partners."

He nodded. Probably wasn't a human in North America who hadn't been subjected to parts of that sex video. It'd been turned into numerous memes.

"Another mother was an asylum-granted scientist from Iran. She left her daughter here and returned to her homeland, carrying state secrets."

Ah, no wonder Fee had sisterly feelings toward these women. These daughters, like her, had been forced to carry the responsibility for their mothers' reputations. Dorothy had been accused, but not convicted, of hiring mercenaries to assassinate a world

*Broken P*

leader. "This pendejo's manifesto ties the daughters to their mothers' crimes?"

"Yep." She sipped her coffee, made a face, then turned toward the coffee pot. It beeped.

She looked back at him. Tears brimmed in her eyes. "You made coffee. That's really…" she paused and he watched her will back the tears, "…nice of you. Thank you."

Could his simple kindness be so unusual in her life that it had brought tears to her eyes? Is that why she fought so hard to seem tough? Did she think her softness made her vulnerable? "De nada."

She dumped the old coffee into the sink and poured fresh mug. "Want some?"

"No. Thanks."

She sat back down. "Anyway, that's why I asked if you'd seen the hashtags. Because #sickosgotapoint and #putmeonthelist are trending this morning."

He processed each hashtag, assumed a meaning for the first. Fuckers. "Put me on the list?"

"Yeah. Apparently, I wasn't the only one to read the manifesto last night."

"Qué?"

"The manifesto is designed to ignite rage or fear, harkening back to Eve and original sin, claiming Eve's genetic evil reappears in certain bloodlines and could be the downfall of society. Again."

He bit back a curse. "Sounds like he's trying to start a real Salem witch hunt."

"Exactly. Anyway, a few big, bold online personalities called out The Puppeteer's misogyny and started using #putmeonthelist hashtag. It's spread like wildfire."

"Women are asking to be put on The Puppeteer's list?"

"Not just asking, arguing for. It's sort of a let-he-who-is-without-sin thing. They're putting out personal stories, reasons they should be on the list, along with the hashtag. It's backfiring big time. Women with any kind of following are now being trolled, threatened, and humiliated. Basically branked."

"Branked?"

She closed her eyes and inhaled the steam as it rose from her mug. "Cinnamon. You remembered."

He nodded, a flush of pleasure spreading through him.

She sipped. "Being branked was a practice in medieval England of silencing women who spoke out of turn. Usually about politics. Part of it involved forcing a large-barbed metal bit into a woman's mouth."

"Mierda. I've never heard the term."

Her gaze turned reflective. She rubbed her thumb along the handle on her mug. "I first heard it in India when Mom explained it to a room filled with mostly female journalists from some of the most repressed countries around the world."

Encouraging those women to speak out... That sounded like Dorothy. "Your mother was an extraordinary woman. She spoke out about injustice and offered solutions for all people. She deserved so much better."

The kitchen grew heavy with the memory of Dorothy's vibrant presence. Her death made him sick with fury.

They stared at one another. He waited for her to

give him the invite, to let him know she wanted to speak of her mother's loss and not just the violence that had taken her life—and taken over the social media world.

She shook her head so slightly he would've missed it if he hadn't been looking for it. Not yet, that signal said. Not yet.

"The hashtag #sickosgotapoint sprung up in direct reaction to #putmeonthelist. People started pasting lines from the manifesto with #sickosgotapoint." She massaged her red eyes with her fingertips. "I'm taking screenshots of the worst threats and sending them to the authorities. I wish these women wouldn't put their stories out there though. I can draw attention from the other women on the list to me with the eulogy at my mom's funeral, but I can't protect—"

"Whoa. Whoa." He put up his hands. Hot alarm shot through him. "Fee? Are you going through with the funeral to say goodbye to your mom or are you putting yourself in danger to protect the other women on the list, your list-sisters?"

*Please don't let it be that last one.*

## CHAPTER SEVEN

The sun shone brightly through the small kitchen window, highlighting Brooks' disbelieving gaze. Sitting across from him, Fee wanted to squirm under the intense stare and his right-to-the-heart-of-it question. She didn't.

She wasn't having the funeral to protect the others. She'd told Meeks the truth. She intended to honor her mother with a funeral. But the added benefit of protecting her list-sisters had occurred to her last night after reading the manifesto. She realized she could use her mom's eulogy to call the fire down on herself.

She'd emailed her boss this morning to get her help with publicizing it. She knew, deep down where it counted, this was the right thing to do, so she easily maintained her stare-down with Brooks. "I have no choice here. This is my—"

"Don't say responsibility. You are knowingly taking on a lunatic. No es tu trabajo."

"Might not be my job, but it's what Mom would've done."

"Let the feds handle this."

If only she believed they would. "The current administration is the one my mom ran against. They have no love for her. Or me. Right now, they're barely putting any resources toward finding The Puppeteer. It'll be worse after the funeral when the media attention dies down. I need to spur him along."

His jaw hardened. He squinted at her. "What did you do?"

This time, she did squirm. Brooks wasn't going to be the only one to give her grief about her decision. "I told my boss, Helen, to arrange to have Mom's funeral carried live on multiple networks. Globally."

Brooks pushed out of his chair, then leaned his fist on the table. "Basically, the exact opposite of what the feds told you to do?"

Despite the plaid pajama bottoms and light gray tee, Brooks looked intimidating. She tried to calm the needle of unease that slid along her skin. He was a big guy, broad of shoulder. With his fist on the table, the corded muscles in his forearm stood out.

"Please...." She worked the fear down her throat. This wasn't Liam. This wasn't a threat. "Would you please sit down?"

His eyes grew wide. He sat with a heavy *thud* and stared at her. *Into* her. He couldn't know. And yet, it felt as if she'd told him Liam had shoved her and given her a concussion. His gaze softened. "Sorry for making you uncomfortable. I forgot myself, being here again. I forgot that you don't really know me anymore, and that you've had eight years of experiences that don't involve me."

His sincerity, his protectiveness made her more uncomfortable than any of his actions. Shutting her laptop, she mentally fumbled to make it better. "No. You're fine. I overreacted. Hyper-awareness comes from growing up in the spotlight."

He rubbed a finger up and down the bridge of his nose—a gesture of unease she hadn't realized she missed until this moment. It wasn't just the gesture. It was all of him. The kindness. And the intensity. And the heat. So hot.

Despite his obvious disquiet, he let it go. "Next time, just roll your eyes at me. Like that adorable picture of you rolling your eyes at President Richards' inauguration speech."

She cringed. That childhood picture was still one of the most used memes online. "That picture taught me not to show any emotion in public."

"And yet, you're moving ahead with televising the funeral, running toward the fire instead of away. Why?"

The weight of his question reminded her heavily of that day, so long ago.

*"You're running scared, Fee. You hate the idea of falling under public scrutiny and being judged not good enough. Or, worse, being branded like your mother. Don't throw us away."*

A barb of shame pierced her. He'd been right. It hadn't only been about her mom and the trial and her fear that the jury pool would be tainted by Brooks' growing outburst. It had also been about her fears of public hate and ridicule directed at him and them.

She'd been an idiot who'd had to learn the hard way. When you run and hide and try to avoid conflict, you end up with a bigger problem.

Like still having unresolved feelings for someone you really didn't know anymore. Sheesh. No matter where the conversation started with him, it always led her back to the past. She thought she'd moved beyond all that pain and regret. So why did it keep stabbing her?

"Because this is the best way. I'm as safe as I've ever been right now." It was *after* the funeral, she worried about. When the police and feds left. Not that she'd tell him that. Despite years of watching her mother do and say whatever she wanted, plowing through the consequences with her rhino skin battered but intact, this was very new to her. If her actions didn't draw the killer out now… If she couldn't protect her list-sisters, as Mom would've done…

She couldn't think about that. It would work. Had to. Her list-sisters needed her to put herself out there, bring this to an end, and keep them safe. "But I don't want you to stand in the line of fire. If—"

"I stand where you stand, my fearless friend."

Air thinned as emotion squeezed her lungs. This man…

Another upsurge of regret streaked across her body. Gulping air, she calmed the attack. She couldn't let the past overwhelm her—and remorse about him was the past. It was too late now. He'd been in love with the woman she'd been. That woman—the hope and optimism of her—was long gone.

Now, all that was left was a determination to make it up to Mom for letting her down, for not calling the police when she'd first suspected something was wrong. She'd kept silent when she should've raised the alarm. She sure as hell would speak up now.

## CHAPTER EIGHT

Beyond the air-conditioned limo Fee shared with Brooks, the sun draped tender arms across Santa Fe's enchanting architecture. The earth tones were a mixture of indigenous, Mexican, and Spanish styles. She'd always loved the combination, but today, it hurt. Like everything about this day.

In the week she'd spent planning the funeral, she'd expected something she didn't feel—a sense of closure. But burying Mom wasn't going to be an act that ended. It stretched like a dark and long road into an invisible and bleak horizon. A forever without her.

A column of spiffed-up newscasters lined the streets, speaking into microphones as camera operators shot footage of the limo passing. Despite the privacy glass, she turned away, feeling so very exposed.

Of course, this was what she wanted—to draw attention to herself, to keep her list-sisters safe. But without Mom's shadow to hide in, she was blinded by the full sun of intense scrutiny and burning hate.

Last night, she'd received threatening texts and emails on an account and cell number she'd kept private for years. The nonstop vile and violent messages rattled her in a way even reading The Puppeteer's manifesto hadn't.

People well and truly hated what they thought her

mother had represented and, thanks to The Puppeteer, that ignorant hate had been transferred to her.

The limo turned a corner. *Bam! Bam! Bam!* hit the doors. Brooks dove, dragging her down and shielding her. Her face paralleled his and their breath mingled. Her pelvis pressed against him as the big car lurched to a stop, her body responding in a way her dismayed mind fought.

Brooks lifted his head. "Don't fucking stop!"

The driver spoke through a speaker. "It's okay. It's okay. Just some idiots throwing tomatoes."

"I don't care. Move."

Three more *thunks*. The car jerked forward. That overly aware sensation slid along her skin, feeling as right as it did wrong. She pushed against Brooks. A moment's hesitation, then he released her from the shelter of his warmth, securing his weapon back in his holster.

Should she have brought her own weapon? It hadn't occurred to her before now. Regretting not having it, she sat back in her seat and smoothed the black silk of her funeral dress with a shaky hand.

He pushed a stray hair from her face. "Are you okay?"

If you didn't count her pounding heart, sweat-soaked hands, and the traitorous tears straining to pour from her eyes, she was fine. "I've had fruit thrown at me before."

Like the gong of an inescapable clock ticking away eight years of hours, minutes, and seconds, a deafening silence descended between them. This was more undeniable proof that she'd been dealing with things like this while he'd lived a quiet life in another country.

"Sorry," he said, picking up her note cards from the floor and handing them to her. He straightened his black tie, adjusted his matching jacket. "I realized it wasn't bullets. Couldn't figure out the sound."

The continued threat of tears and sobs that wouldn't stop rose up and up. She clenched her jaw. A knot of cold determination cemented her. She was putting herself out there for a reason. She'd take the hits to keep the others safe. The blur across her eyes dried up. She took the eulogy cards and tucked them into her clutch.

Clicking the silver clasp closed, she exhaled a breath that did nothing to ease the tightness in her shoulders. "My one goal today is to get through the eulogy without breaking down in front of millions of people."

She had no idea how many people would see the broadcast, but millions were a given. She'd focus on those who loved and championed Mom, not those who'd worked to put her behind bars and besmirch her name.

The sleek, black limo pulled up to the stone stairs that cut through the retaining wall surrounding the raised St. Francis Cathedral. The architectural details, including the arches, squared north and south towers, and Corinthian columns built out of yellow limestone, comforted like a bit of home. She and Mom had come here a lot.

The limo driver got out of the car and wiped the tomato-slick sides down before opening her door.

Tucking the clutch under her arm, she slipped out into the warming day.

She walked up the steps to the church courtyard.

Except for the occasional lizard scurrying about, the tight security meant the usually busy area was empty.

A *tap, tap, tap* from her heels bounced off the dry stones as they passed the bronze statue of Saint Francis of Assisi. Hot wind blew, molding her dress against her thighs and a strand of hair across her lips. She pushed the hair behind her ear.

Looking every bit the capable professional, Brooks scanned the area. Her friend. Her protector.

They neared the church's bronze doors where Father Perez waited. He was a small man with brown skin, sparse brown hair, and soft brown eyes. He greeted Brooks and embraced her. His cassock, warmed by the sun, smelled like herbal tea and incense.

He squeezed her hand with a hand as dry as the weather. "She was one of the bravest souls I have ever met."

The certainty of his words waved a banner at her loss. Grief tied itself around her neck and squeezed.

Massaging her throat, she said, "She adored you, Father. Thank you for meeting me here so early."

"Don't thank me, my dear." His shaking fingers fitted an unusually large key into the lock of the bronze doors. Mom had loved those doors, inlaid with intricate and beautiful tiles depicting the history of this church. He pushed them open. "It is my greatest honor to give you time alone to say goodbye to your mother before the ceremony."

A crack of splintering wood and a gruesome figure plunged from the rafters into the doorway.

Faster than she could react, Brooks shoved her behind him and drew his weapon.

Clenched fists of panic thundered against her ribcage as she struggled to see past him. What was that?

"Madre de Díos." Father stumbled backward and ran off. "¡Policia!"

Brooks lowered his weapon, spun, and grabbed her by her upper arms. "Don't look."

Too late. A figure suspended at odd angles dangled in the open doorway. A woman. A wig. A short, green plaid skirt. Blood dripped down stocking covered legs, over square-toed, patent leather shoes and onto the wood floor, pooling beneath her body.

She recognized the bloody face. The wires. The horror. Felicity screamed and tried to push past him. "Mom! No! Mom!"

Brooks tightened his grip on her arms, leaned his face closer to hers. "Not her. Not her. Look at me, Felicity."

She looked at him, watched his lips repeating the words. His voice broke as he said them again and again, "Listen to me. Please. It's not her. *Not* her."

She couldn't stop calling for Mom. She couldn't feel her lips. She detached from her babbling wails. Brooks' reassurance. The creak of ropes. The wind rocking the suspended corpse. The pounding footsteps and shouts from Santa Fe police officers.

Her mind wrestled with a question in complete calm. If not Mom who? If not Mom, who?

Oh.

Of course.

One of the seven. Her list-sisters. She'd failed them. She'd failed Mom.

Again.

## CHAPTER NINE

Inside the ambulance, Fee's shock was beginning to subside. At least, the shaking and babbling had stopped. The pain in her chest... not so much. But she could think more clearly.

Outside the open ambulance door, the police—many borrowed from the state and neighboring towns for today's event—were everywhere. Red and blue lights played across the church walls. Police radios crackled down the street. Helicopters buzzed overhead, but without the same rushed feel that had occurred directly after they'd found... the body.

Because no one had known if the killer was still in the area, there had been a flurry of activity. Screaming moments of sirens as Fee had been guided—nearly carried—by Brooks across the courtyard.

The police had quickly cordoned off blocks as part of the crime scene so she wasn't surprised to now see Liam—the very last person she wanted to talk to—wending his way toward the ambulance.

Slumping on the paper-wrapped gurney, she lowered her head and stared down at her bare feet. Her shiny black shoes lay helter-skelter on the floor.

"Back off, Delgado." *Gah*. Liam. Overly loud, Overly confident—overly compensating for his lack of a personality. What had she ever seen in him?

She glanced up. Brooks stepped in front of her ex. "She's being evaluated by the EMT. Give her a sec—"

"This is my investigation. I need to speak with her."

Brooks put a hand on Liam's shoulder, halting him.

A sneer curling his lip, Liam looked down at the hand. "Don't make this personal."

Brooks didn't budge. "There is nothing—not one thing about any of this—that I don't take personally."

Great. Total stare down.

Fee groaned to her feet. Strobes of dark dizziness blinked the world away. Antiseptic burned her nose.

Instead of knocking Brooks off—karate-chopping a steel bar might've been easier—Liam met her eyes. "You okay to come out here, Fee? Walk me through some things?"

His tone said it'd be selfish, maybe even irresponsible, not to talk to him right this minute. Hard to believe there was a time when she hadn't seen through his blatant manipulations. She saw them now. But since there was no way to avoid giving in without causing a fight, she'd at least use it to her advantage.

"Can you take this getup off?" she asked the paramedic.

The woman glanced disapprovingly at Liam, but nodded and removed the blood pressure device, the pulse monitor, and unhooked the fluids—though she left in the IV line.

Leaning against the gurney for support, Fee slipped on her shoes and glanced up at Liam. "Who was the woman in the church? Do you have her name?"

Brooks dropped his hand. Liam puffed up. "She wasn't on the list. That's all we know."

*Broken P*

She wasn't? What did that mean?

She trod down the metal steps. Brooks moved to help her, but she waved him off.

Another detective came up behind him. "Excuse me, Mr. Delgado. I'd like to ask you some questions about what happened here today."

Brooks flashed the detective a *one-sec* finger without turning away from Fee. "I'm right here. Not going far."

Her pulse quickened. "Thanks, Brooks."

He walked a few steps away, talking to the detective while keeping one eye on her.

Liam's face took on soft concern as she stepped over to him. Oh, sure. Now that he'd gotten his way, he'd act like he cared.

Shielding her eyes from the sun, she noticed police officers standing nearby glancing over at her. Her skin crawled. There was the sudden and unmistakable feeling of being watched and judged and evaluated. God, she was so exposed without Mom. Why had she thought she could handle all this attention? She ground her teeth. "Where's Meeks?"

Liam pointed at the church. "Chewing out whoever was in charge of securing the church. Might be awhile. Would you rather talk to her?"

She would. But why drag this out? "How do you know the woman in the church wasn't on the list?"

"We've contacted all of the women. They're all okay."

That should've been a relief. It was and wasn't. There was a sick game being played around her and her list-sisters, a sick game in which all women were in danger. "The woman in the chur—"

He pointed to the body-cam attached to his suit jacket. "You're being recorded so it's better if you let me ask the questions. That way, you can go home and get some rest."

Better for him, he meant. "Okay. Ask."

In addition to the recording, he took out a notepad. "Can you describe the events of this morning?"

She did. He asked questions. Really good questions. Liam might be an ass, but he was good at his job. Did she see anything unusual on her way into the church or on the street?

He probed her when she mentioned the tomatoes being thrown. It was likely irrelevant, but he didn't drop it. He got every detail, radioed to the officer working that side of the block, and asked the officer to come see him later.

And then he shifted gears. She answered everything, and even though it didn't seem important, she told him about the threatening texts and phone calls.

His pale cheeks pinkened. "I'm going to need your cell. And the password."

Giving your ex your cell seemed stupid, but it wasn't personal. Especially in this instance, it wasn't. She quickly catalogued what was on her phone. Nothing she needed for work. She'd worked almost exclusively on her mom's PR, for the same company Mom had employed since her trial. Her boss, Helen, was probably biding her time until she could fire her.

"Felicity?" Liam said.

She handed him her phone. He put it into his pocket. "I'll get it back to you ASAP."

"No rush. There's nothing on there I need."

He reached up blindly, flicked off his body-cam,

*Broken P*

then glanced back at Brooks, his gaze running over the big man in an evaluative, can-I-take-him way. He leaned closer. His cologne smelled like a day at the ocean. And deceit.

"Not even phone numbers, Fee? You seem to have forgotten mine."

"Really? You're going to do this now?"

He rubbed at his jaw with the tip of his pen leaving behind a blue line. "You sent the ring back without even a note. I'd had it specially made."

It was all she could do not to roll her eyes. He'd had it fitted. Not like the ring she'd had made for Brooks. *That* had been specially made.

"I texted you repeatedly. No answer. You wouldn't let me explain. Not even once."

So frustrating. This was what he always did: focused on her actions to steer away from his own. There'd been a time when she would've let him get away with this, because her upbringing under a critical public spotlight had made her hyper-focused on every small mistake *she* made. And her flaws always seemed a thousand times more damning than everyone else's. Especially Liam's. The golden boy.

He met her eyes. "It never went beyond sexting, Fee. I swear."

Ha! As if she hadn't seen it with her own eyes. Accidentally. She'd never have looked at his cell otherwise. She'd been borrowing his car. He'd left his cell inside the cup holder. She'd picked up the phone to run it inside. A text had flashed on the screen. He'd been typing to the other woman from his computer. Inside *her* house.

Stomach turning as their conversation had

scrolled across the screen, her hands shook. The texts were raunchy enough to leave no doubt. Her ears burned. Now, she felt nothing but a flat need to keep away from him. "Any more questions?"

He clicked his pen closed and slipped it into his pocket with a sigh. "Are you ever going to forgive me?"

"Oh, I forgive you. But I'm not going to waste any more time on you. Not in anger. Not in words. Not in texts."

His nostrils flared and he bared his teeth. The switch in his demeanor forced her to take a step back. He laughed with an edge that pulled at her skin, shredding her poise like a serrated knife. "There's little FeeRocious. Only you would throw away two years of a relationship after one mistake. But I guess that's your MO. First Brooks, now me. Does he know how hard you like it? How dirty you are?"

His piercing comments and the belittling nickname hit its mark. It made her feel small and guilty. Shame spider-crawled across her belly.

*No. Stop. It's not about you. It's about him.* Once again, his focus fell on her actions in some egotistical attempt to diminish his own. Not today. Never again. "Just do your job, Detective."

Hands shaking, she climbed back into the ambulance and told the EMT, "Take this thing out." She tugged the IV line. "I need to go home. Now."

## CHAPTER TEN

Crossed-legged on her bed, Fee stared at her laptop. Ten tabs open, her bedroom door closed, her eyes streaming tears, she dashed off another anonymous and angry reply to a computer troll. Anonymous, because, now, she was terrified.

After returning from the church, she'd locked herself in her bedroom. Brooks grudgingly accepted her need to be alone.

If only everyone was so understanding. She ignored the multiple emails from her boss. Helen had a hundred questions and as many angles for what she called, "this unfolding story" and the "dynamic and misunderstood women" on the list.

Bullshit. Helen wanted Fee to be a liaison between her and the other women. And although she longed to speak with her list-sisters—at this point she'd learned almost everything else there was to know about them: names, ages, what they looked like, where they lived—she had no intention of drawing them into the spotlight.

Still, her attempt to keep them safe hadn't stopped at least one of her list-sisters from taking the spotlight. Weaver Jukes, a nineteen-year-old beauty with a sharp tongue, was boldly blasting online trolls.

The trolls were loving it. Fresh meat.

What was *with* these people? This was a woman on a *kill list,* defending a woman who'd been viciously murdered.

Unfortunately, a lot of people didn't see it. They were actually *blaming* Kelly Smith, the woman in the church, for her own murder. As if she deserved it because she'd spoken out.

Kelly hadn't even been on the list. She'd put herself on the list. Twenty-six and a social media influencer, known for her trash talk, Kelly Smith had started the #putmeonthelist hashtag.

Now the trending social media hashtag was #youtoo. Fee clicked that tab. Her stomach dropped. Sweat beaded on her upper lip. The thread had grown.

Some demented human on Reddit had actually reposted The Puppeteer's list and begun adding names to it. He'd added Kelly Smith and all the prominent women—celebrities, activist, and politicians—who used the #putmeonthelist hashtag on social media.

A bunch of nuts were following suit, adding old girlfriends or women they hated.

Could Meeks look into each one? Probably not. No wonder no women felt safe right now. Women scrambled to delete their #putmeonthelist posts. At least one celebrity had closed her social media accounts.

Yanking a tissue from the overturned box on her bed, Fee wiped her eyes and running nose. By killing Kelly and Mom, this guy had wanted to kill boldness. He wanted to kill outspokenness. He wanted to kill fearlessness.

For a lot of women, he had.

She fisted the tissue, unable to stop crying, grinding her teeth, and looking for ways to lash out because she felt so unbearably heartbroken, so put in her place, and so very damn afraid. Her head ached, a thousand pounds of hot, snotty mess. Her eyes were swollen. Her nose burned.

And every time she blinked, her mind's eye brought forth details from the church she would've sworn a thousand times she hadn't had time to see. The frizzy blonde wig, hands frozen into claws, gory, lidless eyes, bloody mouth, baby-doll dress, white leggings, and the unnatural bend of broken arms and legs. Cruel. Mocking. Humiliating.

*Oh, Kelly.* She deserved so much better for her outspokenness. She'd tried to stand up for what was right.

The vicious words on the screen blurred. What could she do against all that hate? *They* should be on a fucking list...

That was it—she was making her own list.

Wiping her eyes, she opened up a spreadsheet, wiped her eyes again and began copying. She put the username of every sicko on the list along with the name of the woman they'd added. Those had to be clues to their identity. Then she added a column for whatever demented thing the user had said like, "Eve started it; we'll finish it."

What did that even mean? It might be useless, but it was better than giving in to the pain that kept insisting that curling into a ball on the bed was her best option.

Twenty minutes in, her search skidded to a stop. She ran down the information she'd compiled. It was uncanny. The similarities in some of the posts... It was like they all had the same marching papers. Or they'd all read from the same script...

*Had* they?

The Puppeteer's manifesto and the writings that had inspired Bart Colson, a man who'd threatened her mother four years ago, were so similar.

Funny, but, back then, the threatening notes her mom found in her office, purse, and car had seemed terrifying. Now, notes in a car seemed... manageable. Especially since, well, the worst had happened. And, back then, she'd still trusted people.

Like Liam. He'd worked her mother's case. Two years later, when Colson had been dead in the ground, Liam had asked her out. She'd been flattered. He was a hero in her eyes. Older. And the man who'd found the person threatening her mother. Granted, that man blew himself up before Liam had the chance to arrest him, but the fact that he'd found him had meant everything.

The feeling of power was short-lived. Colson, like the dog Cerberus that guarded the gates of Hell, was just replaced by another drooling, growling head of hate. And since The Puppeteer put out his manifesto, it seemed those heads had multiplied. They were feeding off each other.

Or were they being fed by someone else?

Opening up her Tor browser, she did something she should've done years ago. She researched on the Deep Dark Web.

She started with her mother's name, along with copying-and-pasting parts of The Puppeteer's manifesto.

The hits came fast and hard. Her guts twisted into a knot and her pulse quickened. Tears dried on her face. Okay. Time to comb through them all.

## CHAPTER ELEVEN

Twenty-nine hours after Dorothy Shields' funeral was to be broadcast live around the world, Brooks paced like a tiger caged in the guest room. Fee was in the bedroom next door. She hadn't come out since they'd gotten home yesterday.

What was she doing in there?

His foot caught the fringe of the blue-and-red area rug laid over the wood flooring. He unhooked it and righted it.

*Cozy.* That's the way Fee had described this cramped room the first time he'd come over. They'd been dating for two weeks and had ended up making love on the floor of the then-empty room. Damn. Seemed like another lifetime.

It now served as a guest room and office, with a full-sized bed, a desk, chair, file cabinet, and—stuffed into the corner—Fee's acoustic guitars. With only two bedrooms in this *cozy* house, there was no way he couldn't hear Fee cursing and typing next door.

She was angry. She had every right to be, but it hurt him down to his soul. This was so wrong. She needed time to grieve her mother. Not this. Hadn't seen her cry once. Seemed to make a point not to cry in front of him. Fuck.

He was moving in circles. He'd cleaned her

whole house. Made her dinner, breakfast, lunch, and dinner. He'd eaten each meal alone, then put everything away. Fixed the unbalanced chair in her kitchen. A squeak in her wood floor. The running toilet in the hall and a bunch of other handyman projects that made him long for the cabin he'd built in the woods. He seriously considered getting onto the roof and fixing some of her broken terracotta shingles.

He pivoted, swiveling the carpet again. He tossed it back into place with a flick of his foot. Wouldn't be right to barge into that room and demand to comfort her. Díos. Or, better yet, for her to come back to Canada with him.

It would be downright intrusive. Didn't make him want to do it any less. But she'd asked for alone time. He'd respect that.

But, on the other hand, how long was *too* long? She had water in her bathroom in there, but did she have food? Had she eaten anything since they'd gotten home? Should he bring her something?

A crash sounded from the next room. *Coño.*

Now she was throwing things. Didn't mean he should barge into her room. But, honestly, her request needed a time limit.

He scanned the room. The back wall of the closet was as close as he could get without ignoring her request.

He swung the door open. The closet was filled with Felicity's clothes, coats, and shoes.

Kneeling down, feeling like an ogre ravaging Narnia, he climbed inside, pushing plastic-wrapped dresses out of his face. He bit off a curse as one of her pointed shoes upended and bit into his knee.

At the back wall, he pressed his ear to the cool drywall. With the smell of Felicity's perfume—a mixture of rose and baby powder— in the air, and the dark cloaking his eyesight, he listened.

The sound of her typing came clearly through the drywall. He'd bet every last dollar she was on social media again, obsessing over the online ghouls who talked trash about her mom.

She cursed again, growling, "They are fucking everywhere."

Not being able to go to her was killing him. The barriers she put up to keep herself safe from the prying eyes of the world were obvious, but it seemed the greater barriers were keeping her safe from any kind of close relationship. That isolation kept her from grieving properly. Kept him from being free to comfort her. Hold her.

The *tap*, *tap*, *tap* of her keyboard increased in speed and volume. Every keystroke traveled through him like a zap from a cattle-prod. Hang back or barge in? What was right here?

Disrespecting her request to be left alone was the old Brooks.

*That* Brooks had needed so desperately to keep her safe, he'd insert himself between her and any danger. Or reporter.

That hadn't worked out. He'd become militant, angry, and out of control.

She'd asked him to dial it back. When he hadn't, she'd asked again and again and again.

Until he'd sent a reporter to the hospital, lost his job, and ended them.

Every time he thought back to that loudmouth

idiot—the man he'd been—he wanted to shake some sense into him. He wanted to say, *"She's asking for a postponement of the wedding, pendejo, so you can have time without the pressure of the media to find a new job and get your life in order. She's asking so that her mother's trial—already a fucking spectacle—doesn't have the added shitshow of a groom constantly flying off the handle. Don't be an idiot. Take the postponement."*

It wouldn't have done any good. It'd taken him four years to calm down enough to stop being angry with her, to stop thinking *she'd* done it to *them*. A year more to realize he was a total ass. That *he*—not *she*—had destroyed their relationship. A year more to admit that he wasn't over the loss of her, that he couldn't continue to face the emptiness of not having her in his life. One minute of an Internet search to discover she was dating Liam Forster. A year later, he'd learned they were engaged.

They weren't engaged anymore. If her anger at Liam when he'd arrived and the manipulation and control he'd displayed today were any indication, she was better off.

He wouldn't let himself contemplate the idea that the man had done something other than manipulation. The thought made him want to tear down the police station one brick at a time and pound each brick into Liam's head.

But he'd done something. Add Liam's bullshit to the soul-crushing loss of her mother and the horrifying murder of Kelly Smith, and Fee had to feel so very alone—*and*, knowing her, responsible.

More than anything, he wanted to be there for her.

She wouldn't let him. It might not be in her anymore to know how to let him in. He was practically a stranger now. He hadn't pushed before the funeral. He thought the funeral would give her that time, give *them* that time.

He was wrong.

The Puppeteer had sent Felicity—*all* women—a message when he'd put Kelly's body in that church. He'd wanted to make women too afraid to speak out. Fee was right. This nut was a terrorist.

And he was succeeding. He'd silenced Felicity and taken her mother's funeral from her. In response, she'd locked her grief and herself into an isolated corner of her home. She needed to bury her mother. She needed to say goodbye.

That was it.

Brooks climbed out of the closet and found his cell phone. This was how he would help Felicity. He'd give her time to grieve. He'd give her a lifeline.

# CHAPTER TWELVE

Inside her bedroom, Felicity stared at her screen, at the documents she'd made, her eyes burning. Her search into The Puppeteer's manifesto had brought forth the same reference again and again—the writings that had inspired Bart Colson.

She wasn't the only one who saw the uncanny similarities between The Puppeteer's writings and a man who called himself The Great One. She reread the screenshot she'd taken.

*Dolf91: The Puppeteer is taking from The Great One's playbook.*
*CAntCarrY: Don't be an idiot, he is The Great One. The revolution is happening.*

Ice crept up her spine. Thank God she'd saved that exchange. It had been deleted since she'd first spotted it... seven hours ago? Hard to remember. She'd fallen asleep at some point, only to wake, pee, grab a granola bar from her purse, then start again.

She couldn't let it go. She *wouldn't. Were* they the same person? Or was The Puppeteer just another Bart Colson, inspired by writings that had been circulating on the Dark Web since her mother's vice presidency?

*Broken P*

The sound of a single knuckle rapping against the door jolted her from the screen. She looked around as if waking from a dream. What time was it? How long had she been doing this? Wiping her eyes, she rolled out of bed. "One sec."

She darted into the bathroom, splashed her face with cold water, patted it dry, then put some cream under her puffy eyes. Ugh, that wasn't helping. A quick spritz with perfume and she opened the door.

Brooks stood before her. The soft concern on his handsome face made her regret not taking more care with her appearance. Crud. She didn't want him to worry. To think she wasn't holding up. Though, in truth, she wasn't. She smoothed her hair.

"Here." He held out a maroon-and-gold Arizona State jacket. "It's chilly tonight. We can get something to eat on the way."

He must've gotten that jacket from the guest room closet. She never wore that old thing. It was too loose. It made her look like a child. "You want to take me out to eat?"

His eyebrows went up. He shook his head. "I've made arrangements with the groundskeeper at the cemetery. They haven't buried your mother yet. If you'd like to…" He seemed to struggle for words. "Don't let this sick fuck take your final goodbye from you."

The only thing that could've gotten her to move, to leave this room and detach from what she was trying to uncover, was the thing Brooks offered her. Saying goodbye to Mom.

Willpower surged, rallying and steeling her nerves. Grabbing a brush from her dresser, Felicity dragged it through her hair. She found socks atop unfolded laundry in a basket on the floor and put them on.

Brooks stepped out of the doorway into her room. She tried to ignore how he took in the intimacies she surrounded herself with—the copper framed king-sized bed, the rumpled turquoise sheets, the distressed white wood dresser, black terracotta jar lamps, and white painted wooden blinds. Then his eyes settled on the distressed wood frame, the painting of yellow flowers in a red vase, hanging over her bed.

"You kept it?"

She told herself she'd kept it because of the splash of color, the way those colors complimented the other colors in the room, but the truth was entirely different. It was the memory. "It's one of my favorite things." *One of my favorite memories.*

His eyebrows lifted. He stared, but not at her. *Into* her. Reading a truth she was much too tired to hide. Yes, her eyes admitted, she'd kept it because it reminded her of him. Yes, every time she walked into this room and saw it, she thought of him, missed him.

He licked his lips, cleared his throat. "The one you gave me hangs in my house, too."

Heat spread through her chest. Silly. But the fact that they'd each kept the other's painting from that night meant so much. Especially since Brooks' painting was a fairly good drawing of a vase and flowers—the man worked with his hands and was no creative slouch—while hers was an abstract, drunken-girl nightmare. "Mine was a disaster. Made worse by Mae's criticisms. Whose idea was it to bring a real artist to a paint-and-wine night?"

He laughed. "She was merciless."

Her closest friend had always been direct to a fault. "Not an ounce of tact, that one."

They laughed. It felt so good—and so very wrong—to laugh.

He said, "How is Mae?"

"A marketing guru at one of the biggest advertising agencies in Germany."

He nodded. "As expected."

"Also married with one son and on bed-rest expecting number two any week now."

"Married with one-point-five kids? *Not* expected."

"No. She always said the second-best thing about being a lesbian was that she could never get accidentally pregnant. I was the one who was supposed to…"

A moment of silence so flat and so long it seemed to interlock time. A dizzying wave of awareness and familiarity washed over her. Her lips parted. His eyebrows rose. What was she doing?

She looked down. Such big shoes. Such long legs. *That* didn't help.

Being toe-to-toe with him jolted her senses. Shortened her breaths. Made her head spin and her pulse pound. She fumbled for steady ground, words. "I guess we can't really decide at twenty-three who we'll be. I'm definitely not the sweet, carefree optimist I was then."

She felt the warmth of his hand reaching toward her, as if to coax her head up, but he didn't touch her. She lifted her chin.

A knuckle of skin was pinched between his creased brows. "Why are you so hard on yourself?"

She was being hard on herself? "I'm being

honest." He should try being in her head for two seconds. "You can try it. I won't break. Trust me, you can tell me whatever you think about me."

She kept her eyes pinned to him, open, inviting, and waiting. Drawing in a deep breath, he reached forward, swept his finger lightly across her forehead, down her cheek. His touch, electric and warm, sizzled through her with breathtaking speed. His pupils dilated. "Querida, you are a song that my heart never stopped singing. And when I'm with you, the music is everywhere."

The rich tone of his voice caressed her senses. Warm delight prickled her skin. She'd meant mean stuff. Kind stuff... well, she had no defense for that. But she would *not* cry. Not in front of him. But maybe... something else she wanted, needed...

Tiptoeing, she did something that, an hour ago, would have seemed unforgivable.

She lifted her face to his and kissed him.

She'd intended to catch and release, but the second she met his smooth, full lips the need that had been burning in her for eight long years erupted. She fisted his shirt, pushed her tongue boldly through his wet lips and into his warm mouth.

A surprised pause was followed by him gently tugging her hands from his shirt.

She let go, put her arms around his neck, and held him in place. So good. So Brooks. So long denied.

The hot heavy length of desire unfurled inside her and she disappeared into that need.

With a groan, he wrapped his arms around her and dragged her closer.

Their low sighs and grinding bodies left no doubt

what would happen next if they kept it up. Maybe that's what she wanted. Maybe, forgetting this way would be best.

He pulled back. "Fee..." Catching his breath, he disentangled her arms from his neck. "I'm sorry. I shouldn't have... I'm sort of seeing someone."

*Oh, my God.* She snatched her hands from inside his. Of course, he was. He was a beautiful man. Kind and... beautiful and... *Oh, my God.*

She covered her hot cheeks with her hands. Why hadn't she asked? Why had she just assumed it was okay to kiss him? She wasn't desperate or aggressive or any of those terrible things Liam had always applied to her. "No. I'm sorry. I..."

His eyes filled. Pity. Regret. Two things she frantically didn't want to see. She didn't know where to look. She snatched the coat he still held in his hand. "Let's go."

She raced down the hall into the foyer, head spinning. Brooks had tried to pull away. She'd forced him to kiss her. Had she lost her mind?

Brooks caught up to her and grasped her arm. "Fee. Wait. Please."

She pulled away. Held up her hand. Shook her head. That motion, along with the overwhelming scent of rose and lily condolence flowers, flipped her stomach. "I can't, Brooks. Whatever it is you need to say about that kiss, about the woman you're dating, about us...." She willed her voice not to break. "I can't. Let just go. Okay?"

A myriad of feelings crossed his face. Too many for her to pick out what he must be thinking.

"Okay. Whatever you want. We can talk later."

He grabbed her keys from the candy dish on the foyer table, then headed through the kitchen to the garage. He looked at her over his shoulder. "We'll have to tell the police we're leaving."

Shrugging into her too-big jacket, unreasonable anger swamped all other emotions. Mom. Kelly Smith. Her list-sisters. The danger that connected them all was greater than anyone had suspected. Did Meeks understand the true menace from The Puppeteer?

How could she not? There was no way the feds hadn't put together what Fee had discovered on her laptop in a few hours. Yeah. Meeks knew. And yet, she hadn't told them.

"No feds. No police. I can hide in the backseat."

Meeks wasn't to be trusted any more than Liam.

## CHAPTER THIRTEEN

The cemetery groundskeeper, a trim older man who spoke little and nodded often, stood on faux grass dotted with dirt clumps. He started the casket down with the push of a button.

Brooks kept one arm over Fee's shoulders, as they stared down at the slowly lowering casket. A squadron of moths darted around the floodlight that illuminated Dorothy's grave. Except for Fee's sniffles, the silence of the cemetery was complete.

The smell of freshly turned earth—fertile soil, earthworms, and stones—tangled with the cool night air. Fee tossed a flower and whispered, "Love you, Mom."

Though she sniffed, she still hadn't cried in front of him. But her puffy, red-ringed eyes when she opened the door to her bedroom said she'd cried. A lot. He couldn't imagine her pain. His own heart lay heavy with a thousand complicated layers of grief.

He didn't want to be out here exposing Fee to the world, but staying in the house meant denying her this goodbye. For what it was worth. Not the best way to say goodbye to such a bright and wonderful woman. God, he hoped Dorothy had realized how much he respected and loved her.

He tossed his final flower onto the casket. *I'm here for her, Dorothy. Rest in Peace. I've got her.*

Fee made a small, choked sound. "I keep seeing her bloody face."

*Ay. Díos.* He squeezed her closer and bent to her ear. "I wish I could say something, *do* something, to make all of this better."

With a telling shrug, she created some distance between them. He dropped his arm. An ache grew in his chest. He'd been an idiota with that kiss. And wished desperately to hold her now.

"No one can make it better. But you wanting to is enough. You being here is enough. You arranging this is enough. It's much more than anyone else has done. Even my own father couldn't be bothered to show up for my mother's funeral. Or call to see how I was."

Her father had sent condolence flowers and a note saying he was unable to leave Amsterdam. Apparently, his young wife had just had a baby. Fee was on her own. But not if *he* had anything to say about it.

"She's here!" The shout came out of the darkness along with a blinding camera light.

*Coño.* Moving with fluid ease, he gripped her to his side, and pivoted them both.

It took only a beat for Fee to gain momentum. They hustled across the grass. Over his shoulder, he saw a photographer stop and snap photos of the lowered casket.

The groundskeeper was waving his arms. "No pictures. This is closed to all but family."

A reporter and a cameraman gave chase. They were fast. Managing an Olympic speed walk despite her high heels, the reporter stretched out an arm and pushed a microphone into Felicity's face. "Miss Shields, how did you feel after finding Kelly Smith's corpse? Was it a mistake to attempt the funeral mass? Do you feel like you're to blame?"

Felicity's feet tangled. With a quick assist to her elbow, he kept her from tripping as they wove around tombstones. The weight of the cameraman's equipment and the reporter's heels helped to ditch them.

At the car, he fished out Felicity's keys, hit unlock, then opened the passenger door. Fee slipped inside, but her eyes drifted behind him.

He draped an arm across the door. "Don't engage. They're baiting you."

She met his eyes. "Mom wouldn't have run. Maybe I should talk—."

"Miss Shields, what do you think of the second list? Do you think The Puppeteer wants to silence women?"

*Coño.* "Don't say anything. You were right all those years ago when you told me I was pouring—"

Fee pushed past him out of the car. "Of course that's what he wants." She took a steadying breath.

Despite his misgivings, Brooks couldn't help the surge of pride.

"This is terrorism. Can you imagine the outrage if some woman went mad, snapped, and began killing men? But this happens and we don't blink an eye. Worse, we blame the women. We caution the women. We put the women on a list. We mock Kelly Smith's bravery and act as if she asked for it, when she was only trying to live her life with the dignity and freedom we all deserve."

"So, you're challenging The Puppeteer? Calling him out?"

*Madre de Díos.* Proud or not, this went too far. Brooks stepped between her and the reporter. "Time to go."

Thankfully, Fee dropped back into the car, shaking now, rubbing her hands together. Not as adept as being as outspoken as her mother, at least she knew when to stop beating her head against an unmovable wall.

Brooks slammed the door shut. The reporter shouted questions as the cameraman filmed Fee through the glass. Why did the need for a scoop turn this human—probably not a pendeja on most days—into a headline-baiting idiot?

He swung around the car, opened his door, and, pounding on the roof, got the reporter and camera operator's attention. "Watch your feet."

Brooks flung himself inside, clicked his seatbelt, then revved the engine.

The cameraman jumped back.

Accelerating down the smooth cemetery blacktop, Brooks glanced in his rearview. No one followed.

It seemed like it would never end. Dorothy and, by association, Fee would always be part of a narrative people used to sell stories or create conflict. Even after Dorothy had been acquitted, press and politicians would wave her name around in situations that had nothing to do with her. She became a red flag for a vicious mentality that charged like a bull, without thought.

Fee put her forehead against her closed window. "The Puppeteer wants everyone to think Mom, Kelly Smith, and I caused his behavior by challenging him."

"It's bullshit."

"He's blaming the victim for the abuser's actions. Switching the narrative. I went to so many talks where Mom spoke about how governments and big business used this tactic, but it wasn't until she sent me books on that mindset in intimate relationships that I saw that same control and intimidation in my own life."

He gripped the steering wheel hard enough to

bend steel. "Why would Dorothy send you books on gaslighting?"

He looked at her, willed her to raise her head, answer him.

She did raise her head. Startled. Pointed. "Look out!"

He jolted his gaze back to the road and slammed his foot on the brake. The car screeched to a complete stop. They jerked against their seatbelts. He saw Fee reach for the glove compartment and the Glock he knew she'd stashed in there.

The woman in the street held up a white poster board with the word STOP painted in glowing letters. Her black hair was crew cut short. She wore dark jeans and a sleeveless shirt that showed off an arm filled with colorful tattoos.

She lowered her sign. Fee's hand fell away from the glove box. She pulled at her seatbelt and massaged her clavicle.

Brooks put a hand on her shoulder. "You okay?"

She nodded and gaped out the window. "It's Weaver Jukes. She's on the list. She's been all over social media in the last twenty-four hours."

He leaned closer to the glass. Fee was right. He'd looked up all the women on the list. Weaver's mother was the famous singer, Skye Jukes—the only mother on the list who wasn't dead, in jail, or otherwise out-of-the picture. "What's she doing here?"

Weaver started toward the car.

"I don't know. But judging by her openness on social media, she's about to tell us."

# CHAPTER FOURTEEN

Fee slid down the car window

Weaver's ruddy skin showed her indigenous heritage. Colorful tattoos covered one arm. She had multiple piercings—ears, nose, eyebrow, and lower lip. She was too young to be branded irredeemable and caught up in this mess.

Weaver flicked her head toward the back door. "Open sesame?"

"Fee?" The concern in Brooks' voice said it all.

Of course, it wasn't a good idea. She was a focal point for the hate. Resisting the need to reach out to the other women on the list kept them safe. In theory. But she'd never had any contact with Kelly Smith.

"It's okay," she said to Brooks. "I've got this." She unlocked the door.

Weaver slid into the car and put her poster board on the floor.

Car headlights hit them from behind. With a wary glance into his rearview, Brooks drove forward.

Fighting the seatbelt for slack, Fee faced their passenger in the back seat, blinking away the glare from the headlights behind them. "You're Weaver Jukes."

Weaver put up a fist. "List-sister."

A smile tugging at her mouth because *of course*

one of the women on the list would make that same connection, she pounded the raised fist.

Weaver dropped her hand with a grin. That smile made her look even younger than nineteen.

"Why are you here?" Fee said. "How did you find me?"

"I had you followed."

Brooks made a sound somewhere between a growl and a curse. "That your guys behind us?"

"Yep."

"What crew?"

"Tate Personal Security."

Brooks grunted derisively. "Call them off. Tate is a small enough outfit that any operators know me. Give them my name. We'll meet them at Plaza Entrada in ten minutes."

Weaver leaned back, pulled out her phone, and texted. The car behind them flashed lights and turned.

"Sorry, dude." Weaver put her phone away. "You were good. You lost the first two."

Felicity swung head and eyes toward Brooks. He hadn't said a word about being followed on the way over.

He shrugged. "Thought they might be reporters."

Weaver snorted. "They're too good to be reporters. My mom hired the very best. Kind of impressed you lost them. But I had someone camped out at the cemetery. Figured, if it had been my mom…."

Her voice trailed off. Her eyes rose to Felicity. "Sorry about your mother. She was kick-ass. I really liked her."

"You've met her?"

Weaver nodded. "We met at an event for world hunger when I was fifteen." She smiled. "My mom couldn't stand Dorothy. Trust me, there is no harsher judge of character than a reformed party girl. It didn't help that Dorothy called Mom by her real name." She rolled her eyes. "Naturally, *I* loved Dorothy."

"Naturally." Weaver probably had *rule-breaker* tattooed on her somewhere. A glance at Weaver's ink revealed a hodgepodge of tattoos woven together by color rather than theme. As if every time she'd had the slightest idea for a tattoo, she'd ran out and had gotten one. "And, naturally, Mom loved you right back."

The side of Weaver's grin quivered then dropped. "She did. I mean, I can smell insincerity a mile off. She was the real deal. We became friends. She helped me get into Stanford."

Warmth flooded Fee's heart as solace bloomed over the barren ground of her loss. So many seeds had been planted. The good Mom did would keep growing.

Brooks slid to a stop at the red light, then looked back at Weaver through the rearview mirror. "Did you tell Meeks you'd met Dorothy?"

Weaver slapped a hand on her jean-clad thigh. "Fuck Meeks. She's a stone-cold idiot. I told her. She said Dorothy was a super-connector and it was probably coincidence. She also said if I endangered myself or her case by trying to contact you and the other women on the list, she'd put me into witness protection."

*Uh-oh.* "Is that why you're here? Because you want to get the women on the list together?"

Weaver let out a breath. "Yeah."

"I'm not certain the other women—"

"Three of the others have already agreed. Two said no, flat-out. You're the last one. And the hardest to get hold of."

*Broken P*

Brooks grimaced and cast a sideways look at Fee. Good thing he didn't know what she suspected about The Puppeteer being The Great One or he'd probably kick Weaver out of the car. She wasn't going to go that far, but she did think it better to limit contact with her list-sisters. Getting together would be risky.

"Weaver, your mom has a point about my mom. I meet people every day in the most banal of places, like the grocery store, who've met my mom or whom my mom helped."

"You agree with her?" Weaver's face fell. She pushed back against the seat and flicked a black ring on her thumb. "I thought you'd be different. More like Dorothy."

Ouch. "Being cautious—"

Weaver shifted between the seats. "Everyone is running scared. My mom wants me to—" air-quotes "—*lie low*, not make trouble. Like this guy's a bumblebee. Don't bother him, and he won't bother you. That's fucked up. Know what kills me?" She flopped back into her seat and growled. "We need Dorothy more than ever and she's gone."

Fee grabbed her chest. A dagger would've hurt less. Weaver was right. This was the exact moment they needed Mom. She'd know what to do. How to phrase things, the tone to use. She'd remind people to focus their ire on the killer and not the women on the list. The ache threatened to overwhelm her. And then… electric determination rushed up her spine.

She was her mother's daughter. Weaver showing up, offering contact with the other women, was an opportunity to do the right thing, the thing Mom would've done.

If Mom had discovered—assuming the facts held up—a connection between The Great One and The Puppeteer, she would've shared that information with the other women.

She sat up straighter. "Like I was saying, I think there's a safe way to meet, but we need to be cautious."

Weaver's eyes grew anime-wide. A teen with her faith in humanity restored. "Yeah. Totally. We'll be super safe. My security can handle everything."

No wonder Mom liked her. Fire and hope, intelligence and boldness. Fee liked her, too.

Brooks said nothing, but she could feel his disapproval. His knuckles whitened on the steering wheel as he pulled into Plaza Entrada. Maneuvering toward a spot in the back, he parked and looked at Fee. "¿Esto es lo que quieres?"

Swallowing over her guilt because she still had to tell him the danger was greater than he knew, she said, "Yes. This is what I want to do."

He exhaled a long, slow breath. "Okay. Then we figure out the right way. Organized and safe. Let's keep this from ending up in the papers as some kind of vigilante meeting."

Weaver snorted. "That's stage two."

Fee laughed. Brooks groaned.

"Relax." Weaver texted something on her phone. "These aren't stupid women. We'll do this right."

## CHAPTER FIFTEEN

Brooks flashed his headlights at Weaver's private security team. When they'd gone, he accelerated through Plaza Entrada. He thought he'd met all Tate's people, but those two were new. Tate's operation was growing big, fast.

Not sure that was the best thing. The outfit, a start-up with three years under their belts, recently upped their package with Delgado. And they needed it. If they'd been doing their job, Brooks wouldn't have been able to spot the tail. Should spend less time promoting themselves to big-name clients and more time training.

Still, knowing the owner meant he could coordinate the meeting Fee wanted. The talk with Weaver had energized her. She practically vibrated in the seat next to him.

Despite not understanding her insistence on this meeting, it made his heart lift to see her so excited. He wished he could leave it at that, but he had to know. "Can I ask you something?

He pulled out onto the road and drove through town. The streetlights cast shadows on Fee's suddenly wary face.

She brushed a strand of hair from her face. "Okay."

The smallness of that word crashed as sharp as a steel blade against his chest. He would tread lightly. "Before Weaver spoke of needing your mom, had you intended to meet the other women?"

She fidgeted, glanced his way and then back out her own window. "Nooo. Actually, I was going to suggest Meeks was right and we shouldn't meet."

He wasn't surprised. "Yo lo pensaba."

She smiled. "Guess you still know me."

He pulled to a stop to let a group of twenty-somethings through the crosswalk. Dressed to go clubbing, they moved as one contiguous group, talking loudly and laughing. The area was busy for nearly midnight. "Why'd you change your mind?"

"Because Mom was never angry like me."

A startled burst of laughter shot from him. "Never *angry*? I've seen Dorothy enraged. It's why so many people put her down—because she showed an emotion many thought shrill."

And another reason why, when he and Fee dated, Fee had made a habit of never showing any negative emotions in public.

"True. But Mom got angry at injustice, at things she could change, and then her anger passed into productivity."

"Unlike you?"

"Unlike me."

He accelerated through the now empty crosswalk. A lot was brewing under those words. He could sense she wanted to discuss it. But though they'd made up some ground, they weren't back to their old talk-for-hours-about-anything closeness. "How are you angry?"

There was a long moment of silence. He gripped the steering wheel. *Please don't shut me out.*

"I'm stealth-angry." She exhaled a breath as heavy as an aircraft carrier. "I'm bottled-up angry. I'm the person who grinds my teeth and creates copy designed *not* to offend and articles meant to paint a rosy picture. I'm so fucking repressed I didn't even know I was angry until I found out Liam cheated on—"

"El es un zurullo sin cerebro." Actually, he was worse than a brainless turd.

She laughed and feathers of heat tickled his chest. Oh, yeah, he was wide awake now. She poked him in the ribs. "The nice Canadian goes mean?"

He turned the corner, grinning at her but unable to ignore his own guilt. Should've told her about Nat. Shouldn't have kissed her. Shouldn't have invited her to kiss him with his words. His actions. "You forget, I'm also part American."

"I didn't forget. That's the best part."

"Hey." He winked at her. "I've got better parts."

She laughed. It was deep and sexy and shot right to his groin. God, she was beautiful. The way her mouth parted slightly, teasing. *Coño.* He was inviting trouble again.

"Here's the thing. Liam cheating was a gift. Not only did I get rid of him, but I came to realize I'd let my fear of offending people become my fear of offending *any*one. I'd let my public relations mantra of "Don't throw gas on the fire" become my life mantra. Liam's action lit the fuse that exposed the anger I'd refused to acknowledge."

Her opening up to him like this felt bueno. And a little heartbreaking. Instead of rolling down the windows, he flicked on the fan, needing to hear everything she had to say. He took the long way to her home. "You're following your mom's example, turning your anger into something productive. That's a good reason."

"Not just that." She fiddled with the edge of the jacket that fell to her fingertips. "I discovered a connection between The Puppeteer's writings and the writings that inspired Bart Colson."

"Bart Colson?" Why did that name sound familiar? "Is that the guy Agent Meeks mentioned? The one who went after your mom a few years ago?"

"Yeah. Him."

"What kind of connection?"

"The kind that makes me think the person who authored the writings that inspired Colson is the same man who wrote The Puppeteer's manifesto."

"Wait. Wait. Slow down." Fear played volleyball against his ribs. "Start from the beginning."

Four years after Brooks left, a man named Bart Colson started putting notes in Fee's mom's car. Then her home. Her office. For a year, that pendejo had made threats to Dorothy. For a year, Liam had worked the case.

"Is that how you met?" It bothered Brooks down to his soul that Liam had been there for Fee and Dorothy when he hadn't.

"Yes. But we didn't start dating until two years after he was first assigned the case—a year after Colson blew himself up."

*Four* years. Fee had known Liam longer than she'd ever known him. They'd only dated for two years before getting engaged—hold on. "He blew himself *up*?"

"Yeah. Liam and his team were outside his home, readying to go in and take him down, when a letter bomb Colson had been preparing for Mom went off. Killed him instantly."

He unclenched his jaw. "If I'd known—"

"It's okay." She put her hand on his thigh.

*Lightning.* A rod of heat landed directly between his legs. A powerful mixture of regret and desire rose up and swamped him. He sat like a stunned animal in the center of this hot deluge.

She slid her hand off, leaving a burning imprint. "You couldn't have known. It didn't make national or international news. Liam worried any media would inspire a copycat. Mom and Liam used their influence to keep the whole thing under wraps. The local stations covered it—an explosion in the center of a neighborhood does tend to attract attention. But Colson was written off as a disgruntled state employee."

Well, that answered another burning question: how she'd ever gotten involved with Liam. It seemed, at least in the beginning, that Liam had wanted to help.

Brooks pulled over to the side of the road at the entrance to her neighborhood. This conversation needed his focus, not questions from the police blocking her street.

"What you're saying is, this isn't one guy alone. This could be one guy with many angry, violent guys on his side. A cult. You need to reconsider everything."

"You mean, *not* meet with the other women?"

Good thing he wasn't driving; he was literally seeing red. "Of course. And not just that, but maybe you should consider coming to Canada with me. Let me protect you at my house with my two badass dogs, weapons, and three hundred acres of wilderness."

She crossed her arms. "Huh. Would you be saying that if my mother was in the car planning this meeting?"

He blinked. Of course, he wouldn't. *Mierda.*

His silence answered her question. She huffed.

"Fee—"

"No, Brooks. Don't. You wouldn't have argued with my mom because you would've trusted her to know what she was up against. Trust me; I'm not the naïve person I was when we dated. Back then, I thought hate needed a reason. And if I didn't give it a reason, it would fade away."

"¿Y ahora?"

"Now? Well, now I understand hate is an emotion looking for a reason, manufacturing reasons. It's tempting to believe the opposite—reasons give rise to hate. Especially when you're the one hating. I could easily fall into that trap with The Puppeteer and let my anger become hate. But I refuse to hate him. Hate is blind. Hate is useless. Often destructive. And never redeeming. Or satisfying. I'm smarter than that."

How could she not hate the man who'd murdered her mother? "You sure you're not back to repressing your anger?"

"I'm not. I know I'm angry. Furious. But I'm using my anger to fuel constructive actions. I'm using it to free me, keep others safe, and hold him accountable."

His internal warning system blinked red alert at her decision. They didn't know enough about this connection, about what or who they were facing.

She'd be safer at his cabin. But that system was flawed. Reactionary. It didn't take into consideration what she'd accomplished. She'd done all this research after dual tragedies and on no sleep. She discovered something meaningful. She wanted to use that information to help others. He was arguing, because he wanted to keep her safe despite what she wanted. So much for not being the old Brooks.

"You're right." He rubbed his face. "I'm sorry. And since I know the guy who runs Weaver's security, I'm going to do all I can to make sure this meeting goes off without a hitch."

Exactly what her tender and open heart deserved.

# CHAPTER SIXTEEN

*Should've taken Fee to Canada.* Tension riding his shoulders, Brooks paced the expensive hotel room in the Four Season's Rancho Encantado. Four days of deep prep for this meeting, and it was already going to hell.

Weaver's security had let him and Fee into the room because Weaver and the other two members of her team were out. She'd texted Fee, "Running late. BIG NEWS. Back soon."

He didn't like it.

Plans were made, remade, checked, and secured. Every detail had been worked out with Tate Security. But Weaver was supposed to be here from the start.

He jerked the French door curtains closed, hiding the beautiful Sangre de Cristo mountains and an outside deck with a hot tub and hammock. Weaver's three-bedroom suite included a large living room with kiva fireplace. Drifting over everything was the delicious aroma of chef-prepared dishes under silver lidded trays. Brooks' stomach growled.

But he couldn't eat. Nerves. More research had only confirmed Fee's theory on The Puppeteer. It was looking more and more certain that the guy Brooks now called TP—because he was such a shit—was actually The Great One. Which meant a lot more unknowns. Many people followed his writings, promoted them, and treated them as gospel.

He turned as Fee glided through the living room. Her pacing mirrored his own tension. Recessed lighting sent flickers of gold through her hair. The wide-sleeved, colorful patchwork sundress highlighted the graceful movements and slim build underneath.

She looked his way as if sensing his gaze. "It means a lot to have you here on my side. Funny, I'm surrounded by people all the time, but no one I'm really close to."

He'd noticed a dearth of people in her life. And with Mae on bed rest and living in another country, another time zone, Fee seemed so very alone. "I'm glad I get to be here."

"You're not missing work?"

Nothing he couldn't make up for. And he didn't have any training workshops until next week. If he had to miss that, his brother and Papí could lead it. He shook his head. "The beauty of owning your own business."

She grabbed her elbows. "Is your girlfriend okay with you being away so long?"

*Madre de Díos*. He ran a finger up the bridge of his nose. "Girlfriend stretches the relationship. She's a friend." *We have sex.* "We're casual enough that I didn't tell her I was coming here."

He'd tried to get hold of Nat a few times since arriving to tell her about Fee—and to call things off. He hadn't been able to reach her. Knowing her and her outback ways, she was probably out of range.

There was a long moment of silence and then she whispered, "How long have you two been... you know."

*Coño.* "About a year and a half."

She cringed. "You should tell her. Sometimes men think things are casual, but women feel differently."

She was wrong. He knew exactly what Nat thought of their arrangement. But the idea of explaining that to her, explaining his casual sexual relationship with another woman, made his balls shrink.

Fee looked toward the door. "What do you think of this thing with Weaver? Do you think she's safe?"

"She has two security professionals with her. Judging only by their rooms, military-clean with a single bag in each, they're buttoned up. But I don't have to judge only by their rooms. Jack Tate, owner of Weaver's private security company, gave me a rundown on them. They know their stuff. Weaver will be fine."

Fee snorted. "If we're judging by rooms, Weaver would definitely qualify as reckless."

Weaver's room had clothes strewn all over, two open jewelry boxes, half-eaten chocolates on the bed, and, on the nightstand, junk food wrappers, a half-smoked joint, and a bottle of Jack. "Probably a lot of college-age people with similar items in their rooms."

"Not me." She laughed. "And definitely not you. Back when we dated, you had such a clean lifestyle, your muscles squeaked when you walked."

She wasn't exaggerating. Thankfully, he'd loosened up. "I'd had a different kind of reckless behavior that involved high-risk sports."

His phone buzzed and he checked the text indicating the first woman from the list had arrived. And, as requested, Decker had texted a photo of herself and her security from the parking lot.

*Broken P*

"That's because Papí taught you cool stuff growing up."

True. He'd learned early and loved it all—scuba, rock climbing, hockey, dirt bikes, and cross-country skiing. All while bouncing from Puerto Rico to Vancouver. "He did. But my addiction to getting my heart rate up is why I couldn't settle down for a long time. It's why I became a stuntman after leaving the MMA tour, and, to be brutally honest, why I'd lost that job."

"I've always blamed myself for that."

"What?" Like *she'd* punched that reporter?

A specialized knock on the door had him walking over to double-check through the peephole. "It's Alia Decker and her security guard."

Their arrival had been precisely choreographed. Brooks opened the door, exchanged a word with one of Weaver's team, then let Alia and her security inside.

A thirty-something woman with golden brown skin, wavy brown hair, and ice blue eyes Dr. Alia Decker was tall. Another few inches and they'd be eye-level. The straight line of her shoulders in a pristine pink shirt suggested someone who'd spent years dancing ballet. Or royalty.

Her security guard was a fair-skinned guy with the contained bearing of ex-Special Forces. Tan tactical pants. Shorn blond hair. Huge shoulders. Blank face. Intense. Scanning the room, he vibrated with an energy that promised a quick and deadly response to any threat. No doubt anyone dumb enough to try would find themselves in a world of hurt.

The guy towered over Fee and had at least three inches on Brooks, which put him at over six-and-a-half feet. Wouldn't want to squeeze that frame into coach.

He was carrying. So was Brooks.

Heat rising into her face, Fee held her hand out to Alia. "Felicity Shields. Fee."

"Dr. Alia Decker. Ali." Instead of taking Fee's offered hand, she threw her arms around her and drew her close. "I'm so very sorry for your loss. And for all that you've been through since then."

For a moment, Fee didn't react to the hug, but then she put her arms around Ali. And the two women, virtual strangers, held each other as if they'd known the other for decades.

A fist rose into his throat. All his worries about the meeting disappeared. This is what she'd needed. And he was intensely grateful to Ali for recognizing it. Maybe, reading people was a psychiatrist thing.

"Thank you," Fee said, pulling back, eyes teary. face red. "You—all of the women on the list—have come to mean so much to me. I know it sounds silly, but I feel like I know you."

Ali shook her head. "It doesn't sound silly. I've wanted to reach out so many times. I worried about causing your more stress. I'm so glad you agreed to this meeting."

Her security guy cleared his throat. Ali's eyes swung to him. She waved in his direction. "This imposing gentleman is Lachlan Sommers, my... uh..."

"East Rock personal security." Lachlan's iron tone left no doubt, but the rise in Ali's shoulders and the sudden glow on her cheeks betrayed more between them.

Brooks shook their hands. "Brooks Delgado. Fee's friend and security advisor." Neither reacted to his pronouncement. If they'd done any kind of research over and above the report issued by Weaver's team on all the players here today, then they were aware he'd once been engaged to Fee.

Let them wonder.

He'd done his own research, but some stuff he'd already known. He met Lachlan's eyes. "Kind of surprised to find you involved with this. East Rock is a global security firm with a reputation for handling extreme cases in extreme countries and situations. Usually war zones."

Lachlan raised a single brow. Not confirmation nor denial. But Brooks got a better look at his heterochromia. His left eye was dark brown. The right was two-toned. The bottom was a brown crescent matching his left eye, but the upper part was honey gold. Never saw anything like it.

Lachlan cleared his throat. "Got a thing for eyes?"

*Coño*. "Only if they're captivating."

Dude almost smiled. "You work for Delgado Land and Sea on Vancouver Island. I've been to Delgado Trading."

"You've been to the store?"

The almost-smile spread, drop-kicking his stern face into an actual human one. "Got some scuba tanks there. Met your dad, Rafael? Spain Special Forces before moving to Canada, right? He's a talker."

*Díos*, he missed home. His family. Even missed his family's outdoor supply store, which they'd started long before the survivalist training. "That's Papí, Grupos de Operaciones Especiales. Taught me everything I know."

"Small world." Ali's soft tone suggested genuine amazement yet bland acceptance. Interesting skill.

"You guys have both been to the wilds of Canada. And Fee and I are both on a madman's kill list."

"Wrong," Lachlan grunted. "To get to you, he has to go through me. That means you're not on the list."

Ali rolled her eyes. Lachlan glanced back to Brooks. "Mind if I search the rooms?"

"Knock yourself out, but they're clean."

"No offense, man." Lachlan went about wasting his time.

This hermano was strung tight. Probably not going to like what Fee had to say about TP. He'd have to run interference for her.

Ali watched Lachlan search with a slight shake of her head. "Sorry. He didn't want me to come to this meeting. Nor did my father. Or Lach's company, East Rock."

From his place checking the security of the back door, Lachlan whispered, "Jesus, Ali."

Brooks had to smile. Dr. Alia Decker wasn't one for holding back. Talk about opposites attracting.

Brooks' phone buzzed with the next set of identifying pictures. He frowned. Both women?

A moment later, Weaver's security knocked twice on the door.

Ali moved to open it. Before she could get there, Lachlan darted over. She let out a huff of frustration. He put his eye to the peep hole. "The other two women from the list."

He lowered his head, shook it. "I thought each was arriving separately. They're laughing. Like they've gone out for tea."

Another level of unease formed in Brooks' gut. They were supposed to arrive separately.

Ali put a hand on Lachlan's arm. "Let them in."

Lachlan blinked, hesitated, as if considering the sanity of that suggestion and finding it insane. The women outside knocked again. "I'm checking the cop. I think she's carrying."

He meant Flor Ortiz. The intel sheet given to each of them mentioned she was a police officer in San Juan.

"Lach." One word, but another multi-layered tone. It was both gentle and suggested no man who liked his balls should ignore it. That tone and her ability to read people probably made her a great psychiatrist. "They've already been through Weaver's security. Please let them in."

The guy hesitated only long enough to prove he actually had balls of steel, before grudgingly doing what Ali said.

## CHAPTER SEVENTEEN

Fee immediately recognized the two women who stepped into Weaver's hotel room. The first one, Flor Ortiz, was twenty-six and a police officer from San Juan.

Flor had curls upon curls of auburn hair, mixed race skin both freckled and tan, green eyes, and curves Beyoncé would envy. She wore white jeans, trendy flats, and a silk red shirt unbuttoned low, showing perfect cleavage.

The second woman, the one in black shorts and a Chambray shirt with the denim sleeves rolled up, was Yasamin Rahmoni. She was twenty-eight and a virologist working at a lab in Virginia. Petite—a good four inches smaller than Fee—Middle Eastern olive skin, long jet-black hair streaked with vibrant blue dye, and almond-shaped midnight-black eyes.

Flor spoke first. "Hola, hermanas demonio! Qué pasa? Patear el patriarcado en las bolas últimamente?"

Brooks' delighted rumble of laughter floated across Fee's skin like warmed silk. Although it took her a second, she translated and laughed along.

Flor winked then proceeded to interpret herself. "Hi, sister-devils. What's up? Kick the patriarchy in the balls lately?"

The other women laughed. Lachlan frowned.

Apparently, he didn't approve of ball-kicking the patriarchy. Or he was still upset that the two women had arrived together.

Yasamin pretended to write on the palm of her hand. "I'll pencil in ball-kicking for later." She looked up. "I'm Yasamin Rahmoni. You can call me Jazz. And this," she motioned to Flor, "is Flor Ortiz."

Both the newcomers exchanged the happy looks of friendship.

"Do you guys know each other?" Ali voiced the exact question Fee had wanted to ask.

Jazz shifted her head from side to side in a *sort of* gesture. "We've never met. But we've talked. When I learned Flor was a police officer, I reached out. Since I couldn't afford security, I thought she could give me pointers."

"The feds didn't offer you security?" Meeks had all but tried to force Fee to accept security.

Jazz blanched. "No. Even if they had, I wouldn't have accepted. After my mom returned to Iran, I was treated like a potential spy. Bugged. Tailed. Put on a no-fly list. I'm still not sure they don't monitor my phone."

Ali exchanged a look with Lachlan. He nodded the slightest bit. "We can help you out," she said. "No charge."

"Going to lend me one of your special forces guys?" Jazz pumped her eyebrows and leered at the two men.

Flor burst into laughter. Lachlan shifted uncomfortably, obviously taking Jazz way too seriously.

Ali grinned and said, "I was actually thinking of a particular woman from Lach's company."

"Boo," Jazz laughed and then added, "I really appreciate it."

A sudden surge of warmth settled Fee's nerves. Ali was so genuinely nice. Jazz and Flor had already bonded. And she felt instantly comfortable with all of them. Getting her list-sisters together had been the right move.

"Weaver will be here soon," she told everyone, pointing toward the room and the lidded trays. "There's food if anyone would like to eat while we wait."

They would. Both Jazz and Flor offered condolences to Fee before they grabbed a plate. And, for the first time since her mother's death, she could feel a near stranger's genuine sincerity. It didn't lessen her pain, but it lessened her feeling of loneliness.

The moment the four women had settled on the dusky-rose couches with their plates of food, the conversation took off. Fee's initial impression of her list-sisters was confirmed by the easy banter that turned serious with Flor's terrifying story.

"Verdad," Flor said, as they all sat forward in rapt attention. "The asshole tried to break into my house in Puerto Rico. Wanted to make my death look like The Puppeteer. Turns out, he'd made a huge bet on me being the next woman killed."

Fee shuddered. She hadn't heard that people were betting on that. Though it shouldn't surprise her.

"I'm so glad you took him out," Jazz said.

Flor grinned. "Pendejo, picked the wrong mujera. His cajones will never be the same."

"I'll drink to that," Ali said, holding up her wine.

Fee picked up her water and clinked glasses with Ali, her couch mate. They toasted and sipped. Fee put her drink on the glass table and checked her phone again.

Nothing. Where the heck was Weaver? Why hadn't she responded to her texts?

"I'll be right back." She rose and grabbed Brooks by the arm—so much muscle—then led him toward the front door. "Weaver isn't answering my texts."

He frowned. "She's a bit punchy, but she'd never miss this."

Her thoughts exactly. She lowered her voice. "I don't want to alarm the others."

"Agreed. Lachlan is—"

"What's going on?"

Fee jumped a mile and gave a little squeak at Lachlan's interruption. A muscle in Brooks' jaw twitched as his eyes pinned Lachlan. The men stared one another down.

Half-smirking, Lachlan dipped his head toward her. "Sorry, Fee. I didn't mean to startle you."

Brooks' jaw relaxed a fraction.

"That's okay." Best to get it out there. "Brooks and I were discussing Weaver's lateness."

Lachlan's granite-face furrowed into a frown. She could almost hear it cracking. "When's the last time she was in contact? Did you check with her security? Is this like her?"

Brooks put up a *one-minute* finger. He leaned down to her ear, and whispered, "Want me to go talk to Weaver's security and take Mr. Thousand-Questions with me?"

"I heard that," Lachlan said.

Brooks winked at her. "Secret's out."

She met his eyes, inhaled his scent. He was doing

this for her, to give her an opportunity to tell the other women what she'd discovered. Her heart ballooned with warmth. "Good idea."

For a moment, their faces remained entirely too close. The look in his eyes was entirely too serious. She couldn't find a word or imagine forcing one out of her hot, tingling mouth. She waited for him to ease back, break eye contact, or say something. He didn't. Her face heated.

Lachlan cleared his throat. Brooks jerked away, extended his hand toward the door, and told Lachlan, "After you."

## CHAPTER EIGHTEEN

Brooks stepped into the hotel corridor still feeling the heat between him and Fee. The attraction was getting harder and harder to resist. But he wasn't going to do anything until he did the right thing of breaking it off with Nat. The last thing he wanted was to remind Fee in any way of her ex, that cheating cabrón.

A quick scan up and down the corridor showed bright windows, photos of New Mexico's spectacular pink-and-orange skies, and a lizard running along the patterned rug. And nada más. Where was Weaver's security?

Having made the same exact scan of the hallway as Brooks, Lachlan grabbed the door. "I'm getting Ali out of here."

Brooks put a hand against his shoulder. "Let's think this out before we set this whole thing on fire."

Lachlan grunted, looked down at Brooks' hand. *This guy.* He dropped his hand. "Look, Ali's safe. And, if you like your balls, I'd suggest you let her talk."

Running a palm over his combat-ready buzz cut, Lachlan nodded.

Well, at least he could be reasoned with. "I'm going to call my contact at Tate Security, Jack Tate. See what's up."

"Isn't it obvious?"

Not to him. "Is it?"

"Their priority is Weaver. She's late. She's gone radio silent. Something's wrong. They've left to help her."

"Maybe." That had been his second biggest worry with this meeting. The fact that Weaver's security worked for her. But he respected Jack. *Like* was a different issue. The former CIA agent had started a personal security outfit three years ago with a single vision.

A lot of industry folks were shocked when his company focused on celebrities and Richie-Riches. Former CIA hadn't seemed the type to be satisfied with babysitting, but Jack made money hand over fist and expanded quickly. Not always easy to deal with clients with reputations or ambition, though.

"Could be something else. Not that she's in danger, but that this is a publicity stunt or—"

"Weaver set something up to get attention?"

"I don't know. Her mother was once a party girl but is now pretty religious. Could also be that she intervened and that's why Weaver isn't answering."

Lachlan cursed. "Weaver's security was set to handle extraction of Jazz and Flor. If they can't now, we'll each have to take one."

This guy was really jumping the gun. But thinking ahead was his job. And he was right. That'd require a lot of changes. "Let's hear directly from the source." He found Jack's number and hit CALL.

Planting himself in front of the room's entrance, Lachlan scanned the hall.

Brooks put the cell on speakerphone. The cell rang and rang.

No answer.

His imagination and his irritation kicked up. They'd spent a lot of time coordinating this event. What'd happened to make the team cut and run?

He hit REDIAL.

Again, no answer.

Lachlan shook his head. "We need to figure out how we're going to get the other two out of here."

Brooks tried one more time. Was Lachlan right? Should he pull the plug? If so, how? No way did he want to put another woman from the list in Fee's car. They shouldn't be seen together. That's why they'd gone through all this trouble.

His cell clicked. "Jack Tate here."

Finally. "Jack, Brooks Delgado. I'm here with Lachlan Sommers from East—

Lachlan shoved closer. "Why did you pull your people. We—"

Brooks waved him off and brought the phone to his mouth. "What's going on?"

Jack exhaled so sharply it sounded like someone had punched him. "Weaver ditched her fucking team at a diner. According to them, kid was texting like mad, asked to use the bathroom, and snuck out a window. Had to pull security from the hotel to fucking go look for her."

Weaver had ditched her team? "She texted Fee about an hour ago saying that she had big news."

"She's so fucking reckless. I wish we'd never accepted Skye as a client. Woman's a walking nightmare."

"Blaming the client? Bad form, Jack." Especially since Brooks suspected Jack had taken the case *specifically* because it was high-profile. The man missed no opportunity to build brand.

"Jesus, Delgado, this isn't a training session. We've done everything your way. A total pain in the balls. And you still got an issue with me?"

Yeah. He did. "A heads-up that you were pulling your team would've been nice."

"Figured we'd be back before you noticed. Didn't want to upset anyone."

Lachlan snorted. "Meaning, you fucked up and didn't want us to know it. You left us with our asses hanging out."

Jack sputtered over an answer and settled on, "An unforefuckingseen circumstance."

Unforeseen or not, Lachlan was right about one thing. They'd lost Weaver and this location could now be compromised. "When are Jazz and Flor scheduled to be escorted out?"

A long pause.

"Jack?"

"The people we pulled were each taking one."

Brook cursed. Lachlan pounded a fist into his hand and met Brooks' gaze. "He can't make this right."

"Don't panic," Jack said.

Lachlan snorted. "Ship's sailed."

"Give me a fucking hour. I'm trying to arrange for two other drivers to come in."

He was? That could take a while. Jack had his priority—and it wasn't the women here.

Worry yanked Brooks' muscles taut. "What about getting Meeks in on this?"

Jack issued a muffled growl. Or a low-grade

snarl. "Give us some time before you pull the fucking feds on us, man. They'll slow us down."

Yep, Jack was covering his ass. But he also happened to be right. The feds *would* slow things down. Better to let Jack have some time. "One hour, Jack. I want to be updated every fifteen."

"Agreed." He hung up.

Brooks exchanged a look with Lachlan, half expecting him to grab Ali and bolt, but he rubbed a hand along his shorn hair and said, "Where's your car?"

"Why?"

"There's a parking lot behind the kitchen. It's used for deliveries. It's a three-minute walk from here. I parked Ali's rental near the dumpster. I want you to take it."

Brooks got his point. "New plan?"

"Yeah. I think I can adapt my exit strategy to include the other women."

"How?"

"The rental is nondescript. It's close. You can easily get there without being seen. Take Flor. She has some experience in self-defense. She's an easier watch. You drive out, watch your six, and make your way to the private airport she was already scheduled to leave out of."

"And you take Fee's car?"

"I take it to her mom's house. I have a helicopter parked there."

Brooks glared. "You *what*?"

Lachlan confessed, "It's not far and was cleared by the authorities recently. Figured Fee had enough on her plate she wasn't going to be there, and if anyone else saw the helo, they'd think it was cops investigating the house. Had one of my local contacts leave the rental car there so there were no ties to me or Ali.

Brooks had to admit it made sense. "Then what?"

"From there, I'll fly Jazz to her airport. Leave Fee's car at her mom's house. I'll arrange to have my guy drop off Fee's car to you and exchange for the rental."

Smart. Flying Jazz was a great option. Taking Flor in a rental was safer than using Fee's. car. He'd run a lengthy surveillance detection route before going back to Fee's. "Might work. But we should do more recon on the hotel."

"I'll go."

"You sure?"

"It's what I do. Rescue and withdrawal work."

"Can you call for backup? You have a team, right?"

Lachlan shook his head. "On my own for this."

Huh. Was that because, as Ali had said, his company hadn't thought the meeting a good idea? No wonder the guy was so uptight. He was risking a lot. First and foremost, the client.

He pulled out his keys, handed them to Lachlan, and gave him detailed instructions on where to find the car.

Lachlan took the keys, pocketed them. He pulled out his cell. "I'm going to give Ali the update."

Brooks nodded and texted Fee. She wouldn't like having to leave early, but it was the safest thing to do.

When Lachlan finished his text, he looked back at the door, then to Brooks. "If anything happens to her, I will—"

"Trust me when I say, if anything happens to her or any of the women in there, it'll be because I'm already dead."

Lachlan full-out grinned. "You'd better be."

This guy was growing on him.

## CHAPTER NINETEEN

After the door clicked closed on Brooks and Lachlan, Fee walked back to the others. She realized she was grinding her teeth at the exact moment she realized she was holding her breath. *Unclench. Exhale.* Where was Weaver?

The others, who'd been chatting amiably, quieted as she took the empty seat next to Ali.

Ali's eyebrow rose quizzically. "Where's Weaver?"

Flor bit into a chocolate chip cookie, crumbs tumbling to her lap. "Sí. ¡Donde? This was all her idea."

*Here we go.* "I don't know where Weaver is. Brooks and Lachlan went to talk to her security and find out."

They bombarded her with questions. She put up a hand. "Honestly, I'm worried, too. And, normally, I'd focus only on Weaver, but I came here to talk to all of you, and I don't know how much longer we have together. Sorry to put it so bluntly."

Ali put down her glass of wine. "Don't apologize for being honest. My mom couldn't stand what she called false positives. People being disingenuous to be nice."

Ali's mom had obviously never worked in politics.

Flor swiped the crumbs from her pants. "Is this the same mom institutionalized after trying to kill you and your father?"

A moment of flat and utter silence. Great. And they'd been getting along so well.

Slanting her head on a long and graceful neck, Ali said, "Just because she tried to kill me doesn't mean she didn't have some good ideas."

Before Fee could figure out if Ali was serious, the woman burst into laughter. Fee found herself smiling. Only in this group could that joke work.

Flor put up her hand apologetically. "Perdón. That was my rude way of pointing out the elephant in the room. Our complicated madres."

"Like I said to Fee, don't apologize." Ali's face turned serious. "And I think you pulled your punches on that last line."

"Qué?"

"According to The Puppeteer," Ali said, "We don't just have complicated mothers, we have *evil* mothers. Each one represents an undeniable sin that corresponds to—as stated in his manifesto—a failing of our DNA. My mother was the murderer. Dorothy was the deceiver. Flor—"

"Mi madre was the thief. She was accused of scamming Puerto Rico out of millions of dollars before she ran off. They still haven't found her. Guess The Puppeteer thinks thievery passes through the genes." Flor shrugged. "It sure didn't pass into my bank account."

"My mother was the traitor," Jazz said. "A rescued scientist who betrayed the U.S. and returned to Iran with state secrets." She pointed a shiny, red-polished nail at the door. "And Weaver's mother is the... is *floozy* still a word?"

Flor snorted. "If you're a hundred. But didn't her mom find Jesus?"

*Broken P*

Jazz pointed her gun at Flor, pretended to fire. "WAPO profile piece?" Flor nodded to indicate she'd read the profile pieces *The Washington Post* had done on the people on the list. Fee had read all but hers. *No thanks.*

Jazz dropped her gun. "Can't believe they compared Weaver's mom to Mary Magdalene."

"Easiest way to rob a woman of her agency," Fee noted, "describe her by her sexuality instead of her humanity."

Flor swept a curl from across her forehead. It stayed put for one-and-a-half seconds before falling back. "Exactamente. Skye's a self-made woman who built an empire on her music. Started her own record label and a connected reality TV show. Has given a fortune to charity, started global initiatives. But, hey, she made sex videos."

Compared to today's standard, very tame sex videos. Or so Fee had read.

Ali's phone buzzed. She glanced down and bit her lip.

A moment later, Fee received a text from Brooks telling her they might have to leave sooner than planned. *Shoot.*

Ali reached into a camel-colored briefcase and pulled out a thick brown folder lined with colorful tabs. "Since Flor brought up the subject of our mothers, I'd like to share some information that I think is relevant."

Jazz clapped her hands together. "Whatcha got, shrinky-dink?"

As much as Fee wanted to hear Ali out, and learn more about what each of them thought of the case, her pulse twitched between bone and tendon. Their time was limited. "I also had info—"

Ali placed a photo on the table. "I've already presented this information to the agent in charge of our case."

Fee's words dried up. In the photo, her mother stood outside on a balcony at night, surrounded by three other women.

The photo, taken from the side, seemed surreptitious. As if the women conversing weren't aware of it. Though younger in the photo, the WAPO profile pieces, which had included photos, helped her identify the other women—the mothers of the women here.

Smoothing her crisp, tan slacks, Ali said, "Our four mothers all knew each other."

Fee shifted back. "You think that matters?"

"You don't?"

Heart pounding, time ticking, she picked up the photo. "The world is a small place, especially if there's a common denominator. Like with Brooks and Lachlan. They're in the security world and share connections through that. Our mothers were all high-powered women involved in global and political work. Their contact doesn't surprise me. Even Weaver and her mother knew my mom."

She handed the photo to Jazz. She examined it, frowned. "That's a lot of connections. But it's true what Fee said. My mom defected during Dorothy's first term as vice president. So that's how they met."

Flor took the photo that Jazz handed to her. "My mom was a banker in Puerto Rico. She was in D.C. a lot. I have photos of her with world leaders going back twenty years." She looked up at Fee. "You say Weaver and her mother knew Dorothy, too?"

Fee nodded. "Meeks told Weaver it was likely coincidence. That my mom was a super-connector. Made sense to me. I've run into people in airport bathrooms who tell me they knew my mom."

"Verdad. Could be coincidence. Pero, it could also mean something. Details matter in any case."

"And this bastard doesn't do things accidentally," Ali said, holding up her brown arm. "Anyone notice our suspect is an equal opportunity killer?"

"Noticed," Jazz said, raising her own dusky arm. "The Puppeteer isn't prejudiced, just misogynistic. But why does that matter?"

"Meeks thinks the killer is sending a message meant to resonate globally," Flor said. "He's targeting the universal ideology of masculinity. That's why Kelly Smith was an important target. She dared to speak up."

"She told you that?" Flor nodded. Fee was a little surprised. The special agent hadn't exactly made her a confidant. "What do you think of her? Meeks?"

"Seems okay for a fed. But I get the impression she's in over her head with no life vest."

"No life vest?"

"A lot of political pressure with no real backup."

Ali fiddled with her folder. Her brow had furrowed. Obviously, this wasn't the group response she'd hoped for. "As much as I respect your opinions. I can't dismiss this photo so easily. After my mother lost touch with reality, I went on to study abnormal psychology. So I'm well aware of what can trigger someone with an anti-social personality disorder. This guy doesn't fit any mold."

"What do you mean?" Flor asked.

"It's like he's manipulating us. Keeping us distracted so that we miss the bigger picture. This photo might be coincidence, but my logic and instinct tell me we need to be looking elsewhere. Not where he's pointing."

Grimacing, Fee rolled her shoulders. She knew what they were missing. It wasn't one man. "I think you're right about that."

Ali and the others looked over, clearly surprised.

"Has anyone here ever heard of The Great One?"

## CHAPTER TWENTY

Forty minutes after he'd gone to make his sweep, Lachlan came back into the corridor where Brooks waited.

They'd stayed in contact. It was all-clear. He appreciated the man's thoroughness. He was good. He didn't overreact. Though, he clearly and dramatically did *not* want Ali here.

She, like Fee, must've insisted. He knew Fee's reasoning. Couldn't help but wonder what Ali's was.

Lachlan grunted in Brooks' general direction. "Hear anything from Weaver's security?"

Brooks shook his head. "Nah. I reached out to Jack a minute ago to tell him if he didn't, I was calling the feds. He agreed to call."

Lachlan swiped a hand across his buzz cut. "Is Weaver the kind of person who would take the I-have-some-candy bait?"

Would she have gone to someone who'd promised her something she wanted? *Coño*. She was nineteen and eager to take on the world. She would've done it. "If it was important, related to what's going on here, yeah."

Lachlan grimaced. A big reaction for someone whose face showed little emotion. His gaze landed on the door. "Checked them recently?"

"Used my key card to dip inside." Only Flor had noticed. She'd reached under her jacket when he'd first come in, but then withdrawn her hand and given him the thumbs up. "They're deep in conversation. What's up? I'm worried about Weaver, but you seem certain something bad has happened."

"Yeah, well, Ali theorized that the killer keeps amping up the tension. Like he's putting on a show. Directing the public's level of anxiety. Grabbing Weaver raises the bar."

Brooks got his point. "Weaver is the only woman on the list, besides Fee, who is well known enough to be recognizable."

"Plus, she has security. Thanks to her selfies on social media, everyone knows it. If he could get her, it would make him seem god-like."

Brooks groaned. The Great One thought of himself that way. Superior. That cabrón might actually have Weaver.

Lachlan met Brooks' eyes. "If I didn't have to keep Ali safe, I'd go after this fucker."

The same thought had crossed Brooks' mind a time or two. But he had a place—a cabin—where he could keep Fee safe. And if the man came looking for her there... "I'd hold off on that. He's not alone, for starters."

Stone-faced, Lachlan waited. Brooks explained, giving him the same basic rundown Fee had given him about The Great One and his writings. How these writings had a Dark Web following, and had resulted in Bart Colson, a man who'd been obsessed with harassing Dorothy, get too close.

"So, Fee thinks The Puppeteer might be another

Colson. That, thanks to having a huge Dark Web following, multiple killers were inspired by the writings of this nut. That it?"

"She doesn't think TP was inspired by The Great One. Her research showed comments on social media and the backlash against #putmeonthelist all contained similar messaging. Like they all came from the same playbook. No way could TP have gained followers like that overnight."

Lachlan's eyes flicked toward the door, concern softening those granite features. Damn. This guy loved the woman he protected. Something else they had in common. "You're suggesting The Great One and The Puppeteer are the same guy?"

"Yeah."

"Fuck."

"Sorry, man. Hate to make you more uptight."

Lachlan grunted. "I was born this way."

Brooks' cell buzzed. He fished it from his pocket and put it on speakerphone. Jack's voice came through anxious and breathy. "They found Weaver's fucking phone. Blood on it. Feds have been contacted. Ordered us to break up this party. Chances are, if this guy has Weaver, he knows about you guys. I have people on the way. Give us thirty."

"Don't bother. We got this." Brooks hung up.

They cursed simultaneously and turned to the hotel room. Time to go.

# CHAPTER TWENTY-ONE

Of all the things Fee had expected when she'd agreed to this meeting in Weaver's hotel room, she'd never expected to want so badly to protect these women that she feared telling them the truth. Her breath was so shallow she wouldn't have been surprised to look down and see a boa constrictor squeezing her ribcage. But keeping them from the truth was a false kind of protection. They needed to know.

Flor put her elbow on her knee and cupped her chin. Her green eyes glowed with interest. "Who is The Great One? A criminal? I work in law enforcement, but this is new to me."

"Fee had access to classified information," Ali said.

"Oh, so your mom told you?" Jazz asked.

The insult hit her before Fee could tamp down her reaction. "My mom didn't randomly share classified information. She didn't try to kill me. Or steal money. Or give away state secrets. She was a good woman."

Everyone went still as the unspoken *Unlike your moms* vibrated around the room.

Crap. But her mom *was* different. Her mom didn't …. Fee closed her eyes. She didn't do that. She didn't make uneducated judgments. "Sorry. It's just—"

Ali put a hand over Fee's. "It's just that you've spent years defending your mother against people who say awful things about her, so you have a hair-trigger sensitivity to criticism of her. Trust me, I know. Can't tell you the number of times I've calmly explained to someone that extreme mental illness doesn't make someone evil. Just mentally ill."

"Claro," Flor said. "No way my mom did what she was accused of. She loved Puerto Rico. It was her island."

"Totally understand," Jazz added. "I keep thinking that my mother is nowhere near as fucked up as some of your mothers."

The others chuckled. Warm affection suffused her body. In a split-second these women had gotten over and understood her outburst. She'd never had this experience before, talking intimately with people who understood what it was like to love a woman so many judged without knowing.

She wished she had more time to get to know them. Or to at least prepare them for what she was about to tell them. But there was no time.

Best to start. "I did learn about The Great One from my mom, but not because she just randomly blurted it out. I learned when Bart Colson, a follower of The Great One's writings, came after her. Mom had been threatened a lot over the years, but no one had really made her afraid, until Colson."

Ali had taken out pad of paper and black Cross pen with a traditional yellow Ferrari emblem on the clip. She looked up from her notes. "What made him different?"

Ali had an intense way of making her feel seen. It wasn't entirely comfortable. "He'd gotten messages into her car, into her office, and even inside her purse. Messages based on bizarre writings by a man who called himself The Great One."

Flor laughed. "The bastardo actually calls *himself* that?"

"Worse than him calling himself that was that people believed it. During the Colson case, I learned Mom had been briefed on top-secret investigations about The Great One when she was VP. Back then, the feds had worried he might be a world leader or someone with enormous power.

"Mom told me she'd been so horrified upon reading the misogynistic writings that, during her presidential run, she went out of her way to put opposing views on her website platform."

Ali looked up from her notes. "Wasn't that the campaign she'd been forced to stop for her trial?"

Shock oozed through Felicity, rooted her feet. Did The Great One have enough influence and power to have her mother accused of a crime she hadn't committed in order, to end her bid for the presidency?

"What happened with Colson?" Flor asked.

"He blew himself up. He was trying to devise a letter bomb for my mom."

"What's the gist of his writings?"

"He believed," Fee said, dismissing—for now—what Ali had suggested, "that the feminization of society has led to its downfall. According to him, only a strong man, an autocrat rising to power, could correct this wayward ship. Basically, his writings are the same as The Puppeteer's."

Ali frowned at her. "You think they're the same man?"

Taking a deep breath, she nodded.

"The same man?" Jazz said. "As in, someone with immense power? Someone who has been around for a long time? Someone who first wrote these crazy writings years ago? Who might've stopped Dorothy's presidential bid? And has now come out of the woodwork and put us on his kill list?"

Ali put down her pen. "This changes so much."

"Sí," Flor said. "If these writings were a power play years ago, and, since then, have been circulating on the Dark Web, lighting fires under incel asses, this guy—this great-one-slash-puppet-man—likely has a whole freakin' army."

Jazz held up a hand. "Hold on. Incels? You think a bunch of angry dudes in online communities follow this guy?"

"Sure," Flor said. "Because *women are cruel and inhuman, stupid and shallow*." The sarcastic tone of Flor's voice practically rolled its eyes.

Jazz groaned, wrapping arms around her middle. "So, he's not one sicko alone, but a rich and powerful sicko with a network of other sickos to turn to. Anyone else freaked out?"

Flor whistled two short bursts. "Esta mujer."

This woman, too. How could they not be freaked out? Colson's case showed that there were many men who followed and acted on these writings.

"But why would The Puppeteer put out a manifesto that matched him with the The Great One?" Ali asked. "He had to know the feds would pick up on that clue."

"It's a dog whistle to others who followed those writings," Flor said. "Knowing The Puppeteer might be The Great One doesn't really do anything to help the feds' investigation. It might actually hinder it. Especially when that brings in so many moving parts."

Fee shuddered. It was so twisted. "That could be why he picked our mothers, women with reputations. Not because they knew each other, but because it feeds the base. Trust me, people wave my mom's name around all the time to elicit a reaction. 'The woman who got away with murder.'"

Jazz spread out her hand, wiggled her fingers. "He's doing what a puppeteer does. He's making us, the women on the list, dance and react. He pulls our strings, so the audience watches the puppet and not the hand-manipulations that make the puppet dance."

"People in Puerto Rico are definitely watching me," Flor said. "This has brought out los que odian. The haters."

Jazz looked at Flor sympathetically. "I can relate. There's no sympathy for the daughter of a traitor."

"We can all relate," Ali added. "Although, so far, the press has treated me as a sympathetic oddity. There are whispers online that I'm like my mom, a once-respected journalist. The suggestion is that I, too, could snap without any provocation or logic."

The sound of someone running a key card through the door had all of them looking up.

Flor stood and pulled a weapon from inside her jacket.

"Whoa. Whoa. Whoa," Brooks said as he entered. "It's us."

Flor didn't put her weapon back. "Qué pasó?"

"We'll explain on the way out," Brooks said. "We've got to move. Now."

## CHAPTER TWENTY-TWO

It was nearly four a.m. and still dark as pitch when Brooks neared Fee's home in a nondescript Mazda rental that smelled of old fries. He'd done an extended detection route after dropping Flor off at the airport. No one had followed them.

Fee put his phone down. "Thanks for letting me use your phone. I left the charger in my car."

"De nada. We'll get it back when Lach's contact drops off your car."

She glanced over at him. "Flor got on her plane. Jazz, too. No word from Ali, but that call with Meeks was bad. She's pissed. And worried."

"I heard her through the cell. Witness protection, huh?"

"Fat chance." She tossed her head back. "I spent eight years of my life—longer—being guarded by Secret Service. It draws attention to you. And I'm still hoping to help these women. In fact, if they haven't found Weaver by tomorrow, I'm going to help look. I'm sick with worry."

Not easy to reassure her when the same growing unease racked him.

They pulled up to her street, stopping behind a car at the barrier. The officer came around to Brooks' window.

He lowered it. "Hey, Marv."

The cop nodded at him.

Fee leaned across Brooks to wave. "Hi, Marv."

Marv shook his head. "You can't keep sneaking out like that."

"Sorry. Last time."

He sighed. "Where'd you get the car?"

"Rental," Brooks said and left it at that.

Marv grimaced. "Go on through. It's been a quiet night."

"I hope you won't have to do this much longer," Fee said. "I know you'd rather be home with the wife and kids."

He shrugged. "It's my job. Besides, I can use the overtime." He banged on the roof of the car. "Take care."

Brooks drove forward, then turned the corner toward her house.

Fee sat back with a sigh. "Not sure how long my neighbors are going to have to put up with all of this. It's not fair to them."

"You don't have to stay here."

"Not sure where else I could go."

He was sure. He'd pictured her there a thousand times. "Why not come to Canada?"

"I couldn't."

"¿Porque no? You'd be free to do as much research as you want without worrying about blocking your neighborhood or having the killer come after you. No one would find you up there."

He pulled into her driveway. She fished the garage door opener from her purse and hit the button. A jarring click and the door jolted into motion.

"It sounds great. But I can't."

*Broken P*

"Consider it. Mi casa es tu casa." In this instance, he meant it. He'd never told her, but the land on which he'd built his home was the wedding gift he'd never gotten to give her. He'd never *not* considered it hers.

"But I need to settle my mom's estate. I need to get back to work. Helen has been patient, but..." She turned her head. "Why is the garage door grinding like that?"

The door slowly jerked up with a weighty *click, click, click*, as if the motor fought to catch. They stared for a long moment. It finally got high enough to reveal jerking, dangling feet.

"Fuck." Brooks grabbed for the remote. He flicked it off as he ran.

Heart thrashing, stomach heaving, he ducked under the half-open door.

"Weaver!" Felicity screamed.

The stench of loosed bowls hit him in the gut. The sight of Weaver froze his blood. Suspended, she jerked and thrashed. Steel wires bit into her neck, cutting off her air supply.

Fuck. Fuck. Fuck. He got under her, wrapped his arms around her legs, and lifted to create slack. She was coated in blood and slippery as hell. He struggled to keep her raised. She jerked in his grasp as if being electrocuted. He nearly slipped in blood. "Fee! Cutters!"

She rushed over to the interior door, reached for the controller on the wall.

"No, Fee. Stop!"

Fee yanked her hand back.

"The wires..." He struggled to hold Weaver's jerking body. "Any movement of the door will strangle her. Cutters. Hurry."

She rushed to the tool cabinet and grabbed heavy-duty pruning shears and a step ladder. Weaver stopped twisting and moving and breathing. Fee scrambled up the ladder, gripped the shears with two hands, snapped the line, shouting outrage. Weaver fell into Brooks' arms.

Her body was so still. Cradling her, he laid her on the ground. She wasn't breathing. He began CPR.

Felicity moved toward the house. "I'm calling an ambulance." She stopped. "Why is the door to the mudroom open?"

*Coño.* "Get away from the door. Get your gun from the car. And my cell!"

She startled away from the door, ran to the car and got his phone. "Brooks, your code?"

He repeated his code. She made a frustrated sound. "No service!"

Even from here he could see how hard her hands shook. She was panicking. Not thinking straight. "Breathe, Fee."

He continued to pump and breathe air into Weaver. So young. So, fucking unfair.

She looked down the street. "I'm going to get Marv."

Hands coated in blood, his palms trembling against what felt like a bird's delicate ribcage, he shook his head. "No. Walk to the end…"

She took off, running up the street.

"Fee!"

God damn it. What was she doing? His heart picked up to double time as his arms strained to pump life into the teenager.

## CHAPTER TWENTY-THREE

Fee tore through her neighborhood. Tears washed down her face. Her legs devoured the distance. Adrenalin galloped through her. Arrowing across open lawns stippled with porch lights, Fee's panic pulsed and screamed through her body. *Weaver. Oh, God. Weaver.*

She pushed herself faster.

A blur of movement. She slanted her head. Bam! A form walloped her, tackling her with a force that sent them both flying. She crashed into the ground and slid a good three feet with his weight burying her.

Flames lacerated her back. Steely pain wrenched her neck. Stars rocked her vision. A cement wall covered her. She managed a worthless, "Help."

His hand boxed her mouth tight enough to crack her jaw and immobilize her head and neck against the ground. His masked face drew closer. The knit strands of his balaclava scratched against her ear. "Shhh. There now."

She convulsively swallowed bile as the smell of turned earth and blood saturated her nostrils and shot panic clear down to her spine. This was how she died.

Terror pursued every muscle. But each flinch, twist, and kick collided with a fortress of flesh. His weight shifted automatically, as if he'd done this a thousand times. "Now, settle down. Can't stop what's coming."

His gloved hand, slick with blood, made it hard to breathe. Her vision started to dim. She struggled for air.

Flaring her nostrils, she drew in a breath and dragged the moisture from his gloves up her nostrils and into her lungs. The cough ripped up her esophagus and stopped dead against his grip. She convulsed.

The world grew dark.

He shoved her jaw which sent her head sideways, pushing her face into the dirt as he jumped off. "Not yet, bitch. This was just a taste."

Gagging and hacking, she rolled, wiping blood and tears from her face. She slumped onto her heels as trembling wracked her. Sucking in air, she twisted her head around frantically.

Gone. He'd gone.

She fought to get up from the ground, but fell back. Her butt hit the earth. Weaver. Had to…

Breathing as if she'd run ten miles, she staggered to her feet. Trembling, she staggered down the middle of the street to Marv.

The moment he saw her, he lifted his radio and called for help as he ran to her.

#

Battered and sore, Fee regretted agreeing to come down to the station to be interviewed. Why were interrogation rooms so intimidating and uncomfortable? Steel table, steel chairs, gray walls, and zero decor. Should've listened to Brooks when he'd pleaded with her to go to the hospital.

Too late. Now that her adrenalin had fully fled, she could feel every ache, scrape, and bruise. The truth was, she'd been so grateful and relieved when the EMT had said Weaver was alive that she would've agreed to anything.

The ambulance had taken Weaver to the hospital, while another ambulance crew had checked Fee out. She was bruised, had a slight nosebleed, and a wrenched neck, but the EMT declared her stable enough to be questioned.

As if the nightmare night couldn't get any worse, Liam had taken over the moment that declaration was made. This time, she hadn't had the energy to fight him. And despite Brooks' objections, she'd agreed to the interview. Biting his tongue, Brooks had followed her lead.

Liam had had them driven to the station in separate police cars. So now, her home was part of the crime scene to be investigated. And maybe she was, too.

She shifted on the hard seat and took note of the cameras stationed around the gray and paneled walls—one round CCTV camera and two rectangular recording cameras. During her time with Liam, she'd learned the two silver vents in the table were actually recording devices.

Bringing her into this room meant Meeks was not messing around. The special agent stood in the doorway, juggling a cup of coffee and a notepad as she pressed the record button on the outside.

Surreal. She'd seen that switch so many times when she'd met Liam here to go out to lunch or dinner. Not once had she ever imagined being inside this room under these lights while being recorded.

Meeks let the door fall closed with a click. The hollow circles under her eyes were almost as dark as her eyes. Wrinkled clothes and short hair stringy, this unwashed condition spoke volumes. Meeks was working her ass off.

She raised the cup. "You look like you could use some?"

Meaning, Fee looked worse. But caffeine was the *last* thing she needed. Her nerves were stretched tight. She shook her head and pointed to the two bottles of water on the table. "Any update on Weaver?"

Was that her voice? She sounded a thousand years old and wrapped in a shroud. Twisting off the blue cap, she gulped water, letting the cool liquid slide down her parched throat.

Meeks placed files and her paper coffee cup on the table. The rich aroma drifted over to her, familiar and normal. A cup of coffee at work. Except *Meeks* was at work. Fee? Not so much.

Meeks slid into one of the metal chairs across from her. "She's critical but likely to live. You okay?"

The unexpected caring in her voice swamped Fee's defenses. Emotions tackled her as tight and unforgiving as the man who'd held her down. He could've—. "As good as I can be considering…"

"Considering all three deaths in this investigation have now been found by you?"

Brutal images and panic rose like a wave, trying to pull her under. "No. I meant considering Weaver nearly died and I was attacked."

Meeks spun her coffee cup, picked it up, then took a sip. "Can you tell me what happened, starting with you sneaking out the very first time?"

*Sneaking out?* Fee massaged her aching neck. Why had Meeks brought her to this room? Why had Liam insisted Fee and Brooks be driven to the station in separate cars? "Am I a suspect?"

Reaching into her blazer pocket, Meeks pulled out a plastic orange tube of ibuprofen. She shook out three and handed them across the table to her.

Wordlessly, Fee took them and swallowed.

Meeks put away the bottle. "Things don't make sense. The man let you go. It's... This whole thing is..." She waved a hand in the air. "Messy. I need to question everything."

The man had let her go. Just as the first man had. Did that make her look suspicious? Didn't matter. She had nothing to hide. Nothing. "It started four days ago." Felicity sat up taller. "When Weaver showed up at the cemetery..."

## CHAPTER TWENTY-FOUR

Two hours after Fee's interrogation started, the special agent studied her exhaustive notes. Fee prayed she wouldn't ask another question. Meeks looked up at her. Damn it.

"Why didn't you tell me you wanted to meet the other women? I could've arranged—"

"Weaver told us you cautioned her against meeting us."

Meeks' eyebrows rose. "Of course. She's a kid. However, if I'd known all of you were onboard, I would've gone out of my way to make sure it happened safely."

A surge of shame seared her face and stiffened her fists. Truth was, because Liam had introduced Meeks, she'd unconsciously distrusted the agent. And there were other reasons. "I wanted to meet with the women to tell them I discovered a connection between The Puppeteer and the man who inspired Bart Colson—the man who called himself The Great One."

Meeks didn't react.

"You knew." Fee struggled to keep her tone calm and even. "Why didn't you tell us you suspected The Puppeteer is The Great One?"

"Because we examined and discarded that conclusion." Meeks closed a folder on the table. "In fact, the BAU believes The Puppeteer doesn't even know The Great One. They think all of this is to gain his attention."

Blinking disbelief, she tried to puzzle out what the agent was saying. "Make that make sense."

"Have you ever read any of The Great One's writings?"

"Not until the last few days. But I wish I had done so long ago."

Meeks sat back, a cross between curiosity and judgment on her face "Why didn't you?"

"After Colson died, I wanted to forget. Not open and examine the Pandora's box of hate." As if seeing it, looking directly at it, would make it more real. She used to believe denying the bad things created an environment of lightness and joy. Like a child crawling under the blanket to keep herself safe from the Boogeyman.

Hadn't worked. The Boogeyman knew that trick. She understood now. Only by looking at hate directly, without fear or triviality, without dismissal or exaggeration, could she exist with it and work, as her mother had, to overcome it. "Back then I'd preferred…" What had Ali called it? "False positives."

"Well," Meeks continued, her tone instructional, "I've become pretty familiar with his writings. Those known to the FBI."

*Known?* "You think there's stuff out there you haven't found yet?"

"There undoubtedly is. He hasn't stopped writing. He's produced an exhaustive study of women using mathematical and scientific models, including data collected through social media and online algorithms.

Revised and updated writings typically appear when outdated versions disappear on the Dark Web."

He hadn't stopped writing? The Great One used data mined online to substantiate his bizarre theories?

"The writings I've studied consider women as a whole—societal roles, habits, evolution—and then zoom in on individuals who typify and substantiate The Great One's points. Your mother is mentioned several times as an example of a bad legacy. In other words, if someone wanted to impress The Great One, going after your mother would be a good place to start."

If the BAU was right, her mother had been a pawn for The Puppeteer, a way to impress his hero.

Saliva flooded her mouth as nausea swayed. "Why tell me this now?"

"Bluntly, things have coalesced quickly in the last twenty-four hours around you. We need to start over with complete honesty. I want to delve deeper into people close to you and to your mother. Your father. Personal relationships. Not just—" Meeks' cell rang. "Hold on," Meeks said. "I have my phone set so that only my daughter can get through."

Grief simultaneously gripped her by the throat and heart. "My mom used to do the same thing."

Meeks nodded. "Her daughter mattered to her as much as mine does to me." She stood up, pulled out her cell, and answered. "Dalia, I'm working. Is this—"

There was a long pause. Fee watched as Meeks paced, lowering her head, grinding her teeth. "That's what happens when you skip."

Another long pause. Meeks wore her frustration with a patience that Fee found admirable. She was a mom trying to juggle a lot. She was exhausted. Meek's eyes skipped to Fee, then darted away. "Put Grandma on."

Meeks turned her back to Fee and faced the corner. Fee looked away, guilt drawing in her shoulders. This woman had a complicated life with an errant daughter.

After a few moments of whispered conversation, Meeks said, "That's it. I'm done. You make the call."

Meeks hung up. There was a long moment of silence. Meeks straightened her jacket, put her cell away. Fee didn't comment on the small insight into her home life. She'd seen her mom do the same thing—juggle family and work—for her entire life. She smiled tiredly at Meeks. "How did you get stuck with this case?"

The sides of Meeks' mouth pulled down, making her look ten years older, though she was probably only a decade older than Fee.

"I mean, it's not like the current administration has an ounce of love for my mom. She tried to run against the current president. He's coming into his final year. The world has come a long way from caring about Dorothy "Never Surrender" Shields."

Meeks straightened her shoulders and lifted her head. "I care, Fee. And, yes, you're right. No one wanted this case. I asked for it."

That sentence stretched the air like an overfull balloon. "Why?"

Meeks closed her eyes long enough to give away just how tired she was. "I never believed that your mom ordered that hit. In fact, I know she didn't."

"You know?"

"I'm not the only one privy to the fact that when

your mom was running for president, there was this smear campaign against her. And that it worked. I mean, even the media has covered it."

"True. But do you have proof?"

"I'll tell you what. When all of this is over, you can ask me anything you want. For now, let's concentrate on your answers, on the woman who was almost murdered, on stopping any more murders, and getting this bastard behind bars."

That was a plan Fee could get behind. She opened the second water. "Okay. Ask me anything you want. And get ready for brutal, uncomfortable honesty."

Meeks took her seat with the same blank face, but with a tinge of hope in her tired eyes. For the first time since this nightmare had started, they were working together.

## CHAPTER TWENTY-FIVE

Sitting in a chair next to Liam's desk, Brooks chomped at the bit to get Fee and get out of here. To take her someplace she could rest and recover. His fists clenched. Some asshole had had his hands on her… Wouldn't happen again.

The police station's high-ceilinged room with tall glass-dividers buzzed like a hive of wasps squirted with RAID. Awash in white recessed lighting, detectives, staff, and cops buzzed here and there as phones rang off the hook.

The Santa Fe PD wasn't happy about being caught in the international media spotlight with another fuck-up. Poor Weaver. He'd been told she'd survive, but she'd have a long road ahead.

He shifted on the coarse fabric chair. At the desk, Liam's fingers mashed the keyboard as he typed Brooks' statement. His desk was jammed with an ergonomic keyboard, two sleek high-definition monitors, an expensive tablet, two cell phones, and an old, unopened jar of gummy bears.

The candy inside looked stale and sweaty. The dusty ribbon and blue construction paper tag attached read, "To Detective Forster. From: Mrs. Tildwell's 3rd Grade Class." It had never been opened. Such bullshit.

How many people had sat in this chair? How

many would've gladly accepted something sweet to help with the telling of their trauma? Probably wouldn't look as nice with the ribbon ripped off and the candy half gone. Superficial ass.

Just another reason, he wanted to punch this guy in the face. Liam's irritated expression, blond eyebrows drawn in, mouth set in a frown didn't help the want-to-punch-his-face situation. If he were flat-out honest, even if Liam had been smiling, Brooks would still want to punch him in the face.

Something had shifted after Weaver was found. That something revealed itself in the disdainful way Liam questioned him. In the suspicious looks the other officers gave him. In how Meeks had appeared, shoulders squared, eyes slitted, as if ready for battle.

Each murder was now connected in some way to Fee. But they couldn't possibly blame her. She had a roomful of alibis. She'd been attacked. And yet... "Why did Meeks ask Fee to be taken into a private interrogation room?"

Exhaling what sounded like a knot of frustration, Liam looked up from typing. "Now, you're thinking?"

Brooks fought down that urge to punch him. If there was any sort of justice in the world, he'd get his chance. First, he'd get some answers. "What does that mean?" *Pendejo.*

Liam rested his wrists against the leather pad that edged his keyboard. The sneer on his face traveled up in a firm line all the way to his eyes. "You had to know that, even dead, Dorothy Shields has zero friends in the current administration. There are powerful people and certain journalists angling to blame her for her own murder. And plenty of stories out there suggesting

Dorothy was involved in something sinister that resulted in her murder. Naturally, people are going to wonder if Fee was also involved. After all, she worked closely with her mother."

Liam's gaze swept over Brooks. Judging. Invasive. "Now another woman was murdered, and a second woman *nearly* murdered in proximity to Fee. It looks suspicious."

"We live in a sick world filled with stupid people."

"That's news to you?"

"How could anyone possibly tie all of this to Fee?"

Liam leaned back and puffed up. "One example. Conspiracy theorists think Fee's part of an assassination cabal started by Dorothy. They're saying the murdered women are all members. And that the deaths are a way to force Fee into telling the truth. That's why Fee wasn't killed at her mom's home... so she'd confess. The theory has spread into high-level media and caught the attention of powerful people."

Jesus. Scary and sick. Conspiracy theorists were tapping into an already existing anger. Hard to tell who might be helping TP from those mindlessly reposting the rumors. "Conspiracy theories are a dime a dozen. Nothing Fee can do about that."

"If you think that, then you're fucking delusional," Liam said, snapping forward with a slide of his chair wheels against the floor. "She could've stopped all of this by staying home and shutting up."

That was a bullshit way to talk about a grown woman. How could this douche blame Fee for a series of events that involved dozens of people and decisions she had no control over? Not to mention, the actions of a psychopath and conspiracists.

"Even with all your resources," Brooks said, "you weren't able to stop him. And that's your fucking job. It's also your job to see past the lies, distortion, and political pressure to the truth. Not Fee's to monitor or stop that bullshit. So who's responsible here?"

Liam's faced reddened. His eyes dipped contemptuously over Brooks. "Fee's actions are inciting this situation. If you won't tell her to shut up and stay home, I will."

This guy thought Fee was just another candy to be kept in a lidded jar on his desk. Fuck that.

Brooks reached forward.

Liam flinched.

Smirking, Brooks grabbed the jar of candy, twisted off the lid, and ate one of those stale fuckers like it was the best thing he'd ever tasted. He grinned a sticky, sweet smile. "Let's be clear, if you dump this bullshit in Fee's lap—"

"Where is she? Where is that bitch?"

At the shrill and desperate voice, Brooks bolted to his feet. A pink-haired woman wearing a matching, full-length jacket pushed her way into the room.

Skye Jukes. Weaver's flamboyant mother.

Tear-streaked mascara halfway down her face, her hair in spiked disarray, Skye's crazed and tear-swollen gaze darted around the room. "Where is she? Where the fuck is that soulless bitch, Felicity Shields?"

## CHAPTER TWENTY-SIX

Meeks put aside her notebook. Thank God. The woman was so thorough even her silences were pushy. Fee was wrung out and she desperately needed to pee. Two bottles of water would do that to you.

Meeks clicked her pen and placed it inside her suit jacket pocket. "Can I ask you something for my own personal curiosity?"

Her bladder sent up a shriek of protest. "Sure."

"What's your honest opinion of Liam Forster?"

She closed her eyes. "He's an asshole. He cheated on me."

Meeks let out a breath. "He seemed very much a part of your life when he let me into your home. Honestly, after that, I'd thought to take him off the case, but his boss, a woman I've worked with and highly admire, claimed it was unnecessary. That you'd been broken up for two months. He has a strong following here."

"Not really two months, but that white lie is proof of the strong following part. Truthfully, I'm glad he's gone from my life."

Meeks kept her gaze focused on Fee. "I saw you flinch when he tried to comfort you that first day at your house. Has he ever been physical with you? Shoved? Hit?"

Her turn to shift. She'd hidden the details even from her mother. "After I found out he cheated, I threw him out of the house. I shoved him toward the door. He shoved me back."

"Harder than you shoved him?"

Fee stared at her. Her eyes drifted to the camera in the room.

"I promise you, no one but me will see these recordings. I will confiscate them immediately after this interview."

She exhaled through her teeth. "He's half foot taller and a hundred pounds heavier. I was trying to move him toward the door. He was trying to hurt me."

"So you fell?"

"Yes." She'd slammed her head so hard she'd seen stars. The breath had been knocked from her. And there'd been a moment, a split second, when she'd seen him towering over him, seen his eyes...

"Did you file a report?"

Go to the station where Liam worked? Report that she'd been pushed by a highly regarded detective after she pushed him first? Yeah, right. "No, I—"

Someone outside the interrogation room was shrieking. Fee heard her name mixed in with the cursing. Meeks stood up as the door opened and Liam leaned through.

"We have a situation." He hitched a thumb over his shoulder.

Meeks rushed to the door. "Wait here. I'll be right back."

Fee stood up as Meeks left. Outside, the shouts for, "That bitch Felicity Shields" continued. She asked Liam, "What's going on?"

*Broken P*

Liam clicked off the camera switch outside the doorway. He let the door close and stood inside it. He stared at her, an unflinching blue gaze that didn't leave her face.

It was so much easier to see his tactics now. That weighty look. The threat of his anger or disapproval had always trembled on the surface of their relationship.

She dropped her shoulders. No more. She deserved better. She hadn't always understood that. Growing up in a world where insults and accusations were thrown at her and her family daily had hardened her to mistreatment. Not just hardened, made her accepting of it. She wasn't that person anymore.

"Never mind." She sat back down. "I'll ask Meeks."

Liam circled the table. "I had a nice talk with your boyfriend. Guess you finally got the man you've been pining for all these years, FeeRocious."

Ugh, that nickname. Hard to believe, she'd once thought it cute. "Knock it off, Liam."

"That's a big guy. Looks brutal enough to get you off. Bet he'll do all those dirty things your dirty mind desires."

She cringed. She hated that she'd ever slept with him. Had ever shared herself with him. Made herself vulnerable to him. And what was so dirty about liking sex fast and hard? *Stop. Not doing this.* "I need to use the bathroom."

"If I were you, I'd wait. Skye Jukes is here looking for the person responsible for her daughter being scalped by a maniac."

Her mind skipped over his words like a rock skipping over the water. *Daughter. Scalped. Maniac.*

The air seemed to chill around her. She shuddered. "You don't mean... Me?" Skye thought *she* was to blame for what happened to Weaver? "That makes no sense."

Liam shot out a laugh that stung like a taunt. "Makes sense to me. Every action you've taken has made the situation worse. By having the funeral, you gave the killer motive to kill Kelly Smith. *And* opportunity to link her death to you. By organizing a meeting with the women on the list—knowing a madman is after all of you—you put the other women in danger, and you handed him a teenage girl."

Oh, Weaver. But that wasn't her fault. As usual, Liam defined her actions in terms of black and white. Good and bad. No shades of gray. This time, she wasn't falling for it. "With or without the funeral, Kelly Smith would still be dead. The killer would've tied her death to me somehow. That's his jam—finding ways to blame the victims. And, as shitty as it is, as much as my heart aches, that's also true for Weaver. She was surrounded by security, and he *still* got her. There's no way I could've guessed that."

He drew out an expertly condescending sigh. "How hard is it to figure out The Puppeteer would go after anyone on the list who had contact with you? You as good as strung Weaver up yourself."

"You're just trying to hurt me. Please leave."

With a shake of his head, he walked to the door and waved a fob over a pad there. "The truth hurts. How can I help you and stop this guy if you keep acting like an idiot?" Hand on the lever, he continued, "I'm leaving this unlocked. You should at least come out and explain your actions to Skye, show her basic human concern. It's what your mom would've done."

*Broken P*

Felicity stared at the door after he closed it behind him. The muffled shrieking that occasionally included her name zapped through her like electricity. Liam was right. Mom would've talked to Skye. But not to accept blame. She would've gotten Skye to understand exactly where the blame needed to be placed.

## CHAPTER TWENTY-SEVEN

An overwhelmed police officer tried to steer the distraught Skye Jukes into a seat. Skye's bejeweled hands shoved her away. Distraught mother or not, if she kept that up, they'd arrest her. Weaver needed—and deserved—to have her mother by her side. Brooks had to do something.

"Ms. Jukes." He approached, hands raised in supplication. Her gaze flashed to him. Anguish. It stabbed him straight through. He couldn't imagine her pain.

Skye's frantic gaze swung back to the officer. "My daughter's security told me that Weaver ran off because she needed to do something for Felicity Shields. And then she was found at her house? Can't you see? She's trying to lure Weaver into her cabal."

"Ms. Jukes." He tried again. "I'm so sorry about your daughter. Felicity and I found Weaver. We helped save her life. I promise you, we both genuinely care for your daughter and are so very sorry this happened."

Hands balled into sparkly fists, Skye spun fully on him. Mascara and eyeliner had flooded out with her tears, sinking into the lines around her brown eyes. "Liar! She's the reason for this. She needs to admit to her crimes, admit about the cabal!"

Her hands flew to her hair, and she began pulling the pink strands. Her anguished sobs silenced the entire room. Brooks moved in and gently took control of her hands. She wrestled away and punched him. It didn't hurt. He was a lot bigger, and she had no follow through.

"Felicity had nothing to do with this," he told her gently. "She's a victim. Like your daughter. Don't let this bastard win by blaming her instead of him."

"He's right, Ms. Jukes." Meeks moved in with a directness that was somehow also laced with caring.

Brooks had no idea how long she'd been watching.

"It's just a coincidence Weaver was at Felicity's home. Felicity wasn't even there."

Skye's posture broke down as she sobbed and mumbled, "He shouldn't have hurt my baby. I'm a good mother. Not like the others."

Brooks pulled out a chair for her and Meeks guided her into it.

Meeks mouthed, "Thank you," to him and put her arm around Skye. She whispered words too low for Brooks to hear, but whatever she said had a calming effect. And Skye was obviously worn out.

Liam Forster strutted toward them. His smugness seemed out of place, even for him, and Brooks got that punch-him-in-the-face feeling again.

Felicity followed, her face and lips pale. Her bruised chin trembled. Her eyes were sunken and deeply sad. But she looked... determined, somehow.

"Ms. Jukes." Fee's kind voice wavered with emotion. "I'm so sorry. I want you to know I had nothing—"

Skye jumped from her seat, reaching over a

startled, kneeling Meeks, and slapped Fee across the face. The crack of sound silenced the entire station. "You're as wicked as your mother."

Brooks was on his feet again. Raising a staying hand, Fee cupped the bloom of red spearing the blackened bruises on her face. "With all due respect," she said, dropping her hand, "you know zero about my mother. And blaming her or me might make you feel better, but it's unfair and exactly what The Puppeteer wants. Don't let him manipulate you."

Skye tried to hit her again, but Meeks intercepted her this time.

"Come on, Fee," Liam whispered hotly. "Don't be so insensitive."

Leveling a rancorous glance at him, Fee said, "Fuck you, Liam," and walked out of the station, head held high.

Torn between wanting to echo Fee's point and wanting to punch Liam's face, Brooks stopped dead at Liam's expression. Face red. Lips thinned. Fee's words had punched him in the face. In front of all his colleagues.

Brooks followed her out.

## CHAPTER TWENTY-EIGHT

Fee woke to a darkened room. She took in details bit by confusing bit. Electronic lights dotted the darkness—clock, DVR, fire alarm. She was tucked under a crisp, white duvet lumpy with feather light goose down. Long drapes covered the only window, blocking the outside.

Oh. Right. The Hilton in Santa Fe.

She rolled over and pain flared. Everything hurt. Neck, arms, legs, hair follicles. Even her chest ached. *Weaver.*

Last night, in her exhaustion, it had been tempting to accept all of the guilt Liam and Skye threw at her, but she'd been able to see it for what it was, while it'd been happening. That was a big deal to her. But it didn't mean the whole thing didn't sting.

She pressed her fingers to her swollen jaw, blinking at the neon green numbers on the clock. 2:48 p.m. She'd only slept three hours. Maybe she should get up and find a cheaper hotel for tomorrow night. A place with a kitchen. Technically, she could go to Mom's. The police had cleared it.

No. Nope. Never. But she definitely couldn't afford to stay long at the Hilton...

Oh.... Yes, she could.

It broke through her like a lance punching

unexpectedly through her middle. A sharp and sudden pain, a sharp and dreadful realization.

She had plenty of money. *Mom's* money.

She reached over, grabbed one of the many white pillows, and shoved it up against her face before the sob could escape and startle Brooks, who was asleep on the couch in the outer room.

She hadn't cried in front of him. Didn't intend to. But the sobs wouldn't stop. They became louder.

She turned away from the door, tossed the suffocating pillow.

Strands of hair stuck across her sweaty, tear-drenched face. Hiccups shook her body. The bed shifted. A warm hand rested against her head.

"Querida."

She rolled toward him, pinned her forehead against his thigh and the edge of his boxer briefs. She sobbed all over his warm skin.

His hands stroked her hair and down her back.

He gathered her up without a word, slipped in beside her, and coaxed her head to his chest. He smelled like home. Like Brooks. Like the woods by the ocean.

His hand continued to rub tenderly down her back. Her muscles relaxed. Her mind quieted. The steady rhythm of his heart soothed her to sleep.

Fee woke up hours later with a heaviness between her legs. It took her a moment to realize she was rubbing her clit against the firm meat of Brooks' thigh. The glorious friction was intense and demanding.

"Fee." Her name came out as a moan on his lips.

Her brain unraveled one cell at a time. She looked

*Broken P*

up at him. And whatever he saw in her face had him rushing to claim her lips.

Electric. The opposite of gentle. Their kiss started hot and steamrolled into open mouths and probing tongues. Hands searched. Bodies throbbed. Glorious. Perfect. She hadn't been rocked with this level of heat in so long. Even before Liam… cheated. Cheater.

Her conscience prodded at her through the lust fog with that word, *cheater*.

*Hold on.* Crud. She eased away. "What about Nat?"

He grimaced. "I haven't gotten hold of her to break it off."

Closing her eyes, inhaling, she tried to calm the desire flooding her. The thick, heavy heat of his hard-on tried to compel her. Gah. This wasn't right. She remembered the pain of having someone cheat on her and she wouldn't do that to anyone else, no matter how casual the attachment.

She threw herself away from him and back against the bed with a growl.

*Must not think of his hard cock still throbbing in his boxer briefs.* Or that everything in her wanted to suck him right through that blue material. Damn. "I think everyone in this situation deserves better, Brooks." Even Nat, who Fee was pretty sure she hated right now. "Don't you?"

A very long pause. "Sí."

She needed a shower. A *cold* shower. "Going to shower." She kicked off the blankets and jumped out of bed.

Brooks inhaled sharply and looked away from the sight of her in only her shirt and thong.

Standing beside the bed, she fought the urge

crawl back in beside him. *No can do.* "I want to head to the hospital to see how Weaver is doing."

He glanced at the clock on the nightstand. "It's five a.m."

*Wow. They'd slept for twelve hours.*

He flung an arm over his eyes. "Go take your shower, querida. We'll get breakfast first."

It was dark with the drapes drawn, but she spotted an outfit, including underwear, on the chair. She picked them up. Tags still on. The right size. It was all such a blur. Maybe Meeks had bought them. No. Brooks had. Sometime between the police station and this room, he'd provided them for her. Just like he provided her safety and comfort.

Her resistance melted as her yearning intensified. Brooks not only made her feel desired, he made her feel something else she hadn't felt in a long time. Eight years to be exact.

Cherished.

She closed the door with a click and placed the clothes in the shelf cabinet under the sink. She took off her shirt and startled at her reflection in the mirror.

The skin under her right eye and cheek. Her chin was bruised. She had a scratch down her neck. The right side of her arm was raw. She twisted in the mirror. A huge bruise stretched from her shoulder to halfway down her back.

A cry bubbled from her lips. She pressed her shirt to her mouth, biting the fabric. Every day the hate got closer and closer. And more vicious.

Was this what she had to offer Brooks? A life of danger? A woman who drew down the fire? He deserved so much better.

That's why she'd sent him away the first time.

# CHAPTER TWENTY-NINE

Outside the cell store, with a clear view of Felicity speaking with a store associate, Brooks took the call from Natalie. Bad timing. If she'd called yesterday, he'd still be in bed with Fee, not out here lusting after her so hard that every glance brought on a hormonal assault. "Hola."

"Hola, guapo. I go camping for two weeks and come back to find you and Felicity Shields all over social media. Seems like you need a lifeline. Or a friend. How're you doing?"

The fact that neither of them had known the other was traveling pretty much summed up their relationship. Still, he was glad she knew where he was and who he was with. "Doing okay. I'm more worried about Fee. She's going through a lot since her mother's death."

"I heard. So crazy." She took a deep breath. "It's nice of you, and so like you, to put yourself out for her."

Sounded like she was fishing. Odd, since they'd always been so direct with each other. "I want to be here, Nat."

"Must be weird though. I mean, you're so different. Woodsy. Isolated."

"What's that mean?"

"Look, I'm better with direct."

"Go for it."

"You're not used to some of the crazy out there.

Isn't that why you moved here? To get away from all that? Don't get caught up in it again."

"Don't get caught up in it or her?"

She huffed a laugh. "Yeah. Both, I guess. I know you were once engaged to her, but I've read... She might not be who you think. She might've changed."

She had changed, but Natalie's suggestion seemed more sinister. "I wouldn't believe anything you read in the media, Nat."

"I'm not talking about the news. I'm talking about things from her friends on social media. Her boss. Co-workers. #FibbingFelicity is trending. They can't all be lying, Brooks."

That hashtag hit him in the gut. That same hashtag had trended after he'd left Fee. Fuck. He ducked his head, as if Fee could possibly hear him. "They *are* lying. Trust me on this."

"O... kay. Why do I feel like I insulted you?"

Because she had. Because he couldn't stand the idea that they were, once again, bashing Fee online with that fucking hashtag. "If you know and trust me, then trust what I'm telling you. Fee is nothing like what they say. I care deeply about her."

There was a long pause. "Brooks, her co-workers and boss are saying she's always been a loner, distant. And she's being accused of some pretty awful shit in the media. Like she's in some kind of killing cabal."

He watched Fee as she leaned toward an electronic pad that the clerk scrolled through. She was so lovely. His heart warmed as she brushed a strand of hair behind her ears. Fuck this. He was done half-assing this situation. "I'm in love with her. And I want to see if I can make this work."

A long pause. He cursed himself. He shouldn't

*Broken P*

have said that. It was an emotional outburst. And a slap to Nat.

"Whoa." Another long pause. "Does she love you?"

He was in it now. "I'm hoping for a one day."

Natalie let out a breath. "This isn't how I expected this call to go."

A moment of silence that indicated she was thinking. "You're a good man, Brooks. I guess if I weren't secretly in love with someone in Washington State, I'd be pretty bummed right now. Though, honestly, I will miss the no-holds-barred sex."

He squirmed as Fee turned to him in the store and held up a bright pink phone. He gave her a thumbs-up. "Pretty sure you won't have a problem warming your bed."

"True. I am damn hot."

There was an awkward moment of disentangling. That was the only way he could think of it.

"Thanks for telling me, Brooks. You're more of a gentleman than I am. In fact, since we're doing confessions, I hooked up with said crush when I was camping in Washington last week."

He understood by her tone the last was meant as a jab, but it honestly made him feel a whole lot better about all of this. "I'm happy for you, Nat."

"Well, it was just a hook-up, but thanks. My lovers tend to be shy about commitment."

*Ouch*. No way to soften that. And though they'd both agreed they didn't want serious, he still felt like a shit. Why had he confessed his love for Fee? "I wish you the best, Nat."

"You, too, Brooks. And if you find yourself with regrets, you know where to find me."

Before he could say another word, she hung up.

## CHAPTER THIRTY

Silver-pink cell in one hand, a bag of burner phones in the other, Fee slipped into the passenger seat of her car.

Tapping her new phone, she began to scroll through and make sure all her content had transferred.

She could feel Brooks' eyes on her as he backed out from the parking space. "You okay?"

Was she? She didn't look up but answered with the truth. "It's been a long time since I've had to deal with this kind of stuff, but the store clerk... he told me he wasn't comfortable selling me all those burner phones. He said... he didn't want to be a party to murder. I had to practically threaten a lawsuit."

He tapped the breaks, turned his head, put his arm across her seat, and shifted the car into reverse. "Fucker. I noticed the tension when I came inside."

She looked up, behind, and then back at him. "Wait. No. I don't need you to defend my honor, Brooks. If you start that again, we'll wind up where we were eight years ago."

He hit the brakes. They stared at each other. The silence yanked forward the two people from the past who'd once had this argument over and over again.

She waited for him to tell her it was his job to protect her. She waited for the fight.

"You're right," he said. "Sorry."

A smile broke across her face. "Really?"

He winked at her. "Yep."

"Pretty easygoing considering you're in the car with an axe murderer."

He snorted and put the car in DRIVE, coasted to the light, then pulled onto the street. He reached for his sunglasses on the dash and put them on. So sexy she wanted to crawl into his lap.

He looked at her. "That clerk was an idiota. Why would an axe murderer need so many burner phones?"

She snorted. "To keep in touch with my cabal of axe murderers, obviously."

Dark humor, but they laughed like it was the funniest thing ever. A release of tension. It sure was a lot different from the fights they used to get into.

Warmth bloomed inside her. This relationship with him… it was as hot as it had been sexually, and so much better emotionally. They'd grown up. Their separate experiences had somehow made them understand each other better and appreciate more what they'd had.

"I think I know why the clerk was acting that way."

"You do?" Uh oh. Couldn't be good. He was squeezing the steering wheel so tightly.

He pulled to a stop at a light. "I spoke with Nat while you were in the store."

"Your friend-with-benefits?"

"Not anymore. I ended things with her."

She didn't want to know but had to ask. "Was she okay?"

He cringed. "You were right. I hurt her."

That stung. And not for the reason she *should* feel

bad. Not because this woman had been hurt. Partly that, but mostly because Natalie hurt because she would miss Brooks. And she would miss Brooks because she'd laughed with him, drank with him, eaten with him, and slept with him. "What does talking to her have to do with the clerk's reaction to me?"

"She told me the hashtag #FibbingFelicity is trending."

Eight years later and her cheeks still heated. They'd given her that nickname after she'd called her mom during that CNN interview. Stories erupted that she'd done it to make her mom look sympathetic. That she was in cahoots with her.

The brutal attacks and manipulating photos came every day after that. The mantra *Fibbing Felicity* became so widespread, she couldn't find a job. It was pretty much the worst time of her life. Losing him and enduring that ridicule and abuse. She'd never felt so worthless.

"We've never talked about it. I guessed that you'd seen…" Ignoring the thoroughbred of doubt galloping around her brain, she dared to ask him that long-held fear. "Did you think it was all a setup? The call?"

"Never."

Not even a moment's hesitation. A pleased glow slid warmly down to her stomach. It mattered. Even eight years later, it mattered.

He let out a breath so long she had to admire the capacity of his lungs. "I knew…" He paused. "I *guessed* what had happened. It was the same day."

The same day she'd called off the wedding. The worst day of her life. A day that had rolled into another worse day. And another.

*Broken P*

The light turned green. He drove forward. Once again, the car grew silent. The past kept springing up to sit between them. All that pain and anger. Hurt and betrayal. But, now, there was something else, too. Joy. Being understood and accepted. He'd known. Even when the world didn't, he had.

"That explains it," she said. "He reminded me of how people used to treat me when Mom was on trial. Remember?"

"Sí. Claro. As if a young woman fresh out of college might know something about the assassination of a world leader."

She tapped into her email. Best to see the blowback for herself. "I hated that they dragged you and your family into it. I should've sued when that awful photo of you and your brother's wife went viral as *Brooks cheats on Felicity*."

At the edges of his sunglasses, she could see the lines around his eyes deepen as he cringed. "My brother was so pissed. The last thing Janelle needed at that time was more stress."

Janelle, who'd gone through a serious cancer scare the year before, had been pregnant at the time. The memory soured in her mouth. Fee twisted her hands in her lap. "That's one of the reasons I'd decided to postpone the wedding. I'd hoped the critics would be less interested in you and your family."

Brooks reached over and squeezed her hand. "Querida."

Warmth shot up her arm.

"It didn't get easier for you, Fee."

It hadn't; the attacks got worse. She'd been so ashamed. Every time she read another disparaging headline, she wanted to crawl in a hole. "True, but it taught me a lot. You can live with people hating you as long as you don't turn that hatred on yourself. Self-hatred is the real killer. After you'd left and all that started, it was hard not to hate myself. Not to think I deserved..."

He grunted. "I'm so sorry, Fee. It took me a long time to realize I'd been blaming you for something that was equally my fault. Maybe even more so."

A tremor of hope and longing eased open a long-closed door in her heart. Even though she no longer blamed herself, it mattered that Brooks had apologized. She hugged tightly that feeling of release. And yet... things were only going to get worse for her. "My boss, Helen, fired me."

He blinked. Accelerating forward from the green. "She fired you? When?"

"Today. I just opened her email." She read part of it to him: "*Sorry to do this via email. Couldn't reach you. Our board has concluded the firm can no longer weather the impact of your scandals.*"

"Gilipollas." He glanced at the phone in her hand. "This is more than just rumors. This is manufactured hate, fear, and danger. You were right when you told Meeks this guy is a terrorist."

She put her phone down. "Yeah. It's also a warning."

"¿Qué?"

"Before Kelly Smith was taken, she was trending on social media. Before Weaver was taken, a negative hashtag about her was trending on social media. Now, I'm trending."

He tensed. "Sounds like you have a theory. Care to explain?"

"Okay. But brace yourself."

## CHAPTER THIRTY-ONE

Turning into the hospital parking lot, Brooks coasted to a stop before the red-and-white arm of the parking gate. Outside the main entrance to the hospital, people stood waving signs of love and support for Skye and Weaver. He'd have to take Fee in through a different entrance. Too much bullshit about her out there right now.

He couldn't keep the anger from flooding his veins. He ground his teeth. The yellow ticket dispenser spit out a rectangular white strip of paper with a *click* and a *tick*. The gate rose. He tucked the ticket into a silver clip on the car's visor and drove forward.

"Let me get this straight. Your name is trending online. And you've noticed a pattern wherein the woman whose name is trending is the next to be killed? Are you sure? Because Lachlan mentioned Ali thinks TP is always trying to direct the public eye by picking recognizable victims. Kelly and Weaver were both very public. And it seems like having your victim trend on social media before you kill her would be an easy giveaway to the feds."

"I'm pretty sure, but Ali could be right. This could be the way he controls the narrative like the way he dreams of controlling women."

He was succeeding. He heard the questions the

reporter at the cemetery asked and saw the way Skye had attacked Fee. "And if you're right?"

"If I'm right... we need to pay attention. Right now, his marketing strategy is zeroing in on me. We can see that. But when he shifts focus to one of the other women, I think we can assume he plans to make his move on me."

He ground his teeth 'til he heard something pop. *Coño.* "We need to tell the others."

"Yeah. But I want to make sure I'm right. I messed up before. Meeks told me she doesn't think my theory that TP and The Great One are the same guy is right."

"She doesn't? She thinks they're two—"

A fist slamming with a *Bang!* against the hood of the car jerked them from their conversation.

A bearded man—white, early forties, with a ponytail—stood by the front of the car, staring at Fee.

Brooks reached for the gun at his waist.

The man brought a heavy fist down onto the hood of Fee's car again. "'Fess up so people stop dying, you crazy bitch."

Fuck the gun. Brooks started to get out.

Without even glancing his way, Fee put a hand on him, stopped him. "Let me do this."

*Coño.* "Careful."

Sliding down the window, she told the man, "Would you like me to explain why you should stop believing every stupid lie you read?"

Ponytail stepped off the strip of grass and onto the blacktop. "Sure. Come on out and explain it."

Before he could stop her, Fee was out of the car. She went toe-to-toe with Ponytail. "First, I'm not part

*Broken P*

of some secret cabal. I don't have that kind of energy. Or hate. And neither did my mom—"

"If that bitch is your proof, stop right now." Ponytail crowded her, fury and intent oozing from every pore.

Brooks jumped out and moved around the car. "Get the fuck out of here."

The man's gaze swung to Brooks, but his gaze hardened. He lifted a hand. Guy wasn't trying to gesticulate or wave Fee off; he wanted violence.

Brooks was on him like a hawk on a rabbit, grabbing his fingers and yanking them down until they touched his shoulder blade.

Though bigger and slightly taller, he gave way to the pressure and his knees buckled.

Brooks held his head down and kneed him in the face. The crack was instant, brutal, and clean. He shoved him to the ground. *Slap.* "I said, get the fuck out of here."

Ponytail caught himself on his palms. There was a moment of stillness.

Brooks waited, wanting the guy to come at him again.

The man tottered to his feet and ran off.

Trembling with rage, Brooks gave way when Fee wrapped her arms around him. She put her head on his chest. "Thanks for the assist. I know how to protect myself, but all that went out the window when that guy raised his hand."

He squeezed her tight. "There was a time when I hadn't been there, but no more. From now on, I have your back. Got it?"

"Brooks—"

"There they are!"

Brooks spun. The man who'd harassed Fee now led three other men and two women. They carried signs he'd assumed were supportive of Weaver and Skye, but, on closer inspection, he saw they were laced with crazy conspiracies and calls to, "Arrest the bitch!"

The flash of rage blinded him. These idiots needed an old-fashioned ass-kicking. He was just the man for the job.

## CHAPTER THIRTY-TWO

She'd done it. Fee had done the one thing she'd told herself from the beginning she wasn't going to do. She'd dragged Brooks back into her crazy life. The mob of people walked forward with the confident swagger of the living dead.

She pulled his arm.

Brooks turned to her. "Get in the car, Fee."

Oh, hell no. Assisting her when she needed him was one thing, dismissing her something else.

Darting back to the car, she opened her glove compartment and took out a weapon she'd been training with since she was a teen.

Brooks stood in front of the car, facing the people walking across the lot.

Breathing hard, hands shaking, Fee aimed the Glock at the grass and pulled the trigger. The recoil traveled up her arms and the concussive sound broke against her ears, muffling noise.

Even Brooks ducked.

One of the women threw herself to the ground. One of the mob-men jumped on top of the lady as if to protect her. The rest of the mob scrambled.

Eyes wide, Brooks spun on her.

Fee flicked her head toward the car. "Time to go."

His eyebrows rose to his hairline.

She pointed the gun at the ground again.

He rolled his eyes. A small smile played at the corner of his mouth. He put up both his hands, gestured to her side of the car. "Sí. Vamanos."

Fee jumped into the passenger seat just as one of the men regained his feet. Brooks pulled out of the parking space, tires squealing. A sign came flying toward them, sliding across the hood as he accelerated away. Then—gunshot. A *thunk* in the side of the car. Brooks hit the gas and didn't stop until they were nearly at the exit.

Something close to hysteria bubbled up from Fee's gut. She shoved her gun back into the glove compartment. The aroma of recently discharged gun powder filled the car. "I can't believe I did that. I don't' randomly shoot. I was taught better."

Her mother had insisted she know how to protect herself. And one of the Secret Service men who'd guarded her at the time had been happy to help.

Lee had taken her to the shooting range on his days off. At fifteen, she hadn't taken it seriously, but Lee had taught her to take it seriously. A nice guy, but he'd never smiled while holding a gun, never smiled while instructing her. He'd smiled the moment they'd gotten back outside. To this day, Fee never smiled while holding a gun. It wasn't a joke; it was a deadly weapon that required deadly focus.

"It was a scary situation. I can read a man pretty well and Ponytail wasn't about yelling at you. He wanted violence. That and the terrifying hell you've been living through these past few weeks, I'd say your reaction was understandable."

"I can't do this. You have to go back to Canada. I can't be responsible for you getting hurt."

"And if I go home, you'll take Meeks up on her offer of protection?"

She repressed a shudder at the idea. She'd spent a huge portion of her childhood guarded by Secret Service. Eight years. And then by private security when her mother ran for president. The thought of going back to that kind of watched existence made her crazy. "I might."

"You're lying."

With a grimace, she shifted in her seat.

"I have an idea. An idea that terrifies me to be honest. But what just happened... I can't keep you safe here, Fee."

Her phone began to buzz. She glanced at the screen.

Flor texted: *I know the truth. And they're the liars.*

Heat rose up her throat and started a fire there. She managed, "What idea?"

"We leave here and do a serious and full surveillance detection route. I have my plane flown to a different airport. We go there and take it to the cabin. Once there, we take two days to rest and recover. On the third day, we coordinate with a group of security professionals. Men who are already scheduled to be out there to train. We organize an ambush. Then we send word to TP to let him know where we are and wait."

"You're saying you want to lure him out to the cabin, use the men who are scheduled to train as our protection, and trap him?"

"And whoever else he might bring."

"It's too dangerous."

He shook his head. "Fee, who's a safer bet—me and a group of professionals with home field advantage or me and you?"

There was something so tempting about this reckless plan. The biggest temptation was to do something—*really* do something—to keep her list-sisters safe. "These trainees... They'd do that?"

"Before any of this happened, I was scheduled to put Jack Tate and six of his men through high-intensity training next week. Assuming The Puppeteer comes, this would be as about as high-intensity as you could get. And Jack is looking to redeem his reputation as well as get payback. It would take next to nothing to convince him."

"What about your family? I don't want to endanger them."

"We wouldn't. They aren't close. I live on that plot of land we looked at years ago. The one way up on the uninhabited northern part of the island. My family has to use a boat or a seaplane to get there. Unless they insist, I wouldn't ask them to take part."

He lived on the land they'd looked at together? Now why did that hurt and feel fantastic all at the same time? But facing his family in Canada terrified her nearly as much as the idea of facing The Puppeteer. "Your family doesn't hate me? I—"

"What? No. They love you. They would've closed up shop and come to the funeral if I hadn't asked them to stay. I figured it would be enough to deal with just me."

She lowered her chin. She liked dealing with just him. "I don't feel right about it."

They drove in silence as it started to rain, the

drops scattering across the windshield like her thoughts. She couldn't run away to Canada... Could she?

Brooks put on the wipers. "After what happened, you know this is the best idea. Either that or we take Meeks up on her offer and go into witness protection. I don't know about you, but I'd much rather be holed up in a picturesque cabin, secured through our own devices than in a hotel room with the feds."

He drove along. The wipers *cha-whooshed, cha-whooshed* into the silence.

They would be safer in Canada. Plus, she couldn't risk another incident like the one back at the hospital. Since she no longer had a job, there wasn't a lot holding her here. *Thanks, Helen.* "I'd have to call the others on the list. And my mom's lawyer."

"Don't tell any of them where you're going. And not Meeks either."

She wouldn't have. Certainly not Meeks. She didn't need the headache.

"What about phones? Can't we be tracked?"

"I'll get us a Faraday bag; it blocks cell signals. We'll take out the phones when we're ready."

"Seems like you might have been thinking about this idea a bit."

"Sí."

Maybe this wasn't such a good idea. She'd be stuck in the wilderness with Brooks Delgado. A fact that made her hyperventilate. And salivate. Yes. This was a terrible idea. But it could save lives and end this nightmare.

"Okay."

## CHAPTER THIRTY-THREE

Ed walked the hospital corridor, disgusted and uneasy. How could people work in this environment? All the sickness, weakness, injury, and despair. Gut-churning.

Keeping people alive was a messy business. More so than killing them. Especially when done incorrectly. Embarrassing. Humiliating. Weaver was practically a child. God damn it.

This couldn't be the thing that ended years of trying to win over The Great One. Thinking of all that had gone into this, all the planning... It was painful.

Since the moment The Great One's writings had crossed over from being an obsession to being a... calling... vocation... religion... Whatever this awakening was termed, every waking hour since then had been spent reading the incredible, mind-shifting writings of this man and, alternatively, obsessively trying to discover his identity.

Needn't have bothered trying to discover the impossible. But all that research left a trail, a purposeful trail that had the desired result. The Great One himself reached out. He'd sent a list of names and two words: *Impress me*.

But not just that. He also sent enough bitcoin to change everything. To take MOTO from Friday-night fringe element to a functioning band of mercenaries.

*Broken P*

But the money didn't matter as much as the words in that first communication between them. And the names. Considering the man's secrecy, it was an incredible gift. A clue.

But, also, a problem. Three of the women on the list were impossible to get to. One was in Iran. One was in a high-security loony bin for the criminally insane. One had vanished after stealing money from Puerto Rico. The solution? Lure them out by going after their daughters. Add a few extra women to the list to confuse investigators and to keep them hopping.

*Impress me.* Not easy to do. But the plans were finally in action and meeting expectations.

Except for Weaver. There could be no errors when the stakes were this high. That The Great One stood out as a man of immense and unquestioned power could be understood by any simpleton who read his writings. That The Great One sought power on a scale heretofore unachieved by any human was discernible only to those with the acumen of the deeply ambitious. They were cut from the same cloth.

When someone with global power and reach pointed to your ass sitting on the bench and shouted with confidence, "Get in there, son!" it elevated every moment of life. Every moment before and after the event. It made it all worth it.

What choice was there but to pick up the ball and win the game? All had been going according to plan, until the idiot MeTooFu soiled that perfection by allowing Weaver to live.

Why get cute with the setup? How many times had they gone over the kill? How many times were the men told to think of it as a PR campaign with a lot of blood? For fuck's sake. Dorothy Shields' educational support of Weaver was enough to tie Felicity to the crime. Enough to feed the conspiracy hawks online. Taking the body to her home? It was too much. And too soon.

MeTooFu was so consumed by his own righteous fury, he'd lost his mind. By failing to kill Weaver, he'd exposed the group to a risk that threatened the entire long-range plan.

Once recovered, Weaver would describe the man who'd tried to kill her. Worse, the snuff video showed the guy had been a talker. A real Austin Powers villain, spilling his plan along with his seed.

Infuriating. And what excuse had the man given when he'd met his own end? *I didn't have enough time. She should have died.*

His excuses had ended when he'd realized there was nothing left to say. The end had been unquestionable. The man had been a noble creature. No blubbering. It was a good death. A death worthy of a soldier.

No one in the group would find that video entertaining. No one would jerk off to it. But they'd watch. And learn.

Walking the syringe of dioxin inside the ICU ward was a volatile risk, but the safest way to eliminate the threat Weaver posed. It would take hours for the slow drip of chemical byproducts to finish her.

Of course, there were easier poisons, mists, and vapors that could trigger fast-acting reactions like an apparent heart attack or organ failure, but the risk of being associated with the deed since cameras were everywhere was too great.

This would be a merciful death. Not so for that whiny bitch, Felicity Shields. She thought she'd escaped.

Not at all. The entire plan hinged on her death. She couldn't contemplate all the steps that had gone into getting her to Canada. Or the army that would defeat her there. The Great One's ultimate plan for global balance would unfold.

*First things first.*

A curt nod to the guard at Weaver's door. If the man was surprised to see someone here this early, he didn't show it. The guard opened the door to Weaver's room and held it open with a respectful nod.

So very accommodating.

# CHAPTER THIRTY-FOUR

Flying back to Canada in his single-engine plane took over eight hours and required multiple stops for fuel. If that'd been the worst of it, it would've been fine. But it was also a bit rocky. Enough so that Brooks had noticed Fee clutching her hands. He found turbulence fun, but, for her, he did his best to smooth out the ride.

By five a.m. when they entered Canadian airspace, she'd calmed down and he was downright happy. Now, lights twinkled in small patches below, but it was the rising sun that allowed the stretch of small islands thick with forests and mazes of winding waterways to be seen.

Her voice clear in his headset, Fee said, "It's so lovely here."

"Thanks. I think so."

He radioed ahead, apprising the controller of his final approach. He descended, the yellow lights lining the small runway of Port Hardy, the northernmost settlement on the island, seemed like a magic carpet leading him back to a life much simpler than the one they'd left.

#

Exiting the airport, Brooks drove through town until he reached a gravel logging road. Light streamed through the branches of the huge fir trees. For long miles, he guided his car around the numerous holes and dips in the dirt and gave plenty of room to the large logging trucks. It was their road, after all.

"Fee, this is…" He looked at her and trailed off. She'd fallen asleep, her head turned toward him, her beautiful features relaxed and untroubled.

Heat and urgency thrummed along his skin. As foolish as it was to love her, to open himself to the possibility of having her again, he wasn't one to delude himself.

Él estaba todo adentro. All in. It didn't matter if he got hurt again. Didn't matter if she rejected him. He was willing to risk that pain, risk that rejection, but he wouldn't walk away again. His ego had made him leave before. The ego of a man nearly a decade younger. So much foolish pride.

He was a fool no longer.

Turning from the logging road to the two-mile private road it had taken him months to clear and build, euphoria sped up his heart.

Fee groaned in her sleep and, without thinking, he dropped his hand into hers, resting palm up on the center console. Her fingers intertwined with his. And though it felt all kinds of wrong to have such joy in the middle of all this tragedy, it wasn't something he could control.

They pulled up to the cabin with a crunch of gravel under the tires. The cabin had never looked so good. The wide steps leading to the wide front porch, the wooden rockers, and the hand carved front door welcomed him home.

He'd designed and built this place with Felicity in mind. Of course, it had taken him years to admit that to himself. One day, he'd just stood back and looked at it—long after he'd gotten over his anger—and had seen the truth. This was a home Fee would love.

Now, here she was. He caressed her soft, warm cheek. "We're here."

She sat up, blinking. Confusion turned to a gasp, her eyes springing wide. "Oh, Brooks. It's..." she trailed off. "This is where I pictured you. When I was broken-hearted. When I regretted letting you go. I pictured you here and happy. That made it easier."

The tag team of exultation and anguish camped out over his vocal cords. He wasn't sure he could speak, but he needed to say it. Needed her to hear it.

He wrestled control back. "You saved me. You were right. I was going down a rabbit hole. If I'd been trapped in that hate, I would've never found a way to this life. Thank you."

She wiped away a tear. "Then it was worth it."

They locked gazes. The rawness of this moment, the honesty, blew him away. He had one more declaration to make. "Now, it's my turn to help you. Take a couple days. Get comfortable. Relax. Grieve. After that, we get to work."

Averting her eyes, she told him, "Thanks, Brooks."

She gestured at the looming trees and dense forest. "I'd forgotten how isolated this land is. I'd assumed it was less so when you mentioned the roads."

Proof she'd slept soundly through those *roads*. "Boat or seaplane is the easiest way into or out of here. This place didn't even have a road up here until I built it."

"You built the road? What about electricity? What about Internet? How do you heat this place? I see satellite and solar panels..."

*Broken P*

He laughed. "Don't get me started on the propane, solar, geothermal, satellite, wind, and water that runs this place. Or what happens when all those things fail."

"Okay. I'll wait 'til we're inside."

He couldn't wait to show her the inside. Would she recognize their shared vision?

# CHAPTER THIRTY-FIVE

Chills rolled down Fee's spine as she stepped into Brooks' beautiful cabin. It was incredible. The open floor plan, vaulted ceiling, the glass chandelier hanging from wooden rafters, the triangular wall of windows looking out onto the inlet and an upward slope of forest... This was the home they'd talked about building all those years ago.

Almost in a daze, she passed the colorful kitchen and the boldly tiled breakfast bar. The cabin was warm and smelled of cinnamon and cedar.

There was a family-sized dining table and a spectacular great room. A hearth fireplace with—she laughed as she noticed her drunken painting over the hearth. It made no sense there. It didn't match the Southwestern decor and the colorful hand-woven rug over lightly stained wood flooring, but he'd placed chunky candles around it, softening its appearance.

A giddy sense of homecoming propelling her, she skirted two tan leather chairs and a dark leather couch. She couldn't imagine how difficult it must've been to get every single piece up here. Which explained why the coffee table seemed to be hewn from the trunk of a tree. She didn't need to ask who'd made the spectacular piece. She could see the exacting skill of Brooks' hands and his creative mind in it.

At the triangular wall of gleaming windows, she took in the inlet, dock, and forest surrounding them. The beauty stretched her awareness, dragged it from her body so that her senses absorbed a thousand nuances—the angle of each tree, the water lapping shoreline, the birds flitting through sky, ocean breeze, salt and sea, warming sun, and thrumming energy.

"This has to be the most picturesque place on earth."

Everything seemed enhanced by the slight elevation of the cabin that sloped gently toward the inlet. A T-shaped dock stretched left and right along the waterline, and straight out into the blue water.

So many places to dock boats and kayaks. And that was exactly what he'd done.

A huge kayak stand stood along the banks, filled with at least a dozen kayaks, and two good-sized fishing boats were tethered to the left side of the dock, right next to the...

"You have a *seaplane*?" She looked at him.

"Mmm." He stood between the bags he'd brought in, smiling and rubbing the center of his chest. "I'll give you a flying tour once you're settled."

"It'll only take me a minute to get settled." She moved to get her bag.

He grinned and suddenly looked all boy. "You're ready to take to the skies with me again?"

"Yep. I want to see it all."

The sound of a boat had him looking over her toward the inlet. "Sounds like Papí's here."

A stab of fear and pain. "I thought you said... Brooks, I don't want your family involved in our plan. It's... it's not right."

"I never said I wouldn't involve them. Papí and Carey are trained professionals. And they'd never forgive me if I tried to exclude them. Not that I could since they're part of the business. I had to tell them."

"But—"

"Don't freak out. We have time to go over all the plans. Time to make sure you're completely comfortable with everything. For now, you're safe here. There's no easy way in. We've already put our phones into the Faraday bag. I turned off the internet, so we stay offline. Later, I'll set up cameras along the woods and on the road."

They were really doing this, luring a serial killer into the woods. Not the smartest plan. But they had backup. Jack Tate had been a "Fuck yeah" when Brooks asked if he wanted to help out. Still... "I want to be part of the plan. Fully part."

"Claro." He waved toward the back. "Come say hi to Papí."

She wanted to, but... "Oh my God. You still have a bladder of steel. Bathroom?"

"Sorry. Through that door."

"Thanks. Out in a sec."

He turned and left. She walked toward the bathroom, running her hand across her forehead. Maybe, she'd be out in two seconds. She needed a breather before she faced Rafael.

## CHAPTER THIRTY-SIX

Squinting at the late morning sun and what promised to be a beautiful day, Brooks quick-footed it down the stairs to the dock. His father pulled up in one of the company boats—a tricked-out Coast Guard Defiant, its steel pilothouse lined with tinted windows. Bad as fuck.

The dock creaked under him as he walked toward the open spot the boat glided into as Papí cut the engine. Hooking a hand around the grab handle, Brooks jumped onto the non-skid deck. He threw the dock line down, and jumped back to tie the line to the cleat hitch.

All the while, his mind mulled over Fee. He wanted to show her every bit of this place. Wanted to show her the trails, the waterways, the waterfalls, and caves. He wanted to take her climbing—

Had to keep a level head, though. Like his mother always said, "You can send the invite, but you can't write the reply."

Letting out a breath, he finished the figure eight and tightened it down. Papí appeared with a wave. A minute later, a white blur jumped from the boat. The German shepherd mix slammed into him, nearly knocking him on his ass. He managed to hold onto the muscular, wriggling, licking beast until the gray

Sappho, a Malamute mixed with wolf, took him out with her large, powerful one-hundred-seventy pounds.

"¿Qué te dije?" Rafael, his papí, jumped from the boat with a cold pack slung over his shoulder. "Too much dog for one man."

Though his father had told him the same thing time and again, Brooks only laughed harder. He liked *too much dog*.

His father offered him a hand, yanked him to his feet, and hugged him fiercely.

At 6'1", Brooks was not a small guy, but Papí—ex-Special Forces, four inches taller, and still lean and mean—was a giant.

Papí released him with a smile. "I spoke with Jack this morning. We've come up with a solid plan based on the hostage rescue scenario. He'll be arriving in a couple days to make it happen."

Brooks dropped his gaze. "Are you sure you and Carey want in on this? It's—"

"If you're suggesting looking after Fee isn't a priority for me and Carey, I will have to ask you, very seriously, if you've lost all respect for us."

Heat pricked up Brooks' neck. He was an idiot. This was the man who'd taught him about self-defense and security. Carey had served in the military with his wife, Janelle. "Lo siento, Papí. Send me the details?"

"Comprendo, mijo. We'll catch this cabrón."

Sappho's sudden growl sounded like the threat it was. She was a fierce warrior, one of the biggest mixed breeds he'd ever seen. She'd chased more than one grizzly from her territory. At the end of the dock, Fee froze.

"Sappho, stay," he said, with the clear, unequivocal voice that'd set her at ease. "She's a friend."

*Broken P*

Following Sappho's example, the blue-eyed Blanco watched Fee intently, but held back at Brooks' command.

To her credit, Fee didn't bound over and try to make friends with them. Perhaps she understood instinctively that these weren't those kinds of dogs. They were protection. They were well-trained, here to offer the security he needed against wolves and grizzlies and sometimes even two-legged predators.

Brooks motioned to her. "You can come down. Let them smell you. The bigger dog is Sappho. Let her go first. The smaller, male dog, is Blanco."

She grinned at him, walking forward cautiously with a wave to Papí. "You named the white dog Blanco? How original."

He laughed. "Smart ass."

She held out her hand, balled into a fist. After they'd smelled their fill, he released them with a whistle. Their caution dissolved. Both dogs wagged their excited-to-meet-you dance.

Well-trained and protective, his dogs were still fury bundles of love.

Fee petted them, accepting their affection with laughter. "Good dogs. So beautiful."

Papí put a hand on Brooks' shoulder because, in addition to being the biggest, baddest man in the woods, he was also extremely empathetic.

"Too much for one man," Papí whispered.

Brooks could only nod. Joy had a stranglehold on his speech.

"I've got this." Papí slung off his cold pack and handed it to Brooks. "¡Mi hermosa hija, you have come home!"

Fee looked up from the dogs and spread out her arms. "Rafael!"

Chills goose-bumped down Brooks' arms as his father swung Fee up and twirled her around with the dogs jumping here and there in celebration. *Ay, Díos.* Not helping. He could not take a full breath.

His father put her down and wiped the tears from his eyes and then from hers. "Mi hermosa hija, lo siento mucho. Your mother was a remarkable woman."

"Gracias, Rafael. Mom loved you." Fee looked at Brooks. "All of you."

"Okay, you two." Brooks waved his hand as if he could sweep away the debris of his emotion. "I'm seconds from crying here."

Papí grabbed him in a one-armed hug, then kissed him on his head. "A big baby, this one."

Fee laughed. "Total softie."

Papí let him go and headed inside with Fee. As if no time had passed, they fell into talking of life and loss. Thankfully, Papí respected Brooks' earlier request to avoid tactless topics, like the wounds on Fee's face, the fact that they were luring a killer up here, or how dangerous all of it was.

Not all reunions and warmth. But he'd promised her two days. And, *Díos le ayude*, he was going to give her that.

"Patrol," he said, adding the two-fingered whistle telling the dogs to do one broad circle and come back. He wanted them close.

They tore around the house and took off into the woods.

## CHAPTER THIRTY-SEVEN

Was it weird that Fee had already grown comfortable at Brooks' cabin? Maybe. She didn't care. She sat on the barstool, elbows on the colorful tiles, talking to Rafael as he moved about the kitchen. "I could help," she offered again.

"No." He waved a hand in dismissal. "You are our guest."

He reached into a cabinet and pulled out a large frying pan and, from a bag sporting the company logo, took out all the fixings for a traditional Spanish omelet.

He directed Brooks, "After you put everything away, start the potatoes."

"Sí, Papí."

She should be starving, but she really wasn't. She should be tired because they'd flown a good part of the night to get here, but she wasn't that either. Maybe it was seeing Papí again.

Who was she kidding? She was hyper-aware of Brooks' every movement as he emptied the rest of the cold pack. The lean lines of his body under his Henley. The smooth way he glided into action. Phew, it was hot in here.

Brooks slipped a jar of what Fee recognized as Papí's homemade sofrito into the fridge. Yum—and not just the sofrito. He then moved to place a glass pan filled with layers of uncooked empanadas in the freezer.

Pushing his wavy salt-and-pepper hair from his gray eyes, Papí pointed. "En la nevera."

Brooks changed destination and put them in the fridge to defrost. "I was going to save them."

"And what would you feed Fee tonight? A can of soup?" Rafael pointed at the fridge, declaring, "Más vacio que el corazón del diablo."

Fee laughed at his pronouncement, *Emptier than the devil's heart.*

Brooks shook his head, peeling potatoes into a silver compost pail. "There's meat in the freezer. And provisions in—"

"Tsk." Papí poured some oil into the pan and pulled out a cutting board. "Mami and I will come by tomorrow night with supplies. Write a list." He began cutting onions and peppers. "We'll make something fresh for you tomorrow. We'll invite your siblings."

Brooks' gaze darted to her, then snapped away. "Give us a couple days before you bring the family."

"We won't bother you."

Oh boy. As much as she'd missed Brooks' family, the idea of seeing them again made her belly shrink to the size of grape. Especially seeing Soledad, Brooks' mother.

Brooks tried again. "Papí—"

"Fee needs familia now," Papí said.

*Family.* Realization locked her jaw shut. Tears brimmed in her eyes.

Brooks glanced at her and moved a potato onto the cutting board. "Papí, *por favor*—"

"And Mami has gems for Fee. She says they ward off evil."

"What?" Unexpected humor tore forward and squelched her distress. She couldn't help the startled laugh. "Soledad? The geologist? Thinks gems ward off evil?"

Papí pointed the cutting knife at her. "She's expanded her horizons into crystal healing."

He wasn't laughing. But Soledad was a no-nonsense geologist who'd grown up in Puerto Rico and had learned the love of geology from her geologist father—who'd worked at the University of Puerto Rico. After she'd gotten her own geology degree, she'd gone on to work for one of the biggest oil companies in the world. Not exactly your typical crystal healer.

A few years later, the research vessel she'd been on had been hijacked. That's how she'd met Rafael. He'd been part of a joint Canadian and U.S. Special Forces task force that had rescued her. Theirs was a romance made for movies and Fee had always thought them the perfect couple.

She looked at Brooks "Really?"

He shrugged and nodded.

Okay then. "What inspired this change?"

Papí started to add a layer of thinly sliced potatoes to the heated pan. "When we first opened the store, she set a section apart to share her love of geology. She'd envisioned teaching people about the Mohs scale, where to dig, and selling hammers, picks, chisels, and collection bags."

Although she had no idea what the Mohs scale was, she nodded for him to continue.

"Pero, people don't want to know about the Earth's mineral makeup. Gente quiere saber the gems' spiritual properties. So, after many years of learning the ins and outs of geology, she turned to the study of the spiritual aspects of gems."

Speechless, she again looked at Brooks for continued confirmation.

Drying his hand on a dishtowel, he said, "She's doing readings now."

"Soledad does readings? Spiritual readings?"

"Verdad. We would not lie to you." Papí added peppers and onions to the dish. "She is very accurate. And believes utterly in what she says."

Brooks grinned, leaning against the counter, long legs stretched out in front of him, his arms crossed.

Dear God. That kind of sexy should be registered as a lethal weapon. Or come with a warning label. *Warning: Do not stare directly at the gorgeous man. Brain will stop operating.*

She blinked away randy images. "Do you guys believe her?"

"Sí." Rafael beat the eggs. "She has a gift. And such insight."

Brooks crossed to the breakfast bar, put his elbow on the counter, leaned toward her. The natural scent of him, the woods and ocean, as compelling as the sun on a cold day, made her inhale.

"I'm not convinced," he said.

"Why not?"

Papí grunted. "She told him that he would marry an old flame and have two children."

"Ay, Díos, Papí."

The kitchen descended into silence. Only the

scrape of the whisk as Papí turned over the eggs in the bowl made any noise.

Fee's face heated like it was too close to the frying pan. "Well," she said. "If anyone can tell my future from stones, I believe Soledad can."

"Bueno." Papí said. "We'll come by tomorrow night. Everyone will be so excited to see you again. I'll text Mami now."

"Papí..."

"Nothing specific. Nothing that mentions you. She'll know anyway."

Brooks opened his mouth to argue again.

Oh boy. He'd stuck up for her enough. This was her job. She'd explain to Rafael that it was too dangerous. That she didn't think it would be smart. That...

She moved to stop Brooks by placing her hand over his. A flush of heat. Oh. He had the best hands.

A surge of need suffused her. She closed her eyes to hide it. *Seriously, it's just a hand. Get control, woman.*

She opened her eyes to find him staring at her lips.

He smiled... and she lost her voice.

"It's all settled," Papí said. "I texted Mami to let her know."

And, great, now she had a dinner date with Brooks' mother to have her fortune read.

## CHAPTER THIRTY-EIGHT

Stepping from the shower, Fee took stock of her bruises in the half-fogged mirror. She turned her shoulder. They seemed slightly better. Yellow was better, right? With a sigh, she grabbed a towel from the rack, dusted it over herself, then wrapped it around her head.

Bruises or not, it had been a great day. After Rafael left, she laid about as Brooks made her tea and snacks, had suggested a book for her to read, chatted with her, laughed with her, and told his dogs to keep her company when he went about doing stuff.

Best day ever. Beyond indulgent. This gorgeous man seeing to her every need... If she'd known this was the treatment, she would've left New Mexico days ago.

Tomorrow, she'd get back to worrying about the list. She'd dive back into social media. Brooks had turned off the WiFi when they'd arrived. She'd worried at first, but eventually agreed that two unconnected days couldn't hurt. One down, one to go. After that... everything would change.

Leaving the bathroom, she pulled on the pink lace thong she'd gotten at a boutique near the airport and walked to the window. The floor-to-ceiling, edge-to-edge wall of windows gave her a gorgeous view of the

*Broken P*

inlet and forest. The deep blue of a still bright sky hovered above an island of green trees.

She'd walked from hell into this wild beauty, a house that embraced and welcomed her like a home. And though her thoughts kept trying to turn back to "What will happen when" and "I am I doing the right thing," she pushed them aside. Two days. She was taking them. Because she had no idea what would happen after that.

Outside on the dock, Brooks was securing his boat, checking kayaks, and stacking life vests. This place was big, and not just the house. It was more like a camp. According to Brooks, it had three roughing-it cabins in the woods, three bunk beds apiece. There were also numerous storage sheds, a boat hanger, and a warehouse that looked more like a big barn. All of the equipment and weapons needed for survivalist training were secured inside the warehouse. Brooks had said he'd give her a tour tomorrow.

Not the only thing she hoped he gave her.

Ah! Seriously, she knew it would be intense being here with him, but she'd had no idea how all-consuming thoughts of sleeping with him would become.

Taking her towel from her head and using it to squeeze out any remaining moisture, she watched him make his way back up the dock. He stopped midway and stared over the cabin into the night sky.

She admired him, the breadth of his form, the efficiency and intensity of him. He was so handsome. He was so... not staring up at the stars.

Oh God. Topless, standing in her panties, ringing out her hair. She should cover up. Hide. But... She dropped the towel, moved closer to the window, and placed her hand against the cold glass.

Brooks put his hand to his chest.

Heat pooled in her belly, dropped to the apex of her thighs. In her mind's eye, she saw him running inside, climbing the stairs to this room, and throwing open the door. She imagined them coming together. Her hot, still wet-from-the-shower body colliding with his cold fresh-from-the-outside one. She imagined kissing him with all her passion and desperate need. All of it unfolding in a bright, beautiful reality.

And then she remembered that, in two days, they were going to try to lure a killer into these woods and her stomach soured. Turning from the window, she made her way back into the bathroom.

#

After dressing and drying her hair, it was tempting to crawl into the big soft bed with its white pillows and lush comforter. Tiredness had been kept at bay all day, but now it tugged at her. Still, she wanted to say goodnight to Brooks. It would be rude not to.

*Okay.*

*Fine.*

She wanted to see him.

Yep, this was a problem. Because they'd literally been apart only for the time it took her to bathe, do her hair, and get changed. Still, it *was* rude not to say goodnight.

Pulling an overly large sweatshirt on over her cami hid her suddenly hard nipples. She headed out of the room.

There were two other rooms along a hallway lined with wildlife photos. And, yet, Brooks, who'd given up this room for her, slept in the one room downstairs.

No need to ask why. Hard enough sleeping in his room—imagine if he'd been on the same floor... *Yikes*.

With a wistful sigh, she descended the stairs and turned into the great room. Brooks sat on the couch, Henley and jeans worn in all the right places, long legs stretched out. His dogs were asleep close by.

She walked over, bouncing a little as she did. So much for being tired. This man zapped her fatigue and replaced it with a buzz of energy and desire.

By the time she made her way to the couch, his eyes were already pinned to her. They swept down her as if seeing underneath, seeing the outline of her in the window. His gaze burned.

Heat flushed through her in a thrilling wave.

She swallowed and nodded to the shot glasses and whiskey on the table. "Drinking alone?"

"No, querida. I've been waiting for you."

That sincerely uttered statement shredded her casual demeanor. The way he'd said it... It sounded... Oh, it sounded as if he'd been waiting for her for *years*.

Warmth hour-glassed into her heart one grain of sand at a time, filling her up, covering over every painful moment that had come before.

"Siéntate aquí," Brooks said, patting the seat beside him.

## CHAPTER THIRTY-NINE

As Fee moved to the couch, Brooks' mind brought forth the image of her nude in the window, so bright and luminous, it burned. She sat close enough to brush his leg with hers. Flames shot through him. So keyed up. Her nearness, her just-showered scent had his awareness thrumming.

She leaned forward and picked up the bottle of whiskey. "Expensive."

"And worth it. This is our tribute to Dorothy."

She crinkled her nose. Adorable. He'd debated this memorial tradition, drinking with her tonight, especially after they'd flown today. But tomorrow would be a full day, ending with Mami and Papí's visit, and the next, they'd start down a road filled with uncertainty and fear. Had to be now. He'd been waiting weeks for this moment, to truly grieve with her.

Still, he didn't want her to be sick in the morning. He'd limit the shots to three. He also had water on the table to take after each shot. And Gatorade for after.

"You want to get drunk as a tribute to my mother? This plan doesn't end up with me in bed under you, does it?"

His brain instantly conjured the image of her turning in the window, the curve of her ass, the sway of her hips. He cleared his throat. *Ayúdame, Díos*.

He poured the whiskey into a shot glass and held it up. The red-amber liquid glinted in the firelight. "I get three. You get three. Make them good ones."

"What's going on?"

"Like this." Memory pressed black and white keys in his mind, creating a melody that he hoped he could always recall. Dorothy's. "To Dorothy. When I came here, after what I saw as a loss that I'd never recover from, you called me."

He kept his eyes on hers, kept himself open, no judgment only sharing. She nodded for him to continue. "You told me, one day I'd realize everything I went through was to advance love. A love, you swore to me, that would never die."

He tipped his head back and drank in one swallow. Tears zigzagged down his cheeks. He didn't wipe them away. He poured another glass slid it over to her.

Wiping her own tears, she picked it up. "To Mom, for showing me what the true meaning of courage was. You considered doing good for others above all things, no matter what it cost you, politically or personally. And that requires a courage few will ever know."

She slammed back the shot. She coughed, blinked, and shed more tears. Picking up the sturdy bottle, she poured another shot, and slid it over to him. "Es bueno."

He smiled. She always was a quick study. He prompted her to drink water and then picked up the glass. "Thank you, Dorothy, for showing me that responsibility was the spice of life, something that added flavor, not something to be avoided."

"That's a good one," Fee said, as he slid her her drink. "To Mom…" She gulped audibly, tears freely flowing. "You warned me when your killer was behind me. You warned me."

His hands curled into fists. This was the first she'd said anything about that day.

"You saved my life with the last of your will. I will be that strong for others. I promise."

She downed the shot. Muscles bunched tension into his fists. He wanted to jump in front of her toast, throw himself in front of it, keep her from the pain that had happened, and from the responsibility of fulfilling her promise.

But he'd just said responsibility was the spice of life and he wouldn't keep Fee from experiencing the fullness of what and who she was.

Instead, he put an arm around her, drew her close to his side, and kissed her on the top of her head.

She leaned into him, accepting the comfort, and whispered, "I want to be that brave."

His arm tightened around her. "You *are* that brave."

"Not yet. But I will be. I'll be part of the plan, right?"

"We'll talk."

"Brooks."

"Two days. Come on, now. You've been in the fight for weeks. Give yourself two days to get your bearings. The fight isn't going anywhere, but that doesn't mean you have to be engaged with it 24/7. Be like the American revolutionaries, pick your battles."

"You think?"

"It's what your mom would've done."

She smiled, wiped her eyes, reached forward, and poured another glass. "She was smart like that." She handed it to him. "Toma."

He took the glass, brushing her warm fingers softly. A small sound escaped her lips. Heat flushed through his blood. They stared into each other's eyes. She tilted up her chin. The offer of a kiss?

*Díos*. He considered it for longer than he should. Not right to take advantage in an emotional moment. The drink was working on her. Her heat was working on him. He kissed her forehead, raised the glass, then made another toast.

When she'd finished her third tribute to their Christmas tradition of going to a soup kitchen, a tradition that had forever changed her view of the holiday, Brooks opened the bottle of Gatorade. "Drink."

"I wanted to do one for Christmas. Mom would…"

"You did that one."

She shook her head and reached for the whiskey. "Yesh. But one more."

He slid the bottle away. "No, querida. That wouldn't be wise. "

"But I like this memorial." She cuddled close and sniffed. "You smell good." She kissed his neck—

And set fire to the desire he'd been tamping down all night.

He closed his eyes, fighting his instinct to get closer, close enough to take this to a satisfying conclusion. "I like it too. But buzzed Felicity is not the Felicity I need to convince."

She ran a hand up his muscular torso. "Tipsy Felicity is a lot easier to convince."

A snort of laughter didn't stop the sudden and intense throbbing of his heart. Or other parts. "*That* I remember."

"Sober Felicity is afraid." She blinked rapidly as if startled that her voice had broken.

He brushed her hair back, looked into her eyes with a sincerity he hoped she grasped. "Then I'll wait until she's a hundred percent comfortable."

"It's easier to wait until she's buzzed."

A light kiss on the tip of her nose. "I'm not here for easy or quick. I'd like to do this the hard way." He winked at her. "As slow and as hard as it needs to be."

She giggled. "How is it you can make me laugh when I started this memorial crying?"

"We always laughed together. Now, drink the Gatorade. Then time for bed."

She drank. "I'd forgotten. Forgotten laughter and fun."

He offered her a hand, and pulled her to standing. He stared at her for a long moment. A million words crowded his tongue, trying to get him to lighten the moment, but none came out.

She tiptoed up to him, threaded her hands behind his neck, and kissed him.

The pleading way her lips and tongue worked against his... The tender sounds she made... Lust swamped his body. Blood pounded in his ears. His breath became labored. And he wasn't even kissing her back.

He eased from her grasp. "I need you of sound mind and body." He met her gaze and tried to ignore the rocket of heat that launched through his groin. "Sleeping with me can't be a mistake. And I sure as hell won't let it be a regret. Okay?"

She frowned. "Are you sure that's it? There's no other reason?"

"What other reason could there be?"

"Liam… uh… said my kissing was too aggressive."

That fucker. He couldn't even… Brooks' gripped her face in his hands, looked at her with the hunger he hoped arrested any doubt. "You are the best, most passionate kisser I've ever had the good fortune to lock lips with. And Liam is a cowardly man who sought control over your mind because he feared for his place in it."

Her cheeks flushed. "I know. It's fine. He's in the past."

"It's not over, Fee. Not if you live a life based on what this person said to you, thought of you, then it's not over."

"I know, I know. Usually, I do. It's… been a long day."

Fury clawed at him. How many cuts had been delivered to make this vibrant, beautiful, and once-confident soul feel such shame? "Come on," he said, looking away. "Let's get you to bed. We have a day of kayaking ahead of us tomorrow."

Two days. He promised her two days, so he'd let go of his anger. But if he ever found that pendejo in an alley somewhere… letting him go would be the last thing he did.

## CHAPTER FORTY

The crisp October air sifted flurries across the dock as Fee secured the Velcro wristbands of the GORE-TEX drysuit. Brooks crouched in front of her, securing her life vest. Eagerness thumped like a rabbit for the day of reprieve from her fears. For the burst of aware energy that stroked her nerve endings with Brooks so close.

His breath was white on the air, swirling in little pockets that floated over her. She breathed in deeply, taking in a part of him like a lovesick teen. Sappho and Blanco sat on the dock, giving her curious looks. Judgy dogs.

Brooks tapped her on her helmet. "Ready?"

"And willing." Good Lord. Flirting felt good. Last night, he'd thought she'd been throwing herself at him like a drunken idiot. Today, she'd show him a sober idiot wanted the same thing. Because two days was now one.

Winking, he extended his hand to the edge of the dock. With his help, she sat into the kayak. Brooks checked the skirt around the cockpit.

How was it that the man looked hot in a drysuit?

Hers looked like a floppy yellow snowsuit. "Are you sure this is my size?"

Brooks kept the kayak steady in the launch with the press of his boot. "Sí. This is a quality operation, querida. We get all different sized men and women out here. They're made to be loose."

Considering the expense of these suits, she was guessing quality meant successful. It didn't surprise her that he'd taken the business his father had started with Delgado Trading and expanded it into topnotch security training.

They'd talked about this idea before they'd broken up. She'd actually suggested it. She'd been dreaming of ways to live after the trial. Back then, every sentence had ended with *after the trial*. At least he'd made his dream come true, though her dream of doing PR for a non-profit hadn't panned out.

She took the paddle he offered. "If only you had panties in that giant shed, I wouldn't had to have gone commando under my thermals."

Brooks choked on a sound. His eyes dropped down over the kayak skirt. She expected him to joke, make things lighter, but he didn't. "Set and secure?"

Hmmm, Flirting Fee was confusing him. Fun. "Yes. Yes. Let's go."

He pressed a button to lower the kayak into the water. Water flooded into the sides of the launch. She unlatched and paddled forward. The still water cradled her, welcomed her. A peace she'd forgotten—a peace she longed for—flooded her. Her muscles loosened and her spirit lifted.

One last day before they tried the most reckless thing she'd ever attempt. One day before she faced a daunting process alongside security professionals.

Smiling, she moved her sleek blue kayak through the dark, still water.

Something in her awoke. Something she'd

thought had died long ago. With a burst of speed, she pulled forward and drew back, going from side to side as easily and quickly as muscle memory allowed.

The air was crisp. The sky blue and endless. All she wanted was the freedom of this day, to forget everything and move her body.

"Querida. Esperas."

Wait? Not likely. She paddled down the inlet.

"Fee. I've got to gear up."

He'd catch up. She wanted to keep moving. This place... oh, the freedom. The trees sloping up the opposite shore dangled snow in filaments of pine. Those trees looked huge from the cabin, but down here in the water, they seemed bigger. Imposing and beautiful.

A hawk cried and circled in the gray blue sky. She cocked her head for a moment and watched the graceful movement, then paddled full tilt toward the open ocean at the end of the inlet.

Brooks came up beside her, outpacing her, and grabbed the front lines on her kayak. With a tug, he first slowed and then gently turned her. He was out of breath. "Didn't you hear me calling you?"

She gnawed on her lip, causing the strap on her helmet to rub her chin. "Maybe."

A smile curving his lips, he pointed right along the shoreline with his paddle. "Let's steer away from the open ocean."

"You don't think I can take being pounded by the hard stuff?"

She flushed. Okay. That flirting was graceless. It was the cold air; it was interfering with her circulation. Obviously, a person needed proper circulation to flirt well.

He angled his head to the side. His eyes filled with pure light and warmth. "Querida. You're coming back to yourself, aren't you?"

Wow. He was right. This was who she'd been. A person who liked adventure. A person who took off for the open sea. A person who flirted and had fun. She took in all the joy she could, soaking it up, because this was her last day. "Let's play, Delgado."

Brooks nodded as if deep in thought, then shoved her kayak backward, giving himself the lead. He broke into a fast paddle and called back, "What's taking you so long, Shields?"

Laughing, she attacked the water with her paddle.

## CHAPTER FORTY-ONE

Paddling along the tributary, Brooks swore he'd had the very best of intentions this morning. Hand to God. He'd woken up determined to give Fee everything her tender heart needed: a safe place, a warm home to help her recover from trauma and grief, and a day of reclaiming her outdoorsy nature.

He'd shoved down every instinctual need to touch, to flirt, to drag her to his bed. And, somehow, he'd created a vacuum. And Señorita Shields had rushed in to fill it with flirting so well-crafted and expertly delivered that he'd spent the last two hours kayaking with a boner. Thankfully, he'd gotten his libido under control. "Want to stop here for lunch?"

"Trying to get me on dry land and have your way with me, Delgado?"

*The very best of intentions. Díos. Por favor. Ayúdame.* He'd need God's help to keep his hands off her.

Paddling hard and fast, he pushed his kayak onto the shoreline. Jumping out, he pulled it out of the way.

Fee followed his lead. When she neared, he grabbed the deck lines on the bow and pulled her safely the rest of the way.

Climbing out, she took off her helmet and attached it to the kayak. "This suit is amazing, but no way am I hiking in it."

"Bueno. It's warmer now anyway." The flurries had stopped. Brooks took off his life vest. Releasing the Velcro straps that tightened around his wrists and ankles, he stripped out of the drysuit.

Done, he turned to see Fee's progress. Still dressed? What was she looking at? He twisted his head. *Nada.* He turned back to her. Her cheeks had grown red. He closed his eyes. Such good intentions. "Fee, were you watching me undress?"

She coughed, looked away, and undid the straps on her suit. "It's not like you're naked under the drysuit."

True. He had on thermal pants and a thermal shirt. As did she.

*And no underwear.*

*Don't think about it. Don't.* He took his pack from storage, unfolded his packable jacket and surreptitiously watched Fee undress. The soft black thermals hugged every delicious curve.

No underwear.

*Don't think about it!*

She finished and looked up at him. "Are *you* watching *me* undress?"

"Yes."

Laughing, she tucked her suit into the kayak's dry compartment, then put on her down jacket.

Slipping into his backpack, he led her up through the trees.

A comfortable silence fell, each lost in the scenery: towering trees, broken limbs, changing leaves, green pines, and birds flitting out from undergrowth. Mostly, he listened to the sound of her moving behind him. Of her walk. They'd been avid hikers when they'd dated.

Listening now to her footfalls, he realized he'd actually missed her stride. *Díos*. He had it bad.

When her footsteps stopped, he turned. Fee had squatted by a tree trunk. He moved back down the slope. "Fee?"

She looked up. Blue eyes dazzling bright. "You'd think it'd be too cold for ants."

He smiled. "These are Canadian ants. They eat cold for breakfast."

She laughed and looked back down.

Memory cracked him against the spine. This used to try his patience. Stopping a hike so Fee could look at bugs or pick up rocks or find mushrooms. A hike was never about getting to the end with her like it had been for him. For her, it'd been about taking in as much as she could.

She stood back up. A smile lit but then died on her face. "You're crying?"

*Coño*. He spun around, wiped his face. "Allergies." He started back up the hill. "Come on. It's getting late."

She whispered, "I missed you, too."

A shiver of heat raced down his torso. He closed the distance and rooted himself before her. The longing between them said a thousand wordless things.

Her cheeks were red from the cold or emotion. Her eyes alight. Her lips parted and waiting.

As he waited.

She nodded.

In the words of his father, it was too much. Too much for one man to resist.

In a hot flash, he took her lips with the ferocious need he could no longer keep in check. He let the ache that had been gaping inside him, fill with the heat of her soft, moist mouth.

He kissed her like she deserved to be kissed, like he wanted to kiss her. Because he had the very best intentions when it came to Felicity Shields.

## CHAPTER FORTY-TWO

Something had shifted between her and Brooks since she'd come to his home. It was as if they'd bridged the distance of eight years in twenty-four hours. The outdoors had always been where they'd spent the most time. So, out here again, her soul had rushed toward him—no matter how much she tried to warn herself against it.

Standing in the woods with his heat nudging her and the forest creaking around them, she wasn't warning herself now. Not at all. She reveled in the press of Brooks' demanding lips. His hands threaded into her hair, angling her head, deepening their kiss. His tongue glided against hers, sweeping her into a state of frenzied desire. She grasped his jacket, fisting it at his sides.

He tugged her closer, locking her tightly against him. His hardness moving against her belly flooded her senses.

She moaned into his mouth, then pulled back. "This seems like a good place for a rest."

His grin stretched across his face. He looked down, toed the ground. "It's perfect."

He shrugged out of his backpack, dug inside, and pulled out two square silver packets. Mylar thermal blankets. He shook the first out and laid it on the ground.

They were on a slope, but there were no roots or rocks. Perfect.

He invited her to sit with a wave of his hand. Shrugging out of her backpack, she sat down. He shook out the next blanket, then spread it over her. As it drifted into place, he darted under, snuggling up to her. "Now, where were we?"

"You were kissing me."

"No." He rolled her on top of him. "*You* were kissing *me*."

She leaned down and gently kissed his lips. More than gentle. It was a chaste kiss.

"That's nice. So warm."

"I'm beginning to think, Brooks Delgado, that you are easy to please."

"That's true only when it comes to you. Díos, *everything* is better with you here."

She kissed him again, deep and wild. A kiss that drove away the woods, the cold, the ground. Everything but the heat and zing between them. She moved against him, writhing.

Breaths heavy, frantic hands roaming, he rolled so she was under him. He thrust his hard-on against her. "¿Puedes sentir cuanto te quiero?"

Hard to deny how much he wanted her. No pun intended. The fabric of their thermals left no room for doubt. The pulse in his cock drummed against her. He kissed her again. A kiss as deep and wet and hot as the ache building between her legs.

When they came up for air, Brooks put his hand over her sex. "Your body is calling to me. Talking to me. Mind if I speak back?"

"Talk is cheap, Delgado. What else do you have in mind?"

He grinned, working her thermals down around her ankles. Her breath caught. Cold broke through with their movement. She shivered.

He kissed her bellybutton. Her thighs. Heat replaced the cold. She arched up... and his mouth descended on her, covering her sex.

She groaned as his warm tongue glided along her delicate, slick, sensitive skin. The sweep of electricity sent tingles through every nerve ending. He whispered something in Spanish and warm vibrations cascaded through her.

She was going to come. "Brooks."

"Mmmm, as sweet as I remembered. Sweeter." His tongue played her like an instrument. And every lick, stroke, and suck stimulated a corresponding chorus of moans and cries and sighs.

She threaded her hands through his dark hair, the blessed oblivion of desire rising and rising, covering all senses until she was mindless. The orgasm crashed through her. She cried out, calling his name, as sensation heaved through her.

Slowly, she came back to earth. Came back to the wilderness. Came back to what she'd just done. And where. Felt too good to care.

Brooks' tongue slowed, sending electric pulses zinging through her core. She was still so primed. She wanted him inside her.

"Brooks..."

His fingers slipped through the wetness between her thighs and into her. His tongue continued to stroke her clit. He met her fierce want with quick and nimble fingers, thrusting in and out. His tongue flicked against her in quick, tormenting pulses. Her hips rocketed against him.

The onslaught of sensation sent energy coiling through her. Pleasure built.... built with squeezing muscles. Built with arching hips and thickening want. She moaned and moved faster against him. It was too much. Too much.

She came. A flash of writhing, white-hot energy that drew cries of ecstasy from her. The orgasm slowed, faded. Collapsing against the blanket, she rejoiced, feeling satiated body and soul. No one had ever made her feel this way. No one but Brooks.

It took several moments of listening to his heavy breaths, of feeling his hard-on pressed to her side, before she came back to herself.

She reached for him but he grabbed her hand. "I want only to be inside you. And even if I'd brought a condom, which I haven't, I want you to understand something."

Meeting his eyes, her breath evening out, she waited for him to finish his thought.

"Your pleasure is enough for me. Giving you pleasure, seeing you pleased, brings me pleasure."

"Really? Seems so unfair."

He shook his head. "Unfair is that you've been told and accepted that you are not good enough. Not quiet enough. Not prim enough. I want you to see that, for me, *you* are more than enough."

Delight swam up her torso, spiraling into and sealing a once-gaping wound. She curled into him. "But don't you want to, uh, finish? I'm clean. Liam always used a condom even though I'm on the pill."

His steady gaze riveted to hers. "I'm clean, too. Always use a condom. But..." his throat worked, "it's not only about *what* I want. It's about *who* I want. This is not where I want to make love to you for the first time after eight years apart. ¿Y tú?"

Uh, no. No. She wanted a bed to roll around in with him, a warm fire, long minutes. Not hurried on a bed of pine needles. "No, you're right." She grinned at him, a bit apologetically. "I'm good. For now."

He laughed, a deep throaty sound that had her sex clenching again with desire. She rubbed her nose against his. "You make it very hard for me to keep my promise to myself not to let you get caught up in my crazy life."

"Ah, see? We have a problem. I made a promise that I would get *completely* caught up in your crazy life."

"I think you're winning."

He smiled. "*We're* winning, querida. Together. We do this together."

## CHAPTER FORTY-THREE

What did one wear to dinner with the fortune-telling mother of the man you still loved, the man whose heart you'd broken, the man whose mother had every right to dislike you? What color was the gemstone of shame and regret?

Fee looked at the sum total of all the clothes she had with her. Four sets of thermals, borrowed from Brooks. Two pairs of jeans. Two yoga pants. Four shirts—only one of which was a long-sleeve. The rest were the same style in different colors. And one black hoodie.

None of this would do. She hadn't seen Brooks' mother, Soledad, his brother, Carey, or his sister-in-law, Janelle, in eight years. Oh, hell. She'd been told jeans went with everything. Jeans it was.

She put on a pair, a white thermal, and topped it with a rose-colored, V-neck tee shirt.

The whirring sound of a boat entering the inlet brought her to the window. A sleek, black vessel with red trim glided to the dock.

Carey jumped out, followed by a boy with dark, curly hair. Had to be Carey's son, Malcolm. Jane had been pregnant the last time Fee had seen her. She'd given birth to Malcolm after the breakup. That would make him around eight.

Inhaling so deeply her shoulders rose and her chest puffed out, she exhaled with a controlled sigh. She hadn't only lost Brooks; she'd lost them all. She'd lost time and relationships she could never get back.

Confident and smiling, Malcolm helped his father tie up the boat. A moment later, Janelle appeared. Her brown, wavy hair whipped in the wind. She wore white pants and a loose, matching shirt. Very loose. Brooks hadn't mentioned Janelle was pregnant again.

Carey helped her off the boat, kissing her the moment her feet hit the deck, as if they'd been apart for years. They were so good together. Deeply in love.

Time to face the music.

From the top of the stairs, she could hear Brooks in the kitchen, the *clink* of wine glasses and the *pop* of a wine bottle being opened.

She closed her eyes. This was someone else's life. Other people lived like this. Normal nights here weren't angry strategy sessions, centered around a takeout box and the latest bad news to be combated.

"Breaking out the good stuff." Carey's good-natured voice drifted up the stairs and into the hall where she stood just out of eyesight. "And, here, I brought your favorite overpriced whiskey."

"Tío Brooks," Malcolm's eager voice cut through the din of greetings. "Look at my shoes."

There was an enthusiastic jumping sound. Brooks said, "Bueno. They light up. After dinner, we can go out and you can show me in the dark."

More voices, laughter, greetings, and then Janelle's sweet voice, "Where's Felicity?"

Awkward and unsure, Fee opened her eyes and let out a breath. Tension clawed her shoulders as she descended the stairs. The eyes of those at the bottom drifted up to her.

The smile pasted on her face trembled. She was so very different from the person who'd once been accepted and loved by everyone here.

Janelle rushed to her before she stepped off the bottom step, threw her arms around her, and squeezed.

Oh. The warm acceptance and affection cascaded through Fee. She squeezed back, held on for dear life, feeling the swell of Janelle's belly between them. They held on for more moments than was socially comfortable, but it was exactly what Fee needed. Tension leaked from her body. Tears leaked from her eyes.

"Missed you, Muff," she whispered, calling her by the old nickname Carey had given her because of the way her hair had grown back after chemo. The "muff" was now long and full.

Janelle barked laughter and squeezed her again. "I'm never getting rid of that nickname, am I?" She tossed that hair now, long and full. "Missed you, too. I'm so very sorry about your mom. Devastated."

Releasing her, Fee wiped her eyes. Carey, a younger version of Rafael, with dark hair and gray eyes, gently moved in and took her into his arms. He smelled the same. Like the ocean. "Sorry, kiddo. So sorry. She was an amazing woman."

Tears came again. This time, they were gentle and grateful. This was what she'd missed when Mom died—the simple act of having others who loved Mom mourn with her in a quiet and non-threatening place.

No sooner did Carey release her than the back door opened and the smell of warm food drifted inside.

Rafael held an insulated carrier that smelled fantastic. He announced the contents as he held the bag up as if it weighed nothing, "Bacalaito, sancocho, y arroz con gandules." And, behind him, came the woman Felicity had dreaded seeing: Brooks' most staunch defender, Soledad.

Their eyes met. Soledad's brown eyes softened as she brushed past her husband and grasped Felicity in the fiercest, most genuine hug Felicity had ever received. Locked in warmth, drawn into love, Fee let it fill her.

"Cariña, you're here."

Felicity couldn't speak. A charge of gratitude swirled along her skin. She hugged her back and finally managed, "My heart didn't know that I was waiting for this moment." Her eyes flooded with tears. "Back. Never fully gone."

Almost the moment she said those words, her logical mind thought of what was to come, the danger she'd brought here, the danger Rafael and Carey would take on. Risking themselves and the hearts of the families that loved them.

Two days had gone by too quickly. Tomorrow, all of this would be at risk. More than anything, she wished she could wrestle back control, keep everyone safe. It was out of her hands. Rafael and Carey wouldn't allow her to make that choice for them. She was doing this to save her list-sisters and end this nightmare. She prayed it was the right choice.

## CHAPTER FORTY-FOUR

The night went about as perfectly as Brooks could've hoped for. The food was amazing. Dessert, better. And though he'd feared the break from the quiet cabin for Fee's sake, the noise and laughter temporarily banished the past few weeks.

Fee needed this. He was an incredibly lucky man to have the family he did. They'd had his back for the last eight years. When he'd left Felicity to come here, he hadn't even had a place to live. Only this property.

When she called off the wedding, he'd built this house. She' had no idea, to this day, that he considered this her property as much as his. Or that every day she was here, the unnamed grief hiding inside him lightened. Right now, it was gone.

Brooks accepted the drink Carey offered him. He touched the rim to his brother's, then his father's glasses. "Gracias."

"De nada. Pero…" He motioned toward the side of the cabin. "Someone is taking trees from the property again."

*Coño.* "Mucho? Donde?"

"Too many. Along the training site."

Brooks let the flash of irritation go. Sometimes people cut trees from his property and floated the logs behind their boats to their homes for wood. It was stealing, but he never reported it. If the opportunity presented itself, he confronted the person. He didn't have time to hunt them down, but he'd have to make a point of keeping them away. Hard to set up an ambush with randoms walking the property.

"I'll do a sweep tomorrow with Tate's men," Carey said. "Secure the area. And begin to map out positions before making our way back to the cabin."

"When do they arrive?" Janelle asked, putting a hand on her belly.

"Tomorrow afternoon."

As the conversation shifted to the arrival and logistics of getting the crew out to the training site, Brooks' attention returned to Fee. Her beautiful face was flushed with wine. She spoke quietly with his mother.

Seeing his eyes move in her direction, she pointed at Malcolm who'd fallen asleep on a chair curled up in a ball, his neck bent awkwardly.

He got her point instantly. Though kids were bendy that way, his neck hurt seeing it. Standing, he went over and scooped Malcolm up. The kid flung an arm out but, otherwise, didn't stir.

Janelle looked up. He told her, "Going to put him in the guest room."

She nodded and went back to her conversation with Carey and Papí.

Brooks walked the length of the great room to the guest bedroom, the only room on this level, and the room he currently occupied. He hadn't wanted Fee to feel pressured.

Who was he kidding? He needed the distance to keep himself from pacing outside her room at night like a starving panther.

*Broken P*

After placing his nephew down, he reached for the folded blanket at the foot of the bed and placed it over Mal. Not because the kid would get cold; he was a furnace, but because it messed with his sensibilities not to toss something over a sleeping person.

Leaving the bedroom, Brooks returned to find his mother handing Fee a black stone. Without interrupting them, he drew closer to listen.

"This is an obsidian worry stone," Mami said. "Rub your thumb against the indent in the center. Sort of like a fidget stick. It's good for grounding and absorbing negative energy."

Fee rubbed the indent with the heel of her thumb. "Might need a bigger stone."

His mother sighed softly. "I don't think I've seen you relax your shoulders once."

He cringed. His family could be too direct. Still, Fee didn't seem bothered.

She dropped her shoulders and continued to rub the stone. "How am I to survive all that hate?"

Brooks tensed. Everything in him wanted to grab her, hold her, and reassure her.

With an understanding nod, his mother said, "How does the flower survive the raging storm? It bends, is malleable in the wind, knowing this, too, will pass. And when the sun comes out, it lifts its face and takes in the sunlight."

Fee's eyes rose to Brooks. She beamed at him. "Thank you, Soledad."

"Bueno," Papí said, startling Brooks as he silently appeared beside him. "I told you that you'd like the stone." His father held a guitar out to Fee. "We've missed you playing."

The room went silent. Felicity's eyes widened.

"Papí," Brooks rushed to, once again, run interference. His family's openness meant they didn't always recognize boundaries.

"It's your choice," Papí said. "No pressure."

His father, a man as wise as he was determined, still held the guitar out.

Felicity put her stone in her pocket and reached for the instrument.

Brooks helped with the assist. He took the guitar and pick and handed them to her. Then he sat back on the arm of her chair as she placed her hand on the strings.

"I can't remember the last time I played."

She no longer played?

"Actually, I do remember. I played for my Mom at Christmas a few years ago." Her lips twitched and she laughed. "Mom tried to sing."

The room erupted in laughter. Even Brooks smiled at the thought. "Sounds painful."

She half-said/ half-laughed, "It was." Positioning the guitar, she strummed the first note of The Jackson 5's *I'll Be There*. She stopped and started again.

As if eight years had never happened... as if they'd been together days ago, sitting around like this, the family began singing, encouraging Fee's strummed notes.

She still played well, despite her protests. Revitalized joy pinkened her cheeks, added a smile to her face and a glow to her eyes.

For his part, Brooks put more than tone to the words of salvation, love, and presence. He weighted them, meant them to welcome her here.

*Broken P*

At the end of that song, she wiped her eyes and then switched to playing another. This one, everyone joined in on Sylvia Rexach's slow and sultry *Olas y Arenas* in Spanish. The beautiful and romantic song settled into his bones.

His mother had taught Fee the song way back when they'd been dating and memories speared grateful emotion into his voice, making it difficult to sing.

The song ended and she shifted gears. Maybe needing to lighten the mood, she played Luis Fonsi's *Despacito*. The music was fast and fun. His mother stood up and swung her hips around as she sung.

Fee picked up the pace of her playing. The rest of them clapped to the increased rhythm, unified in their joy, as Mami kept up brilliantly.

# CHAPTER FORTY-FIVE

Fee watched from the window inside her room as Carey's boat pulled away from the dock. Grief, she'd discovered, lessened when you spoke of the person who'd died. For a moment tonight, they'd brought Mom back to life. And that had put a wonderful end to a perfect two days. Brooks' family, their acceptance of her, the kayaking and time with him had broken through the fog of grief and the wall of her anger.

The lights from the boat disappeared. Brooks headed toward the cabin. To her. She'd asked him to come up after he finished outside. His smile had said that he'd intended to do that anyway, but she was glad she'd made it clear. Two days had turned into one had turned into a single night. Hours left. Time was so precious. Fleeting. She wasn't going to let it slip away without making the very most of it.

The knock came on her bedroom door. Fire traveled down her body, purred in her stomach, groaned between her thighs. She smoothed her sweaty palms along the Delgado Land, Sea, and Air t-shirt she wore. "Come on in."

Brooks opened the door, stood in the doorway all casual in his jeans and tee. Lust jumped up, did a backflip, and started to drool. *Breathe, Fee. Just breathe.*

As she scanned him, a smile lit his face. And his gaze, which had been resolutely on her face, dropped down—followed by a small, choked sound.

She wore only the borrowed t-shirt.

He stalked forward.

Was it possible to be completely panicked and completely turned on at the same time?

Check. And check.

He reached out but dropped his hand without touching her. "You're nervous?"

"Like a heart attack."

His soft laughter pushed his warm breath against her face. "How about we go slow... until you decide you no longer want slow."

Felicity's heart already raced as she nodded.

He tilted up her chin. "Is this okay?"

"Yes. Great. Sure. Perfect."

He smiled and dipped to her lips. "And if I kiss you?"

"Yes." *Please*.

He kissed her. It was gentle at first, a probing, a remembering, am-I-welcome kiss. But as her breath increased, as she moaned and opened her mouth and tangled her tongue with his, he deepened it.

She slipped her hands under his shirt. Ran trembling fingers along his smooth, hard muscles. Her breathing became labored. Her limbs trembled. Nipples stiffened. Moisture pooled.

Brooks pulled back. He ran a hand along her face. "Querida, tu tienes mi corazón."

She stared into his eyes. They were lit with lust and something softer. Something that made her legs wobbly. She had his *heart*? "I do? Still?"

"You brought it back to me. Before that moment I saw you at your home, I hadn't been fully myself for so long."

A small, pained sound escaped her. "Me, too."

He bent to her mouth again. His tongue slipped inside, warm and wet and searching. His hands went down her back to her butt. He squeezed, arched her back, kissing her, drawing out moans and heat.

He whispered, "This is me talking, querida. Can you hear what I'm asking?"

She could. "The answer is yes."

The heat of Brooks' skilled kisses overpowered her. His mouth welcomed her home to his heart, his life, and his body. Her soul stretched with joy as she rocked with eager need. She pulled at his shirt. "Off."

Reaching behind his neck, he flipped the shirt off and tossed it away. The sharply muscled line of abs, his thick corded forearms, the powerful cut of his biceps made her mouth go dry.

He'd always been in great shape, but this wasn't the pumped body of a man who only worked out. This was the muscularly nuanced and edged physique of a man who used layers of muscle every day during working hours.

Her delighted hands ran across taut abs, over his broad shoulders, and down his tan and toned biceps. She went up on her tiptoes to whisper, "You feel so good."

"'Bout to feel a whole lot better."

She licked his ear, bit his earlobe. "Promise?"

They both froze for a moment. This wasn't like the desperate moment when she'd found her mother. This was... different. She felt her cheeks heat. She hadn't meant…. It was too soon.

His gaze pinned her. "Take your clothes off." He reached for the button on his jeans. "I want you naked on that bed."

She snorted. "Awfully bossy."

His hands stilled. His eyes became deadly serious. "If you need me to stop, tell me. Anytime..." The look he sent her caused a flood of want between her legs.

He ran a hand along her exposed stomach. "But you told me to take you at your word, to trust what comes out of your mouth, and I intend to do that. Until you can't see straight. Until you scream my name. Until I have reacquainted myself with every inch of you."

That heavy vow tingled along her skin, tightened and pooled between her legs. Giddy with the aroma and heat of him, she stripped out of her clothes, moved up against the pillows, and let hunger and desire take over thought.

Naked and perfect, hot and hard, he crawled onto the bed. His skin contacted hers, singed her. She groaned.

He echoed her. "Spread your legs."

She did. His hard cock pressed against her soft wet center. He kissed her neck, alternating between light kisses and sucking deeply. It was driving her mad. "Brooks."

He thrust just enough to let her know what was coming. "I've been wanting to welcome you home properly since the moment you walked that pert ass through my front door."

She could feel the perfectly sculpted, thick and hard member, erect and ready to enter her. "Please. Please."

"I said every inch of you. I'm a man of my word." And then he ravished her, licking and sucking her breasts until she lost herself to the ministrations of his hands, his tongue, the way his knees kept her legs apart, kept her open and ready for him.

She writhed with wanting. A madness that repeated on her lips. "Take me hard. Hurry. Please."

"So quick, querida?" He sucked her nipple back into his mouth with a fierce tug.

She tossed her head back and opened her legs wide. "Yes. Quick."

Hooking her leg around him, she drew him nearer. "Oh, Brooks. Please. It has to happen now."

"Open your eyes. Look at me."

She did... just as his big, sure body thrust. His cock entered her with a power alien to her. Her delighted moan lingered in the air as the overstretched pressure filled her core. The look on his face, in his eyes, was one of pure lust and joy.

His thrusts came faster, drove deeper. Swift. Expert strokes. Tingles of arousal jumped through every nerve. His hand gripped her hair, sharp and stinging, angling her head so that she kept eye contact. This. Was. Everything. "Yes. Don't stop."

The pressure of his hands on her hair increased as he kissed her fiercely. His hands tied her to him, tied her to his needs. The thrust of his hips quickened. She could barely keep up, rocking to catch each powerful thrust.

Sensation unraveled her. The tight tug on her hair. His tongue in her mouth. His rapid and forceful thrusts. The slap of their bodies. The moans and gasps for breaths.

Each delicious feeling edged her nearer insensibility. The tension heightened, tightened.

She broke apart, crying out into his mouth, against the sweep of his tongue, a kiss that assured her it was okay, that it was all right, perfect. That, right now, he was her everything. And that was exactly how he wanted it.

No sooner had she come than his already frantic pace increased. He took her with blind and demanding speed that left her helpless to do anything but accept the pounding. He broke inside her with a rush of warmth, groaning hotly against her ear.

His hips slowed and the climax ended. He made a sound, half-growl/half-pain, as he fell across her as heavy as a tree.

It wasn't an unconscious move. She saw that. He wanted her there, pinned beneath his weight. For a moment, she was stunned by the command in the heavy feel of him. She was also stunned by what she'd just experienced. Not just hot sex. So much more. The connection... He'd opened her in every way possible. She still loved Brooks Delgado. Deeply. Intensely.

After a moment, he whispered in her ear, "You feel so good, I hate to leave."

He kissed her, rolled off, then drew her to his side. He whispered again, "The way you moaned. Loud and high. Low and throaty. It was music. It filled me. It wrecked me. You played me such a beautiful song."

Oh, he was making a point. Telling her that, for him, she was perfect.

She placed her hand against his cheek. "This is not a night or two nights. This is us. Continuing. Where we should never have left off."

His eyes pinned her, deadly serious and a bit lost. "Promise?"

Chills and warmth braided down her spine. So right. So good. The wonder of her undoing drifted languidly into her satiated mind. She'd never stopped loving him. In that way, she'd kept her word. "Promise forever."

And she hoped that was a promise she got to keep. She prayed that the risk they were taking wouldn't force her to break it.

## CHAPTER FORTY-SIX

Brooks stood by the windows, listening to the sounds of Fee in the shower. He could drop and do a thousand pushups or run for twenty miles through the woods, his body was so primed. Pumped. Their connection transcended logic. It was elevated. Physical. Emotional. Spiritual. All three had avalanched onto him as he'd poured himself inside her. It felt like healing. It felt like finding home.

This morning before breakfast had been... another layer of good. Her pleasure had been the only thing he'd let guide how forcefully he thrusted into her. And she liked it.

The *grrr* of a boat lifted his gaze. Carey pulled up to the dock. *Coño*. Time had truly gotten away from him, but it stopped now. Their two days were over. But if they did this right, the rest of their lives together was only beginning.

"He's here?" Fee scrubbed her hair with a towel as she walked out of the bathroom wearing *nada*. Wishing he hadn't already dressed, he smiled at her.

"Don't get distracted," she said. "There's a lot to do."

Easier said than done. What had she asked him? Oh, right. "Sí. Carey. He's here for equipment. He'll bring it out to the training site, where Papí will meet him with Tate's men."

She frowned, slipping on underwear. "It seems like you guys have already planned some things?"

Why did women think talking as they dressed wasn't distracting? What had she asked? *Mierda.* "Uh... Yeah. We had to schedule some things so that we'd have the needed equipment for Jack and his men."

"But—"

The dogs' barking announced Carey had docked. "Get dressed. We have time to discuss all the details. I didn't leave you out of the final decision. That's yours. Much of what they've planned follows a drill we've done here before. A hostage rescue from enemy territory. It's a solid scenario. Worked out over many sessions."

She put on her bra. "Okay. I'm ready to do whatever needs doing."

He ran his eyes down her body. What needed doing would have to wait.

At the bottom of the steps, Brooks found Carey in the kitchen working on his secure tablet with half a protein bar sticking out of his mouth. "Did you know your WiFi was off?"

Brooks cringed and looked back up the stairs. He'd meant to turn it on this morning but had gotten distracted. "I'll fix it."

"Already did. I needed to text Janelle and test the cameras you set up." He tapped the screen. "A few need to be repositioned. Nothing but leaves."

He's set them up the first day while Fee rested but hadn't checked them. "Thanks. Which ones?"

Carey took the bar from his mouth. "I can walk the property and do it. No reason to leave Fee alone. I'll meet you in the warehouse when I'm done. You and Fee can help me load the equipment onto the boat."

"Thanks. I appreciate… all of this. I know it's costing us…" Jack had agreed to help out, but only if they refunded his training session money. It was costing the business over a hundred thousand dollars. Not that he'd tell Fee that.

"It's worth it. Whatever we have to pay to keep her safe."

"Brooks, is this costing you money?"

The back of his neck grew warm. His brother shifted his gaze to Brooks, who shook his head slightly. *Don't.*

"Good to see you, Fee." Carey swept past Brooks to give her a kiss on her cheek. "Have you been out on the water yet?"

"The other day. Did I hear you say this is costing your family money?"

Tongue-tied silence on both their parts. Fee put her hands on her hips. "I want to be included in all the details. If there's a money issue—"

His brother cleared his throat before opening the door. "I'm going to get to work."

"Bueno," Brooks said.

"Brooks?" Fee placed her hands on his chest. "Is it?"

Moving his hands down to the belt straps on her jeans, he pulled her closer. "Did you know that I built this cabin on land I purchased for you?"

"What?"

"It's yours. I purchased it to give to you on our wedding day, as part of my vows. I put the deed in both of our names. It belongs not only to me. It belongs to you. Should I reimburse you for it now?"

"Brooks, that's... beautiful... and so touching." She fumbled with a strand of hair, cleared her throat. "I had a ring made for you. From that meteorite we found while hiking in New Mexico."

His heart. "You always did thoughtful things like that."

"It's gone now. I should've saved it." She reddened, as if realizing what she'd said, and shook her head. "All of that's different from what I meant. I'm costing you money. Your family. Your business. I need to pay you back."

"This business you're so concerned about was your idea, remember? You wanted to help me find work that I could do and love. You've never taken money for that. What would your finder's fee be for helping secure a business that has been a boon to me and my family for eight years?"

She still pretended to be angry, but her eyes gleamed. "I'm glad it's been so successful."

"You've given me so many gifts." Including a love he couldn't begin to measure. "Please don't try to keep me from giving something back to you. And, so we're clear, that includes this property."

"The property?"

He took her hand, bent low, and brought it to his lips. He kissed her knuckles, inhaling the soft scent that he'd missed like air. "Mi case es tu casa. For as long as you want it."

"Promise?" she whispered.

He lifted his head, stared into her eyes for a long, long time before he found his voice. "I love you, Fee. And that's forever."

## CHAPTER FORTY-SEVEN

Risk without reward was what got stupid people caught. Momma always said, "Stupid is as stupid does." Ed watched as Liam Forster met his destiny with his dick and his hat in his hands.

Well, his dick in his tight black leather pants and his bondage hat in his hands. Enhancing the images on the screen, Ed watched the recording. Again.

It got better every damn time. This guy was gold. An obviously aroused Liam Forster entered the BDSM room at the private club, his heavy boner outlined in the thick leather pants.

*Ready to burst before the first whip falls, Liam? Wait until your dominant finds out.* Ed laughed. It didn't ruin anything, already knowing what would happen.

Liam approached the rack filled with whips, ball-gags, belts, spikes, dildos, and cuffs. Ringing his bondage hood in his hands, he waited like an obedient schoolboy even as he shook with anticipation. His kink would be his undoing. Few plans in life worked out this perfectly.

It had taken years and lots of manipulation, but, eighteen months ago, Liam Forster had started snooping around, looking for The Great One, hoping to promote his ambitions. He hadn't been the first. But then the detective had stumbled onto MOTO. And Ed's defenses went up. A background check revealed Liam Forster was dating none other than Felicity Shields.

This had prompted intense research. Discovering Liam had a deep dark sexual secret and bold political ambitions... well, you could be a lot of things in politics, but you couldn't be a fag and a freak with a female fiancée. Well, actually, you could. You just couldn't do it if you didn't want to be blackmailed.

It'd been a no-brainer to string Liam along, make him think he was part of the real MOTO, and make him the fall guy. Over the year, the detective was fed lead after lead into The Great One. None of it real. But Foster thought himself on the verge of discovering who The Great One was. He thought this would launch his political career. He'd walked into a trap that made him look more guilty than sane.

And the detective hadn't shared any of this uncovered information with anyone. Nope. Why would he share when he wanted all the glory and credit for himself?

Stupid is as stupid does.

Liam imagined himself as the one who'd capture The Great One, earn the love of the girl, and the political backing of her mother. Even before Ed's interference, it hadn't been working out.

Dorothy had seen right through Liam. She'd seen how he treated her daughter, and strongly suspected he dated Fee for the political connections. If she'd known the full truth, she would've exposed him.

Ed had kept that from happening by misleading the investigator Dorothy had sent to research Liam. She'd been a smart old broad. She'd suspected Liam so deeply that she wouldn't have let it go but for the fact that her daughter had insisted she stop.

Oh, what she'd would've seen had she not respected her daughter's wishes.

On the computer screen, the door opened and in stepped a man clad from head to toe in leather. Except for the proud area surrounding his erection. Liam flinched.

Again laughter bubbled up. It had taken a bit of maneuvering to see that this particular paid consort had found his way to Liam's attention. He was worth the money. Every inch worth.

Ladies and gentleman, today the part of dominant will be played by Jason, a man chosen specifically for one qualifying characteristic—an enormously large penis.

Jason bound Liam with expert and jerking tugs, securing his wrists above his head. He stared at Liam's arousal. "Did I give permission for that?"

No, you did not. Snort.

Liam trembled, shook his head, whimpered.

"You'll pay the price then." Jason slipped on Liam's bondage mask. "What's the word?"

"Strawberry," Liam spoke the pre-arranged word that would stop the action if Jason went too far.

Jason grabbed Liam's hard-on, tweaked it. Liam stiffened, threw back his head, said nothing. Jason grunted and proceeded to violently and explosively redden Liam's fine chap-outlined ass.

Kind of a turn-on.

For Liam too, judging by his throbbing erection.

The chiming of a cell phone. This was it. Mouth suddenly dry, Ed answered, "Good evening, Great One."

"Mmmm," the voice purred, obviously liking the

attribute. "You've played an impressive game." His Southern accent released a torrent of excitement. An instant and open reaction to power and perhaps the sexually charged show. Liam moaned as Jason worked him deeply and cruelly.

"But there is a value here you might not realize you've stumbled upon."

"I'm not sure I understand."

"You're not meant to understand yet, Edwina. Finish the job. Kill Felicity Shields. Frame Liam Forster as the leader of your group. If you do all of that, you will be welcome in my organization."

The fact that The Great One understood the plan down to every unspoken detail, including her real name, wasn't a surprise. The man was a genius. And this offer... It was everything. What it had all been about.

The grooming of the men. The setting up of the group. The killing of the women. All of it had been to get the job, to correct the wayward ship that was allowing society to upend. But why only kill Felicity? "And what of the others?"

"From this moment on, I will take care of them."

A surge of anger. Taking them all out was the dream. It took effort, but she let it go. To be a believer in The Great One's writings meant obedience. That devotion came from seeing firsthand what had happened in a world where women forgot how to be safe.

Her daughter had paid the price. It was beyond heartbreaking. All it took was common sense and the basic instinct of an animal to stay away from predators, but women wanted to keep perpetrating the lie that they were victims. Did the lamb accuse the lion? No, it ran.

The Great One... History, and logic proved that some led while others followed. Some killed while others died. Ed believed wholly in the plan that would shape and save the world. The world needed homogeny. And discipline. It needed clearly defined roles. "It'll be done soon. It's already in the works."

"Can Detective Forster do the deed? If he can't, it will be much harder to frame him for all of this."

As little as three months ago, the answer would've been *no*. No way Liam Forster would kill Felicity Shields. Now...

"I have a video," she said, eyes glued to the intense pounding Liam was taking, "that will assure that the detective does exactly what is asked of him."

"Good. You don't have to worry about confining the actions to her. The rest of the family can be removed, too. This has to look like a group of misogynist terrorists led by a vindictive and scorned man."

It basically was. Except for the part about being led by Liam. Not that he'd survive long enough to deny it. "I've got this. This will spark the war, the copycat groups that your writings speak of, forcing women to seek safety from the plague, revealing the fallacy of their position in the workforce, and allowing the autocrat to rise to power and initiate the global cleansing."

The strong survive, like in nature.

There was a long moment of silence. A thread of discomfort.

The Great One finally spoke again. "If you fail...."

"I won't fail."

"Good. After Liam is framed and Felicity Shields is dead, I'll come for you. Trust me on that. Do not doubt it. You belong to me now."

He hung up. Chills rolled down her skin. It was done. This was the dream. To be wedded to a powerful man.

On the screen, Liam came explosively, shuddering and jerking in his restrains. Well, at least he'd had fun. "Buckle up, detective," Edwina purred. "That's not the only way you're going to get screwed."

## CHAPTER FORTY-EIGHT

Catching a serial killer called for long sleeves, waterproof pants, and sturdy boots. Fee was clomping down the stairs in the gear Brooks had provided, ready to join him and Carey in the warehouse, when her cell rang. Stopping on the last step, she answered. "Hey, Flor."

"Finally. I've been trying to call you for the last two days."

Fee's cheeks grew warm. "I was offline. What's up?"

"Weaver is dead."

Fee jerked. She sunk onto the step, blindly gripping the phone. Blackness pinched the edges of her vision. Weaver, a nineteen-year-old child. She'd been vulnerable, hurt already. She should've been protected. Fee dared not speak. Vomit would spurt form her mouth.

She cried, and, on the other end, Flor cried, too. For long moments, neither one of them said anything. Finally, Flor sniffed. "I never met her. We only spoke on the phone, but she was one of us. You know?"

Tears flooded her eyes and rolled down her cheeks. "How?"

"Something to do with her heart. Must've given out from the trauma. But so young. It's insane. And, hold tight, Skye Jukes is blaming you. She's telling people you poisoned Weaver."

Saliva pooled in her mouth and her head spun. She caught hold of the railing and lumbered to her feet. "That makes no sense. I've been out of the country for two days."

"And offline."

"So?"

"Hermana, you're all over the Internet. There's a video of you threatening people with a gun outside Weaver's hospital. Meeks is looking for you."

"She can't think that I...."

"Who knows what she thinks? But I don't. This is social media manipulation. Like what you described after we met. The thing is, it's not just you. Suspicion and accusations are being thrown at all of us."

Taking a deep breath, Fee wiped the tears from her eyes. Her stomach hollowed out. Her heart broke. "All of the women on the list simultaneously?"

"Just those of us who met."

"Are they still saying we're in a cabal?"

"Exactamente. The coverage has slipped from us as victims to us as criminals. Here in Puerto Rico, there is obsessive coverage on my mom, of how much money she took, how that impacted the island's finances and cost lives. Those facts are veering into crazy theories. Like maybe my mom was part of the cabal. And maybe I know where she's run off to. Maybe I've been biding my time, waiting to join her."

This was insane. How did people even believe this stuff? "I'm so sorry."

"Me, too. Some are even suggesting that my mom is The Puppeteer. That maybe this is all a ruse so I can leave Puerto Rico without drawing suspicion about where I've gone. I lost my job because of the coverage."

"I lost my job, too."

There was a long moment of silence, each of them grappling with being caught in this web. Fee could hardly wrap her head around it. It was supposed to be one person at a time. Now, all of the women were experiencing the social media spotlight that signaled they were next.

A long, considered pause. "¿Qué vas a hacer?"

"I have no idea what I'm going to do." She couldn't reach out to Meeks. "Look, it seems we're all being neutralized."

"Feels more like we're being targeted. Jazz lost security clearance for her work. I can't get hold of Ali. This is really bad."

She was right. Strings were being pulled. It felt like being a puppet. "Anything else?"

The dog barked again. Flor shushed him. "Someone put a bounty out on my mom. Some rich asshole. How long before people show up at my door asking me to 'fess up?"

A bounty on her mother? "Does Meeks know?"

"She knows. She's begged me to go into protective custody."

"Maybe you should."

"No. I can't hide and do nothing."

Fee cringed. Shouldn't have taken so long for herself. Not in the middle of all this. "What's your plan?"

"Find my mom. Get answers, like why our mothers met. Prove my mom innocent. And make this a-hole pay *me* the ten-mil."

"And if you can't prove your mother is innocent?"

"*If* she did what they say," Flor took long deep breath, "I'll turn her in."

Fee closed her eyes and tried to imagine being caught in a great race for her own mother, all in the hopes of proving her innocent. God, she hoped Flor *could* prove it. What she was attempting was beyond dangerous. "I want to help."

"How?"

"I'll keep track of stories on social media. I'll do research. I'll start right away. You're right about our mothers knowing each other. Maybe, there's something we're missing."

"Agreed. Gracias."

"Be careful, my sister."

"Y tu, hermana," Flor said and hung up.

The world was going mad. She needed to go online and start tracking trending stories. First, she needed to speak to the others.

Shoulders in knots, Fee called Jazz. She didn't answer. Crap. She tried Ali.

"Hello?"

Thank God. "It's me."

"Fee?" Ali said, talking loudly into the phone. In the background, helicopter blades chopped the air.

"Yeah." She elevated her own voice, gripping her phone tighter, pressing it to her ear.

"Where have you been? Never mind. I'm running," Ali said, but Lachlan's voice corrected, "Tactical retreat."

The pounding whoosh of blades through the phone made it hard to hear. She put her finger in her other ear as Ali continued, "My mom sent me a message. She claimed to be…" Her words were lost. "…a warning about The Great One."

"Your mother sent you a message? How?"

"Didn't you hear? It's all over the news. She's escaped her high-security facility." Her voice broke into a laugh that sounded wholly unglued. "Could be a real clue or it could be she feels like it's her job to kill me before The Puppeteer does."

"I'm so sorry, Ali."

This was insane. The Puppeteer had unleashed all the barely held pieces of each of these women's lives. What was the end goal?

Maybe his game was designed to create a mess for investigators, for Meeks. A mess that just kept getting bigger, making it harder to keep the women on the list safe. Or maybe there was a piece of the puzzle she was missing, something that would make this all make sense. "Ali, I'm going to do research. We're missing something. Keep—"

"We're going," Lachlan said. "Hang up."

"Don't tell me what to—"

Helicopter blades? Or a scuffle? Whatever it was, the line went dead.

## CHAPTER FORTY-NINE

The warehouse's overhead lighting, strung along the rafters, blinked yellow over the large, chilly open space. The wonky, solar-dependent system gave the area an impending-doom, horror-movie feel.

Nah. It wasn't the lights. Brooks' knotted gut said Fee was taking way too long to get out there. She had to be safe. Sappho and Blanco had three commands for three different parameters. Patrol was the widest. Guard was smaller, a half-kilometer radius. And Set was the smallest, the house and the visible property. They would've been all over an intruder. He still wished he was up at the house with her. Wished for one more day.

"¿Qué pasa?" Carey asked.

Nothing was up. So said the dogs and the surveillance cameras' feed on his tablet. Absolutely nothing. Except, his gut. "Nada."

The warehouse setup was similar to a barn with different stalls and sections for survival gear, weapons, ATVs, climbing gear. Grabbing another box of equipment from the survival gear section, he walked out and set it on the ATV trailer.

Cold, windy air gusted against him, wafting his open jacket behind him. The weather had shifted. Rarely snowed this time of year, but damn sure snowing now.

*Broken P*

Big, wet flakes. He two-finger whistled and relaxed a fraction at Sappho's barked, *all-clear* response.

Fee was fine. Rubbing heat into his hands, he tied the final box, securing it with the others. Finishing, he looked toward the house. It wasn't only fear for her safety.

As a young man, he'd been so sure they'd be together forever. He hadn't cherished every moment with her. When they'd lost each other, he'd lived a darker life, the day-to-day torment of losing her. Those minutes had ticked by with agonizing slowness. The time he spent with her now whisked by so quickly, it was like jumping forward in time.

"I can handle this last batch," Carey said. "I'll take the boat around and meet Papí and the group at the site. You and Fee can join us when you're ready."

"You sure?"

Carey let out a gust of air. "Yeah. I know what it's like to love someone and come close to losing them, only to have them delivered back. After Janelle survived her cancer, I didn't want to let her go to the bathroom without me."

Brooks smiled. "That's a bit more intense than I am."

"Well, to be fair, for a while I had to help her go to the bathroom, so when she could do that for herself, I was a wreck. Would she fall? Would she need me but not want to ask? And there was also the fear that she wouldn't need me anymore."

Brooks had never realized that Carey had gone through all of that. It meant something to him, his brother sharing this now. They'd both come a long way these past eight years.

Carey checked the lines on the boxes. "My point is everything is under control. This guy, and whatever idiotas follow him, have no idea yet where we are. Even if they did know, no one is getting near your place with the dogs and security cameras."

"Verdad. Pero—"

"We don't need you to give these guys the lay of the outlying land. I've done it as many times as you have. Take a two-way. We'll give you updates on our progress and meet you back here in a few hours."

Feeling like shit about it didn't mean he was going to keep arguing. He handed him the iPad. "Gracias."

Before Carey could even respond, Brooks and his tactical boots were eating up ground. Snow whipped into his face and onto his hat. His workpants swished as he jogged up the steps, drawing both dogs. They came around the house, but, too well-trained to give him more than a glance, went right back to their jobs.

Inside the cabin, Fee sat at the table, laptop open, her face scrunched in pain. Tears washed down her cheeks.

His heart doubled its pace. "What's going on?"

She swiped under her eyes. "Weaver is dead."

Grief, hot and painful, stiffened his stride over to her. "Coño." She'd been fine. Hurt and healing, but out of danger. "How? I thought she was stable."

"The rumor is heart attack. Skye is blaming me. Saying I poisoned her. Worse, the stories about Weaver being a fledgling recruit for my so-called cabal are everywhere."

"You're trending?"

"Not just me." She waved toward the computer.

"The Internet is saturated with stories involving women from the list."

Shaking the snow from his all-weather jacket, he hung it on the chair next to her, then rubbed her back. Despite the hollow sadness inside, the reality of her delicate shoulders cupped in his palm calmed him. "All of the women? At the same time?"

"Just the ones who met with me. My so-called cabal." She clicked through several open tabs and stopped. "According to this article, Jazz's mom is a mad scientist who raised her daughter to be a bioterrorist."

"Have you contacted her? Is she okay?"

"I called her. Flor called her. No answer."

His gut tightened. He thought of Jazz's optimism. Her blue streak of hair. The way she talked with her hands. *Please let her be okay. Let them all be okay.*

Fee clicked another tab. "Ali's mom escaped from her hospital for the criminally insane in Los Angeles."

He took the seat next to her. "I read Ali's mom was unresponsive, showing little reaction to stimuli in years."

"Well, she somehow escaped and sent her daughter a message."

Cold doubt swept along his nerves. "Or *someone* took her from the state hospital and sent the message."

"Maybe. When we spoke, Ali said she and Lachlan were in hiding, trying to figure out what's going on."

This was why. His gut had known. Something bad was happening. "And Flor?"

She rolled her head on her neck, cracked her

knuckles, then clicked on another tab. "An anonymous person put a ten-million-dollar bounty on her mom."

Like they'd gone from playing checkers to chess with none of the right pieces. "Díos. She's going to have a lot of people creeping around her."

"Yeah. I thought what we were doing would help them, but even if we publicized where I am today, luring TP up here could take time." She wrung her hands together. "But I have a way of finding information that could help everyone and tell us what investigators know." She looked him in the eyes. "It's illegal."

He placed his steadying hand back on her shoulder. Really, it helped ground him, too. "¿Qué?"

Her face blushed pink then red. "I'm going to look on Liam's computer. At his work files."

Brooks' hand slipped from her shoulder. "How can you can do that?"

"Like this," she said, and started hitting keys.

## CHAPTER FIFTY

The rumble of Carey's boat starting up and driving away buzzed in Fee's ears. Her earlier guilt about money was forgotten. Sitting at the table next to Brooks, she focused solely on helping her list-sisters.

"Before I got engaged," she told him, clicking and typing, "my mom made no secret of the fact that she didn't like Liam."

"A direct woman."

"And a careful woman. She saw the changes in my personality. She asked me questions, brought over reading material about gaslighting." Fee closed her eyes against the onslaught of guilt. Her fingers on the keyboard paused. She'd practically thrown her mother out for her efforts. But Mom hadn't given up. "Of course, she'd already done a background check on him that turned up nothing. And since I kept my mouth shut about our deeper issues... What could she do?

"After my engagement, she lost it. Came right out and told me she didn't trust him and that, although she hadn't looked, she'd set up a backdoor on Liam's computer. She said it was my choice and she'd respect it. But before I married him, I should go in and see if her instinct about him was correct."

Brooks lifted his head to the ceiling, blew a kiss to Heaven, and looked back at her. "You never used it?"

"No."

"Never told him?"

"God no." The thought horrified her. "It's a complete invasion of privacy. And illegal. He would've been rightfully enraged."

Worse, Liam would have felt justified in using that knowledge to get a concession or political endorsement from her mom. He'd made no secret that he was interested in running for state senate. "I figured, because I would never use it, the existence of the backdoor was irrelevant."

Brooks nodded at her laptop. "And you can access it from here?"

"Yes." Her fingers paused on the keyboard. "This is very illegal. Internationally illegal. There could be ramifications. Maybe, I shouldn't do this here. I could go into town—"

He moved his arm from her shoulder to the back of her chair, leaned closer. "Open it."

She clicked into applications. "Mom set up the backdoor so it would be as simple as possible."

She clicked on a square green icon. It whirred, led her through a series of steps and asked for the password. She remembered it easily. Her birthday. She entered it. The computer whirred and the program popped open full screen.

Her mother appeared on screen. Short blonde hair, soft blue eyes, laugh lines around her mouth. Fee gasped.

Mom crooked her head. "I think that's working." And looked directly into the camera.

"Did you know?"

"No." She couldn't whisper another word. This

was different from other videos of Mom she'd seen since she'd passed. This was a message meant for her.

"Fee, darling. It was my hope that one day you'd come to look in this file. I know that whatever is happening in your life right now must be truly difficult. I'm so sorry. But you've made the right decision."

Fee took a tissue and wiped her eyes. Mom to the rescue. Again. "Whatever you discover, I want you to remember that you're strong enough to handle this. No matter what, it's better to know the truth than to spend a lifetime with someone who doesn't deserve, and can never return, your love. It'll be okay, Fee. You will always have my love."

An anguished sob exploded from her. Brooks reached to pause it.

"No, please." Tucking down her grief, she gathered her composure. "I'm... I'm okay."

The image of her mom disappeared. The computer beeped. A message appeared:

View weekly recordings? Y or N?
Press Esc to exit.

What was this? "I assumed Mom had given me the ability to search his computer. I never asked... should I exit?"

"No. You'll still be able to see what he's been working on."

True. She pressed Y.

A series of dated and time-stamped images came up. She picked randomly from the list, a few days ago, and they began to make their way through the videos.

Three hours later, Fee was beginning to think this had been a terrible idea. Not only was it boring, but they'd learned nothing of any real value. Except that Liam had a compulsive need to look her up on social media.

Brooks returned from making her tea and set it beside her.

She clicked another video. It opened to Liam going through his personal email. He clicked and discarded. A new email came in. He clicked it. Hit the attachment. "Oh my God."

"Porn," Brooks said.

Aggressive porn. Gay porn. The man on screen was tied up, hooded, being violently fucked by a man dressed in all black. The room was filled with tools and….

A telltale birthmark caught her attention on the hooded man's shoulder. Fee's face burned. Her hand rose of its own accord to her mouth and clamped down on her jaw.

"Could this be work related?" Brooks asked.

Those texts she'd seen. She'd assumed it was a woman. She'd never once thought…. She spoke through her fingers. "That man, the one tied up, is Liam."

Brooks leaned closer. "How can you tell?"

She pointed to the birth mark. "Liam stopped sleeping with me two months after I agreed to marry him, but I'd know that birthmark anywhere."

"He stopped sleeping with you? And you weren't even a little suspicious?"

"He gave me a list of excuses. We should wait for the wedding. Absence makes… yadda yadda. And, of course, the ones that simply blamed me. Not sure who he lied more to, me or himself. What an asshole."

Brooks squeezed her closer. "Verdad. The guy tortured you. You weren't sexually compatible and, rather than face that fact, he made it your fault."

The tension in her shoulders caused a sudden and sharp pain. There was a lot to unpack there. But all the ways Liam's denial and self-loathing had hurt her wasn't something she could deal with right now. Rolling her shoulders, she moved to exit the video.

Brooks grabbed her hand. "Wait."

An email notification had popped up. In the recording, Liam paused the video. He opened the message and clicked on the link. Something that looked like Google Earth opened in another window.

An overview of the world switched to North America. Canada. Realization tapped her awareness and all the blood in her body froze. The image zoomed in on British Columbia. Her stomach clenched. The image tightened on Vancouver.

Brooks hit the table. "That cabrón."

The image that appeared was Vancouver Island. And not *just* Vancouver Island, but a satellite view of the very house they sat inside. The dock. The boats. The seaplane. The trees and wildness of the area.

It shouldn't matter that Liam knew where she was. He was a detective working on her case. He was aware of Brooks. It wouldn't have been hard for him to put together where she'd gone. And kinky sex didn't make Liam any different from the average person.

Except Liam had been lying to her for years. Lying about his love for her that he obviously never had had. Lying about their relationship. He'd cheated on her. Lying about what he wanted from her. Too aggressive, right? So, she had to ask herself, what *else* was he lying about?

As she watched, dumbstruck, Liam researched Delgado Land, Sea, and Air Tours. He went to the company website, clicked on the calendar, clicked on the schedule.

Fee gripped the table. Liam searched the calendar. He clicked on this week's tour. The instructors were listed as Brooks Delgado and Carey Delgado. The schedule hadn't been changed for obvious reasons. Which meant that it seemed like Fee was here alone. A shudder racked her.

Brooks squeezed her shoulder. "Look at me."

She turned to him, stared into his honey-brown eyes. He ran a finger along her cheek. "Is Liam capable of killing you?"

"Yes." The answer came before she could think about it, but it felt right. "It kind of makes sense. Liam was exposed to The Great One's writings during the Bart Colson case. He could've been radicalized. And he could've easily gotten into my mom's home. He had access to the women on the list, their numbers and addresses. He'd could've lured Weaver away with the promise of information. He can be charming. She would've been comfortable ditching her security to meet him."

The evidence left her trembling. Who was this man she'd lived with? Had he ever cared for her? "What are we going to do?"

Brooks exhaled, rubbed a finger up and down the bridge of his nose. "It's sooner than we'd planned, but this is what we wanted. We have men in the woods ready for this exact scenario. Let him come."

"But... I don't want to kill him. Or anyone. And we have clues here, information that could get him arrested."

"No. There isn't time to go through all these files in the hope of finding proof that Liam is The Puppeteer. Without it, getting in touch with Meeks is pointless. Hell, getting any kind of law enforcement up here would take time we don't have."

She looked around. "Do you think he'll come tonight?"

"Doubtful. But within the next four days. The nights that the training is supposed to run."

"We need to alert the others."

"Yeah. And that means we get you someplace safe now."

"Me? We talked about this. I want to be part of this plan. I'm the bait. He needs to see me, moving about the house. That way, he'll relax and make his move."

"He doesn't need to *see* you. He'll see the lights on. He'll assume you are alone. I have six highly-trained men, plus Papí and Carey. When he comes here, we'll take care of him."

His family? But not her? Oh, hell no. "Together. Remember?" She placed her hand over his heart. "You promised."

## CHAPTER FIFTY-ONE

Standing beside the dining room table in his great room, Brooks shivered at Fee's words. He'd promised her they would tackle this together. But now that this moment was here, now that he'd seen Liam's obsession with Fee—the guy checked her updates on social media every two minutes—and knew that that shit was coming here... He wanted this fucker. And wanted, needed, Fee to be nowhere near this.

He had to convince her. He placed his hand atop hers. "You once sent me away to protect me. It saved my life. I want to return the favor. I need you to go—"

"Hell, no. I grew up with Secret Service. I learned self-defense before I learned to drive. I can shoot. If he comes here, he needs to see the bait. Like you said, we have a plan. This is even better. He'll think you're in the woods with Carey and the others. We can trap him."

"Querida, there is another way. Why risk you unnecessar—"

"This isn't your choice." She snatched her hand back. "I invited him into my home, my bed, and my mind. There is only one way out of this for me. I need to stand up for myself. I need to face him. I need to end this. And I need you to believe I can."

*Mierda.* If he fought her on this, he was saying he

didn't trust her. Even while she stood there and told him she once again trusted herself. Something he understood had been hard-won for her. As much as he wanted to protect her, his lack of faith would destroy her. Loving her, supporting her, meant being okay with her decision, with her being her true self.

Every cell in him growled with despair.

Brooks brushed a hand along her forehead, down the side of her face, tucking strands of soft blonde hair behind her ear. He ached with love for her. Was it possible to love someone so much that you'd stand beside her in the face of danger instead of putting yourself before her?

He brushed his lips across her forehead. "I'd wondered what I could do to get him out of your head." He rested his lips there. "I'd wondered how I could push into that spot," he kissed her forehead, "that he'd taken over. I guess I didn't realize getting rid of him wasn't my job."

"I guess I didn't realize it either," she said. "Not Mom's, not yours. Mine."

He drew in a breath that pricked like thorns in his lungs. Pulling her into his arms, placing his chin on top of her head, he held her as tightly if he feared she'd float away. "We do this together. We wait for him to come here, wait for him to pose a threat, reveal himself, and then we take him out. Together."

She eased away, her face brighter, hopeful, but with a touch of worry. "Like I said, I don't want to kill him. Or anyone."

*Díos.* "And if he doesn't give us a choice?"

Felicity's gaze snapped to him. The confident angle of her shoulders reminded him so strongly of her mother that a pang of pride pierced him. "The truth is, I don't want to, but I can. I will. And I don't need hate to do it. I have other motivations. The women this man would silence. The women he has already silenced. Your family. You and me. Don't doubt it. If he won't yield, I will stop him permanently."

Liam would never get close enough for her to have to make that choice. He'd make sure of it. "I'm going out to the warehouse to get supplies. We need to tighten this place up and prepare. I'll get a long-range two-way, so I can connect with the others."

He grabbed his tactical jacket from the back of his chair. "I have bulletproof vests in the warehouse. You will be wearing it."

"Bring two. You'll be wearing one, too."

Damn straight. "Be right back."

## CHAPTER FIFTY-TWO

Brooks stepped out onto the porch. The winds had increased, the tremble and chug were freight-train-loud against his cold ears.

The moon glowed yellow and full, highlighting the snow falling sideways. A two-fingered whistle called Sappho and Blanco to Brooks. He wasn't leaving Fee alone, even for a minute.

Where were the dogs? He tried again, whistling louder into the driving wind. The glowing screen of his watch showed a minute passed. Snowflakes beaded on the glass. Two minutes. This had never happened before.

He strained to hear the slightest bark over the wind. His pulse ticked like a time bomb in his neck. Easing back into the house, he locked the door and took out his sidearm.

Forcing calm, he stalked through each room, and checked the locks on the back doors and windows. Security was working. He checked his cell. Extender on. He slipped up the stairs and into their bedroom. Fee came out of the bathroom, gaze zooming in on the Glock. He held a finger to his mouth. The house had been empty for an entire day while they'd kayaked. He'd never thought about checking for bugs so someone could be listening. He didn't dare go out to the warehouse to get detectors. The dogs weren't responding for a reason. Fuck.

"Problem?" Fee's gaze was wide and terrified.

"No problemo. Nada." He gave her a look that said the exact opposite. "But I need help in the warehouse."

She drew in an audible breath. "Right. Let me get my boots."

As she slipped into her jacket and tightened her boots, he moved to the closet. At the back wall, he pushed aside flannel shirts and pressed his thumb to the biometric rifle safe. It popped open with a beep and double flash of a small green light.

Fee joined him in the walk-in closet. She pressed close. "Qué pasó?"

Smart, speaking in Spanish. He took out a rifle and told her about the dogs. "Los perros no vinieron cuando silbé."

Leaning the rifle against the wall, he took two semiautomatic handguns from the shelf. He clipped one of the holstered weapons to his pants, then pocketed extra ammo and two of the four full clips.

He unholstered the other weapon, pointed it at the closet wall, squeezed the trigger enough to demonstrate. The red laser dot appeared on the sleeve of a flannel. Fee nodded. He handed her the holstered weapon. She opened the conceal carry pocket in her pants. He stopped her and attached the weapon securely to her tactical belt then slipped the remaining two full clips and ammo into her pocket. The lights blinked off. A crash sounded from downstairs but no alarm. They'd taken out his electricity. No extender. No cell.

He waited for the backup generator. It didn't kick on. *Coño.* He pushed her out the closet. "La ventana. Ahora."

*Broken P*

Hustling across the room, he locked the bedroom door and slid his desk chair under the handle while Fee navigated the darkness. Downstairs, men, at least three by the sound of it, moved around. Crashing, doors being kicked open, and then boots on stairs.

Sweat beading his forehead, he ran to the window. Fee had it open and was already leaning out.

He tapped her back. She turned, and he pointed to the roof access ladder secured on against the house, used for roof repairs and satellite issues. Never thought he'd need it to escape.

In a blink, she climbed out and disappeared from his site, as soundlessly as a person running for her life.

Ducking through the window, he swung an arm out. The wind and snow had really picked up. Heavy, wet clumps assaulted his face. His grip secure around the rusting metal rung, he pulled himself over. Anchoring a foot, he reached for and quietly pushed the window closed.

The unmistakable sound of the bedroom door crashing open sent him climbing.

Nearly at the top, Fee froze, pointed down. Shifting his gaze, Brooks' throat went dry. His pulse thundered. The howling wind had masked its motors. Papí's Defiant was docked at the pier.

Two men outfitted in black stood guard at the boat as silent as shadows.

Hands gripping cold steel, he watched the men. Big. Business-like. Confident. They wore Delgado training helmets and night vision goggles.

That reality hit him like an open hand. Sharp. Stinging. Humiliating. These were Tate's men, the ones his father had just brought in. Why bother bringing weapons, ammo, night vision goggles when your victims could provide it? Carey had arrived with all of that at the drop site.

These were the men his father had brought into the area, the ones who were supposed to help. They knew the plan. They knew how to get past the security system, past the cameras. They knew everything they needed to know about the cabin.

Fuck. He needed to get to the training site and make sure his family was okay.

Above, Fee hoisted herself over the top. He climbed after, cursing again. This had been in the works a long time. The four-day training session had been thoroughly vetted, planned, and cost $100,000. Liam didn't have that kind of money.

But Tate did.

Scrambling onto the roof, the tip of his boot caught the steel gutter. The tinny gong sounded exactly like what it was—someone climbing on the roof.

Down below, there was the crackle of a two-way. "Check the roof."

Crouched and running, he spotted Fee at the edge that dropped onto the garage. She stood waiting, gun in hand. He waved for her to keep going.

No time to waste. He imagined the two men below already racing around the house. They'd know the garage roof was the easiest way down, the closest to the ground.

He scrambled after her. The coarse, wet shingles scraped his palms. To her credit, she only paused again to make sure he followed before quietly lowering herself off the roof.

He followed behind her, silent as a panther. Better late than never.

## CHAPTER FIFTY-THREE

Fee dropped from the garage roof onto the snow-dusted ground. Fear pounded her ribs like frantic fists against a coffin lid. Gun out, she scanned the dark. Clear. She headed straight for the woods. The traction on her boots helped her navigate the slippery, uneven property.

"There they are!" A shout in the dark. Two men between the warehouse and the cabin. One glance was all she got. Brooks came up on her right, blocking her sightline and providing her the cover.

"Faster, Fee," he whispered hotly. Raising his gun, he fired.

Another shout in the dark. "Kill that fucker!"

A series of shots blasted around them and heated the air. One bit the ground at her feet. She yelped and pushed harder, her boots digging earth.

They made it to the shelter of the tree line beyond the warehouse. Hair saturated, ears ringing with gunfire, she rocked with the terrain, slipping and sliding but never falling.

Brooks pulled her down behind a large tree. Yanking the hat from his head, he shoved it down over her wet hair, tucking in her hair. "You're blonde."

She tucked the rest, exposing her neck to the cold. Little pellets of ice flicked against her skin. Hail. What next?

She blew into her frozen hands. Her jacket, tactical pants, and boots kept the rest of her warm, but she'd give anything for gloves. Give anything for this not to be happening. She wouldn't dare to speak a word, even if she could. And there was Brooks. Calm. Calculating.

He gestured, *Go!* with a drop of his finger. She hesitated for a split-second. As far as she knew, the training ground, with Papí and Carey, was the opposite direction. Tearing out at a crouch, she followed his instruction.

Her feet stamped the snowy ground. Tremor-wracked, cold hands struggled to hold her gun secure. Breath expanded her lungs, and air rushed out in heavy drafts. The growl of ATVs chasing them through the woods made every panicked nerve twitch and jump. They couldn't outrun them.

The bright light of an ATV cut through the woods, landing nearly on her. She veered away and lost her balance. Her hands sunk into snowy mud. Brooks lifted her up by an elbow, dragging her until she regained her feet. They ran another fifty feet before he signaled for her to drop behind a tree.

Panting heavily, she peered around the trunk. The night smelled of snow, mud, and guns. Kneeling beside her, Brooks grabbed the rifle strapped across his back. Aimed. Fired.

The shot crashed like cymbals against her ears. The ATV driver toppled off. The vehicle's speed kept it going. The man on the back tried to get control. A crash of metal. A crack of wood. A scream.

The ATV hit a tree and fell back onto the still-screaming man, his leg twisted unnaturally. "Get it off! My leg!"

The men on the other ATV swooshed past him.

Coming right at them.

Hands quivering, Fee wiped her soil-caked hands against her tactical pants. She looked through the scope of her weapon.

Breathing deeply, she focused her laser on the man driving the second ATV. Tears washed down her face. She shot. The gun jerked in her hand. The gunfire cracked alongside her ears muffling sound beneath a shrill buzzing.

For a perfect moment in time, she couldn't hear a thing, as if the world had been paused. And then someone pressed PLAY again.

The wind whipped in fury, scattering the blood that rocketed from the man's head. The other man dove from the vehicle. The ATV guttered to a halt. Fee's gut churned. Killer. Murderer. She was going to vomit.

Brooks took her face in his cold hands. "Can you run?"

She swiped her tongue over numb lips. The ATV engine revved back to life.

Felicity ran.

#

The moonlight provided enough light to navigate but the snow complicated matters. Compensating for the slick and uneven forest, they twisted, jumped, and avoided fallen branches. She couldn't hear her breath over the wind. But she could feel it tear up her esophagus. The temperature had dropped. The snow came faster now. The wind howled like it had a mission to conquer all other sound.

Brooks signaled her to slow down. They staggered forward. Fee strained to hear ATVs, screams or people chasing.

Nothing.

She caught her breath. Brooks squatted down, scooped up a handful of snow, and handed it to her. "Here. Water. It'll melt in your mouth."

Setting her safety, she slipped the gun into her coat pocket and took the snow. She thought her hands couldn't get colder. The icy water moistened her throat, and sent a shiver down to her toes.

She'd killed someone. Or maybe he wasn't dead. Maybe his buddy took him to get help. Out of necessity, she eased the guilt from her mind. With her breath evening out, she was finally able to talk. "The last guy must have doubled back."

"Might've gone for reinforcements."

True. A million questions about Tate Security, Carey, and Rafael pushed into her head. She dismissed them all. Those questions wouldn't solve their problems. And they had a lot of problems. They had no way to communicate with the outside world, they couldn't walk out of here, and they had no idea where Rafael and Carey were. But Brooks had brought her this way for a reason, so he must have... "What's the plan?"

He looked over her head into the distance. "We sneak in from behind the cabin and grab a boat. It's a quick boat ride to the drop site. We can call the Coast Guard on the way." He cursed. "Papí mentioned seeing trees taken in that area Should've paid more attention. I dismissed it as locals."

She chewed on that for a moment. Chewed on it

with chattering teeth. "You think the trees were taken by men camped out there waiting for the others?"

He nodded.

Oh, God. A shiver ice-picked down her spine. "And if your father brought six guys in for training, there are more than six men out there?"

"Yeah. I counted five at the cabin. If they sent that many, my guess is that they have at least five more out there. Our best bet to find Carey and Papí is to go to the drop site."

Ten men. They'd shot two. One had been injured by the ATV fall. That left at least seven out there. Maybe more. But, *if* they could get a boat, they'd have the Coast Guard. "How do we take a boat without those men spotting us?"

"We go around the inlet and up one of the more moderate climbs we have set up for training."

A climb in the dark with snow didn't sound moderate. "Anchors?"

"Embedded in the rocks the whole way up. Easy to grab and spot."

She couldn't imagine grabbing anything with her cold hands, but she could picture the climb based on what she'd seen from the cabin. "We'll have to go down a fairly steep grade after that, right?"

"Yeah. We end up across the inlet from the cabin. Once there, we can swim—"

"It's freezing."

"It's not. But even with waterproof jacket, pants, and boots it's cold enough, challenging enough, that they won't expect us to attempt it. They'll be covering the ground. Once across, you sneak into Papí's boat. There's an extra key taped to the pilot's seat."

"What will you be doing?"

"I'll be disabling the other boats so they don't follow. And firing on anyone who gets near you."

"This sounds like a horrible plan."

"It's the safest and fastest way. Once we're onboard, we'll call the Coast Guard, and whoever else we can reach while making our way to the drop zone. We need to rescue Papí and Carey."

"Okay." None of this sounded okay. Not hiking through the frigid dark, not climbing at night with no equipment, not a death-defying swim, or stealing a boat moored at a guarded dock. And all of that before they could even *attempt* what she prayed was a rescue operation. Not okay at all.

## CHAPTER FIFTY-FOUR

Brooks shifted his gun from his right to his left, placing his free hand in his pocket to warm his frozen fingers. The cold, unrelenting wind burrowed into his ears. The chill clawed so far down, even his jaw ached. His eyes watered.

The swaying forest branches, whipped by the wind, blocked the moonlight off and on, dancing shadows on the snow. It made the trek over the rocky ground at the foot of the climb more treacherous.

He navigated across and sheltered against the cliff. Fee caught up with him, and he pulled her close. They glanced up at the looming, snow-slicked cliff. It might as well have been a thousand feet high in this wind, with frozen hands, and no equipment.

"Doesn't look so bad," she said.

He looked back at her. "Piece of cake. I'll lead. Twenty feet from the top, there is a fissure cut through the rocks, more like a chimney. It's an easy reach from side to side. We can press back and legs to opposite sides to brace, resting for split seconds as we finish the climb." Brooks kissed her softly. "Te quiero."

Placing her wet, shivering hands on his face, she stared into his eyes. "I love you, too."

Her words warmed yet chilled him. Everything he'd always wanted. And all of it was in danger.

Cupping her hands in his, he drew them to his lips, heated them with his breath. After rubbing circulation into his own hands, he started up. He found the first anchor easily enough, and, once he got going, muscle memory took over.

He checked on Fee's position, heartened to find her keeping up. She'd always been the better climber. He picked up his pace.

His tactical boots weren't the most flexible and didn't provide the best feel. He had to rely more on his upper body strength. Not good when snow coated every edge and ledge. The anchors helped. Coming to a wide crack, he squatted there, rested both knees inside, then balanced back to shake out his arms before continuing up.

He was seriously impressed by how quickly her skills had come back. At the chimney base, a flat area big enough for them both, he waited for her to catch up then nodded when she asked to take the lead.

This might just fucking work.

Once cocooned inside the rocky fissure, the wind lessened. The rocks weren't as slippery and there were multiple points to use body pressure—knees, feet, legs or back—against stone to leverage up. Fee managed the rest of the climb with ease. He breathed a sigh of relief as she scrambled over the top.

Ten feet below her as he reached for another handhold, Fee screamed. The terrified sound sent the hairs on the back of his neck standing.

Concentration wrecked, his hand came down on a sharp edge of stone. He pulled himself up despite the searing stab. A large shadow blocked the moonlight. A figure—bracing something heavy over his head.

Brooks flattened against the stones, But not quickly enough. The boulder smashed against his shoulder, the force knocking him free.

They'd walked into a trap. Or climbed into one. Held in place by a large hand over her mouth and a knife to her jugular, Fee watched in horror as another man lifted an enormous rock over his head and threw it down at Brooks.

Her attacker's hand muffled her scream, but not the horrible, tumbling sounds, or the jarring crash that followed.

The man who'd thrown the boulder flipped down night vision goggles and peered over the edge. "That fucker's still moving."

"Just shoot him," Knife-to-her-jugular said.

With a shrug, boulder man unslung his rifle and aimed.

Jerking and twisting, she struggled to free herself. The knife dug into her skin. Warm blood ran down her neck.

Knife-to-jugular jerked the blade away, tightened his hand against her mouth. "Stop squirming. I need you alive."

She struggled harder. A gloved finger slipped between her lips. She bit.

"Bitch." He hammered the hilt of the knife into her stomach.

She gagged. Her vision swam. Her mouth watered. Vomit spurted out of her mouth and between the guy's gloved fingers.

"Fuck!" He dropped her.

She hit the ground running, nearly tumbling down

the incline that led to the water's edge. They started shooting at her, cursing at one another, before giving chase. Even through her fear, she felt triumphant. Better they chased her than shoot Brooks. *Please be okay, Brooks. Please be okay.*

She careened down the hill, darting around trees. Her jacket and pants swished. Her feet clipped rocks and roots. She stayed upright then slid and smacked into a tree. She bounced off and kept going.

The men's footsteps pounded behind, racing, searching. Not shooting. Guns down. They wanted her alive. *Advantage—Fee.*

For now, anyway.

Diving to the ground, she fumbled in her jacket for her gun, and aimed. "Stop!"

The men kept walking.

Her throat already hot and sour tightened with determination. "I will fucking stop you if you don't stop yourselves."

This time they did stop. Knife-to-jugular brought his gun up. A fraction of time, a fraction of effort from her cold, sore fingers against the trigger. A split second that saved her and doomed him.

*Crack.*

His neck burst open.

Her elbow slammed back.

An electric zing punched up her arm.

He dropped, arched, fell. Gurgling choking sounds impossibly loud and clear in her ears.

Boulder man, the man who might've hurt Brooks, dodged to the side, slipped to one knee, the tip of his gun jamming into the ground. Fee shot. Missed.

Ears muffled with the recoil, she shot again. The

sound slapped against her head. Jerked her. Blood poured down her face. Not sound. She spun.

The man was only a blur as he knocked the gun from her hand. He grabbed her arm, twisted, and shoved a knee into her stomach .

Pain wracked her. She struggled to see through the warm blood pouring from the wound in her temple, sliding down her face. She fought, rocking and bucking. Nausea and dizziness made her attempt weak and ineffective. Mud and snow coated her face and eyes.

The man rolled her, zip-tied her hands behind her back. "Stupid, bitch. We put a tracker in your boot. I've been sitting by the water drinking coffee while your dumbass made that climb."

She cried out and a gag was quickly and forcefully tied across her open mouth. Her tongue pushed against the dirty, muddy fabric. The man hoisted her over his shoulder as if she weighed no more than a sack of flour and headed down the mountain to the water.

## CHAPTER FIFTY-FIVE

Brooks dropped down the rocky fissure, his arms snapping out mechanically. His wrist slammed stone, exploded with pain. And then something jerked him to a stop, wrenching hard against his ribcage.

His legs shot out, rooting him. Catching his breath, he tried to work a finger through the rifle strap braced across his chest. The butt and tip of the rifle had lodged between the sides of the chimney. It had stopped his fall, but his ribs, pressed against the rifle strap, hurt like they'd been kicked by a mule.

"Fucker's still moving," a man said from above.

"Just shoot him."

Brooks reached for his gun. His hand trembled against his holster and refused to work. Fuck. He reached across with his left hand and pulled out his weapon. Keeping his feet braced, angling his torso, he pointed upward.

He needed a miracle shot while the guy above him was shooting fish in a barrel.

The wind whipped down. His jacket, ripped open in the fall, bucked and filled with air. He pressed his knees against stone and tightened his one-handed grip. No one came.

No time to wonder. Fee was up there. With whoever was supposed to shoot him.

He tucked his gun, latched onto rock, and tried to climb. His rifle, wedged good between the rock walls, stopped him. *Mierda.*

He unhooked himself from the strap, used the rifle like a pull-up bar to raise himself up. Pain shot through his wrist. He leaned into it, struggled past the weapon. Breath hot, legs quivering like the St. Lawrence fault, he kept moving. Every torturous ascending moment echoed his heart's rallying cry. *Fee! Fee!*

Blood, sweat, and snow dripped into his eyes. Probably had a concussion.

Shots fired.

Bunching his strength in his legs, he launched upward, then threw out his feet to stop from falling back.

At the top, he pushed again with his legs and flew up through the opening. He slanted his body, arching into the turn, and pointing his gun. He landed on his bad side, with his gun shaking but ready to shoot—

No one.

Scrambling to his feet, he crept toward the woods and the descent that led to the inlet. Fee wouldn't have run along the cliff. She'd have headed for the cabin, the water, the boats. Like they'd planned.

"I left the boyfriend on a cliff. Definitely injured. Dropped a boulder on him."

He ducked behind a tree. Two men walked up from the inlet. Below, a boat took off.

One of them snorted. "Still can't believe she killed Damon."

"Fuck, dude. Not cool."

Laughter. "It's funny as shit. He was a moron.

And she's about to feel some shit a lot worse than being shot. Karma. Man, she'll get hers."

Weapons focused ahead, night vision goggles on, they finally employed a caution they'd obviously thought unnecessary. Now who was the moron?

Like the calm in the center of an emotional typhoon, he focused the night-vision scope on his semiautomatic on the guy who'd claimed to have dropped a boulder on him. Fired. The crack echoed through the trees, across the water, echoed by another explosive sound more like the popping of a massive cork.

The man dropped. The other crouched, using his friend's corpse as cover. He poked his head up. Brooks shot. The guy's head jerked back, never to pop up again.

Brooks ran to the water. The massive popping sound was, in fact, the pontoons of his plane now going under.

Securing his useless wrist, he got into the inflatable no longer needed by the men he'd killed, and one-arm paddled across to the other side.

He angled for the dock ladder, grabbed hold, and swung up as the boat slipped from under him. He climbed.

Breathing heavily, he looked for the fastest way to Fee. They'd taken out his seaplane and stolen his other two boats. They only had the two ATVs up here. One was blown up. The other somewhere in the woods. Assuming they hadn't taken it. Quicker by land than rowing one-armed to the training site—and he had no doubt that's where they'd gone. He'd have to run.

Jogging up the dock, he surveyed the area. Abandoned. No intruders. No assholes. No Fee. And no… Spotting Sappho and Blanco just beyond the dock, he ran across the snow to their prone bodies.

Swallowing down the cry of outrage, he bent to them. Still breathing. His legs nearly gave out. Tranquilized. Not dead. *Gracias a Díos*.

"Brooks," a voice called softly from the darkness.

Relief tackled his ass and drove him to his knees. It took him a moment to stand. He lowered his weapon. "Carey."

Carey appeared soaking wet, shivering, breathing heavily. Brooks scanned the dark for a sign of anyone else. No one. No boat coming back. He ran over to his brother, embraced him. The man was shivering, but he had on his shell, GORE-TEX drysuit, so he was a damn sight better than he could've been. "Fuck. What happened?"

"Unloading the boat. Hit from behind. Tossed into the water. Should've drowned. The rock I cracked my head on also kept it out of the water and allowed me to breathe."

"Jesus." Brooks could barely bear to ask. "Papí?"

Carey inhaled deeply, shook his head. "When I woke up, I humped it over to the training site. About two miles. Some of the trainees were there, along with about six other guys. Building something. No Papí."

"Let's get the dogs into the house. Get some more weapons from the warehouse. You good to run back?"

In answer, Carey scooped up Sappho and headed for the house. Brooks lifted Blanco and hurried after him.

## CHAPTER FIFTY-SIX

Fee awoke shivering against the snowy ground, trembling so violently, her muscles spasmed. Dark. Moonlight. Freezing. She tried to move and couldn't. Secured at wrists and ankles by ropes, she was attached to spikes driven into the ground. Snow whipped onto and around her.

They'd taken off her hat and jacket. Smoke rose on the air. The whir and rasp of construction. Laughter? She lifted her head. Strands of wet hair blew across her trembling lips. Her vision slanted and spun.

The moon spotlighted the clearing. Snow swirled in eddies, thrashed around stacks of weapons and equipment crates.

She counted the men. Two on ATVs stood on the opposite side of the camp beside a fire. Four men diagonal to her feet. They were building something. Two stood sentry along the clearing. From this distance, they seemed more like long, thin shadows, waiting in the wings. Eight men. That she could see.

Bile rose in her throat. She dropped her head onto the cold ground, blinking away snow and tears.

Above her, a wooden scaffolding loomed like a giant wooden spider. Two crossbeams jutted from the belly piece. Wires hung from them, draped to the ground near her. It took her a moment to recognize what it was. A huge controller for a marionette.

Wild panic thrashed against her like a whip, demanding she move, run, hide. Terror pounded blood into her ears. She pulled on her restraints. The ropes tightened.

Synthetic fibers bit her wrist, trapping blood in her throbbing hands and feet. She was going to die here.

And Brooks.

Oh, God. Brooks. He had to have survived his fall. *Had* to. If not...?

A desperate wail of fear, rage, and helplessness broke from her mouth. Visceral and loud it echoed into the night.

One of the men working nearby yelled, "I want to live. I want to live," in a shrill mocking voice. Laughter erupted from the other men. A figure moved to her right.

Liam. Standing there as if he'd just arrived from the slopes, wearing the expensive, black Ushanka parka he'd ordered from Russia, and the hunter-green Dolomite boots she'd fucking bought him last Christmas. He was examining a braided blonde wig, held over the fist of one hand. Snow covered the top and sides. The braids hung down past his elbow and ended in neatly tied red bows.

"Hi, my name's FeeRocious," he said, moving his fist up and down so the wig bounced.

He giggled, circling closer. His long eyelashes were wet with snow, his cheeks red, his mouth grim and determined.

"Dddid..." Felicity forced the rage-fueled question from her trembling mouth, "kkkill mmmy mother?"

Liam licked his lips. He squatted beside her and

tucked the wig under his arm. He looked at the men securing one of the structure's leg. Their work sent piles of snow plopping to the ground around her. "No."

"Liar."

"Why would I lie? Look at where we are. Look at what I'm being made to do."

"Made? You chose this. You chose to lie to me. You p..p..retended you loved me."

"I do love you—"

"B..b..bullshit. You killed M..Mom." She coughed as cold and snow flew into her mouth. "And Kelly. Weaver."

Liam kept his head turned toward the men working to secure a leg of the scaffolding. One of them was standing. Watching.

Liam leaned closer. He smelled like Liam. His honey soap, dandruff shampoo, and ocean breeze deodorant. His blue eyes flicked to her. "I was trying to find The Great One. I was trying to expose him. For you. For your mom. To prove to you both I was worthy of you."

"For your political career."

He shrugged. "That, too. People do things for their own best interests. If it helps someone else as well, all the better."

"Why propose?"

Liam barked a laugh. "Why did you accept my proposal when you were in love with another man?"

Even with the cold and chill, the truth of his statement sent a hot pang of shame through her. He smiled. "Exactly. Because you benefited from my *in* with the community and with law enforcement. I gave you the respectability you craved. You gave me the political connections and clout I needed. That doesn't mean we loved each other any less. You have to admit we had some fun times."

Liam shook his head, almost sadly. "Your sacrifice is going to matter, Fee. I'm going to help people. I'm going to make a difference."

She spat at him, and it landed on his perfectly square jaw.

He drew back with raised eyebrows and wiped the smudge with his equally wet jacket.

"Hey," a large man carrying a rifle and wearing a balaclava came up behind Liam. "We're done. You're up."

Liam remained where he was. The man shoved his foot against Liam's back. Liam pitched forward, catching himself against Fee's ribcage. Pain and revulsion speared through her.

Grunting, he pushed off her, sending a sickening wave of hot pain spiraling through her stomach and up her throat. Her ribs were damaged from earlier. Carefully, she sipped stuttering, delicate breaths.

Liam picked up the wig that had fallen out from under his arm. He dusted the snow from it.

The man with the rifle faded back. Liam shifted on his haunches and looked at Fee for a long, sad moment. "I'm going to name my daughter after you."

He was insane. "After you kill me?"

"What gave it away?" He put the wig over his fist again, moved it up and down. "Was it me?"

Fear snaked along her skin, leathery and unavoidable. "You've gone insane."

"That's the sanest way to do something insane." He shoved the wig back into his coat. The red-ribboned braids swayed from his pocket like a scalp. "Did you know berserkers were warriors who used to psyche themselves up, hit themselves, curse, growl, and stomp before battle? It's what they needed to do to get in the right mindset. It's where the word *berserk* comes from."

Liam would do this. He'd detached himself from who and what he was in order to kill her.

She gulped air and struggled against her bindings. They seared her frozen skin. "Please don't do this."

Liam looked away. "Like I have a fucking choice."

"You do. Use the knife to cut me free. We can run into the woods." Probably wouldn't make it, but any chance—*any*thing—was better than doing nothing.

He picked up a snow-covered knife from the ground, holding it and staring at it like an actor in *Hamlet* examining Yurick's skull. He took deep, fortifying breaths. "These guys aren't here for you."

All four men were watching now. One pointed his rifle at Liam. "Get on with it!"

Liam's head spun from them to her, from her to them. Roaring like the berserker he imagined he was, Liam lifted the blade, and stabbed it through the palm of her hand.

She screamed, ear-splitting and anguished. Pain ripped through her. Shards of heat tore muscle and ligaments, penetrated nerves, blood vessels, skin bone.

"Shh. Fee, it's okay." He put his weight on the device, driving the sharp metal through her hand and into the ground. "It's okay. Please stop screaming. It's fine."

# CHAPTER FIFTY-SEVEN

For the second time in one night, Brooks full-out ran through the woods. This time he was running toward something instead of away. He barely acknowledged the cold. His focus was on balance, the deer path, scurries and chirps in the woods, and, most importantly, their progress.

They moved at top speed, even with the equipment on their backs and the slick conditions. He cursed the precious time they'd had to take to gather weapons and don bulletproof vests and combat helmets. Tactical advantage was crucial. Carey said there were at least ten men at the training site. Bad odds.

He made up for lost time by taping his aching wrist as they ran. The bite of the tape chafed. Sharp stabs drilled to his shoulder every time a foot hit the ground wrong. Fuck. A hairline fracture at the least.

He was keenly aware of every footfall. Heel. Toe. Heel Toe. Two steps closer to Fee. Two steps closer to keeping his promise.

He held a semi-automatic 9mm Glock 19 in his good hand, safety off. Shoot to kill. Alert to every suspect sound, Brooks prayed they'd find Papí. But they'd seen no one. That didn't mean they were alone, though. Someone had a fire going. He smelled it on the crisp air, wafting with the driven snow.

That fire told him Fee's kidnappers were more concerned with frostbite than Brooks. Stupid would get them killed.

And, yeah, he knew they were well-trained enough to be silently stalking him, but his senses and logic told him they weren't out this far.

Raising his fist, he signaled Carey to stop. They'd run enough training drills to coordinate without speaking. They slowed to a walk, catching their breaths.

Leaving the deer trail, they stalked toward the camp site. It was less than a quarter mile away. Totally isolated. These guys wouldn't waste manpower watching this far out.

A sharp *crack*. He and Carey turned to the sound as one. A fallen tree branch. They never slowed their pace. This was a familiar sound.

Carey put up a gloved hand, pointed. A clearing, no more than a hundred yards, just ahead, was bathed in that fire's glow. They slipped behind trees. Brooks stowed his semi-automatic, and took out the case containing the Nighthawk, a high-powered rifle with a night vision scope. Shielding the weapon from the snow, he put it together in record time.

As silent as his rage, he trekked through the last few feet of woods, scanning through the night vision scope.

When they were within fifty feet, he could see the fire, the scaffolding, and a figure tied to stakes in the ground. *Fee.*

Dropping behind a tree, he scanned with his weapon, marking each man before returning his gaze to Fee—*and* the man squatting beside her. Liam Forster.

He swung back to her to see her struggling against her restraints. Liam was talking. Brooks swept his scope to Liam's head. He could do it. He could put a bullet in the man's skull right now.

Blood pounded in his ears. He put his rage into his furnace, let that burn fuel him without overwhelming him. Mindless anger had no place here. That would get Fee killed. He had to stick with the plan.

Carey signaled, and they were off again. Five men each, if his tally was right. Brooks could see two astride ATVs by the fire, four by Fee, and two at the edge of the clearing. Two were missing.

And... something was off about the scenery. He spent ninety percent of his time during training, stalking these woods. It was part of what he taught trainees—to recognize useful marks in the land, useful plants, useful poisons. So he knew that bush beside a large tree did not belong there. He inched forward to check it out.

Carey put up a finger and pointed to a man walking through the woods, searching the perimeter with a rifle at his side. Weapon down. Moved like he didn't expect trouble. Brooks had a clear shot, but he couldn't take it without alerting others close by. His rifle's silencer still made a definite and knowable *thwuck!*

The scout's trajectory would bring him right into Brooks' path. Better to wait, grab him as he passed. He and Carey stayed hidden behind trees.

The scout got closer.

Closer.

Brooks tensed. Ready.

The bush rose up.

*Not* a bush.

Papí covered the man's mouth, taking him out with a quick and brutal stab that severed his carotid. Blood spurted as he laid the guy gently onto the ground.

Despite the camouflage and his size, Papí advanced through the woods as quietly as a dove. He nodded to them both, eyes barely visible through the twigs and brush that covered him. They moved away soundlessly, and squatted by a tree. Using their practiced hand signals and a map in the snow, Papí laid out his plan.

*Get the men on the perimeter. One down. Three left. One man for each of them to take out.* Papí marked each, showing their last location on his map. The plan was simple but complicated by all that would undoubtedly go wrong. All they couldn't see yet.

Papí directed Carey to move right, signing *Careful, quiet.* It was an instruction his father had given them a thousand times over the years as they moved through the woods.

With another hand signal, Papí directed Brooks up the center. His father went left. They spread out and moved in on the three men scouting the perimeter.

Finding his target though his scope, he continued to count off the minutes. They'd coordinate timing as much as possible.

Fee screamed, desperate and anguished. The sound ripped a hole through the windy night. *And* his soul. Caution went out the fucking window. Weapon raised, he ran straight into hell.

## CHAPTER FIFTY-EIGHT

Snow whipped and men taunted as Fee writhed against the pain. Pinned to the ground by her right hand, she screamed as Liam tugged the knife, trying to jerk it free of the earth, bone, or muscle it was caught on.

"Fuck, fuck, fuck," he said. "I'm sorry."

The four men around them watched, rapt by the twisting of the knife sending electric spasms slicing through her. Fee screamed until her voice broke. She tasted bile and blackness.

"Yo, dumbass," one man said. "It needs to go through her wrists. No bone in her hand strong enough to support her."

Another supplied, "We can rig something for that side."

"Stop moaning." Liam reprimanded. With a heave, he finally pulled the knife free. For a blessed moment all she could feel was gratitude. The pain lessened to a tender ache.

She sobbed. She was going to die in the same horrible way her mother did. *Oh, Mom, I'm so sorry.* The wind whipped her hair against her face, strands sticking to her tears.

Liam stepped over her. A muscle in his jaw twitched. He avoided looking at her as he knelt by her other hand. For a moment, he seemed to hesitate.

"Please," she whispered, voice raw. "Don't."

"Cut her tongue next. That'll quiet her."

Liam flinched, looked away, then back, focusing on her mouth. She saw it then, the decision made. He bent lower, reaching for her jaw.

Every bit of anger and pain inside her reared up and she slammed her forehead into his nose. Bones cracked, the sound snapping in her ears, roiling the acid in her stomach.

Liam shot to his feet, hands flying to his nose, dropping the knife, which missed her wrist by an inch. Blood poured through his cupped fingers as he staggered back and fell on his ass, dazed.

The other men were laughing. Loudly. A *thwuck* of sound and the tall one fell over, a cavernous hunk torn through his hat and right temple.

The others scrambled. A second man cried out and fell, clutching his middle. So close, she could almost touch him.

He blinked and his blue eyes emptied of all life. Around her, all hell broke loose. The two remaining men split in different directions. She watched the closest jolt then grab his thigh. Blood trailed behind him in the snow.

The last man standing managed to get to the relative safety of the scaffolding. Squatting, he fired at someone sprinting across the clearing.

Brooks raced forward. Snow and wind whipped around him as gunfire gobbled up Fee's sob of gratitude and grief.

Brooks jerked as the shot slammed into his leg. Diving to his right, he took cover behind a stack of crates. More gunfire erupted along the wood line from the men on ATVs. The air stank of gunpowder. The

*Broken P*

shots appeared as pops of light in the darkness, coming from a thousand directions.

"Brooks!" Fee yanked on the ropes with all her might. The one binding her right hand slackened. She tugged again. It slackened more. Fee whipped her head to the side and she saw it through strands of bloody blonde.

The knife Liam had dropped.

It'd speared the rope. Her tugging was fraying the rest of the rope. She yanked again and again, loosening and tugging, creating friction.

Shots snapped the air and rolled over her. Shit. The rope was frayed but not enough. She sawed her hand back and forth. Tears of pain and frustration rolled down her face. *Mom, I need you.*

Her hand jolted free. A burst of relief spun her into action. Grabbing the knife, she rolled to her other side. A tremor-laced flick against the bloodied rope strangling her other wrist freed her. Switching the weapon to her left hand, she freed her ankles with the same, savage speed.

She stumbled to her feet to find Liam, face bloody, hunched over and searching one of the dead men, taking his weapon. With a cry of rage, she lunged toward him.

He spun, knocking aside her blade, and brought his own weapon around, firing at her.

But—merely a *click*.

His eyebrows rose. *Misfire*. He swiftly tapped the magazine with his palm, moved to re-rack the slide.

There was a deafening shot... but no pain.

Lowering her hands, she found Liam holding his bleeding bicep. He rolled away and ran for cover.

Pitching to her feet, she grabbed a gun from Dead Blue-Eyes and ran after Liam. This ended. Now.

## CHAPTER FIFTY-NINE

The bulletproof vest didn't prevent Brooks' ribs from burning like they'd been doused with gasoline and lit on fire as he dove behind the trainee gear stacked in crates. His breaths were so shallow his vision started to cloud. He pulled in more air with conscious effort and crawled to the edge of the stack. His right leg shook and slid out from under him. Shit. That shot had fucked up his leg.

Digging his elbows into the ground, he hauled himself forward. Gunfire erupted from the woods. Papí and Carey, at least, had followed the plan. They'd taken out the perimeter, despite Brooks' rashness.

They fired on the remaining men. Papí exchanged gunfire with the ATV riders. One dove behind his vehicle. The other stood in front, legs spread wide in a firing stance, with both hands on his gun. Practically invisible at the tree line, Carey shot the idiot center forehead. His body jerked and fell.

Using his scope, Brooks zoomed in on Fee just in time to see Liam spin on her with a weapon.

Focused, breathing deeply, assuming the bastard had on a bulletproof vest, Brooks aimed for the only clear shot he had. Right shoulder.

Liam roared. Grasping his arm, he crouched low and ran.

Brooks tracked him through his scope. His wrist

burned, causing him to miss the fucker darting into the woods.

A shift of snowy wind, a gap of gunfire, a moment that allowed him to hear sound. Someone was sneaking up on him. Brooks rolled. Not fast enough to fire his weapon, but fast enough to catch the wrists of a big block of man who fell on him like a tree, knife raised.

Buzzed tight brown hair. Sharp black eyes. Full beard. Jack Tate. Cabrón was heavy. "Would've been safer to shoot," Brooks hissed.

Saliva dripped in long threads from Jack's mouth across his beard. The blade inched closer. "I've wanted to do this for two fucking years, asshole."

His injured hand trembled as Brooks pressed up with his triceps, hoping to throw Jack off. And then, his wrist snapped and gave out. Pain exploded as all the action shifted left.

Jack's bulky build played against him. He jolted to the side, burying his knife in the ground beside Brooks' throat.

Using Jack's falling momentum, Brooks drove him to the ground. Wrenching the knife out, he slammed it deep into Jack's neck. *Thwuck.*

Jack's eyes went wide. He blinked. And died.

Adrenalin coursing through him, Brooks pushed off, and stood up. His leg nearly buckled. Gunshot. Soaked in blood. He bit off a curse, forced himself to move. Grabbing his weapon, he ran for the woods. Next up, Liam.

## CHAPTER SIXTY

Fee followed Liam's trail through the moonlit woods. The blood. The footsteps in the snow. She didn't stop to think. Didn't ask what she'd do if she caught him. She simply went.

The wind whipped against her. The land sloped. She found him. Slumped against the trunk of a tree, eyes closed. A gun rested in his lap.

Body trembling, gun poised to shoot, she inched closer. Liam opened his eyes. He didn't seem surprised to find her there with a gun trained on him. He licked snow from his lips. "Put that down. We both know you won't kill me."

Yes. Yes, she fucking would. The gun in her left hand ached to fire. It burned. "You killed Mom."

"She never liked me."

Bastard. She tightened her grip. "You admit it?"

He shook his head. "I didn't kill your mom. I couldn't do that. Help me. My shoulder—"

"Liar!" She held up her injured hand, cold fury rolling through her. "I'm living proof what you're capable of. You tried to shoot me. You were going to cut out my tongue. I saw it."

He inhaled deeply, a ragged sound. "Think, Felicity. Did I appear to be in charge of those men? Look like I knew what I was doing? I didn't kill

Dorothy. I swear. Her killers, the ones who killed Kelly and Weaver, they blackmailed me. I'm a victim too."

She lowered her gun. His reputation, his ego, meant enough to him that he'd be the perfect target for blackmail. The video was the kind of thing he'd kill to keep hidden. Victim? Maybe. But he was a killer too, or would be to save his own skin.

"I saw the video. The one they're blackmailing you with."

His drooping eyes opened wide. And then he smiled, almost condescending. Like it was a joke she was too stupid to get. "The irony is that wasn't me. It was doctored. Deep fake."

"It was you. Admit it."

"Don't be disgusting."

"Kink isn't disgusting, Liam. Killing people to hide it is."

Liam fingered the gun in his lap. She brought up her own weapon. His hand fell away from his gun. "It became an addiction."

"The sex?"

"Hating you. Making you hate yourself."

A shiver passed through her. She hadn't expected that. Honesty. He'd used her. Just like alcohol or drugs. A way to numb the pain inside. A way to exist, if just for a moment, without the searing agony of self-hatred. "I'm going to need you to hand me your gun."

"Don't tell them about the video, Fee. My parents...my dad...everyone...I can't."

Even now. Even here. With gunshots cracking the night. And the future uncertain. He'd ask her to sacrifice her truth for his ego. No fucking thank you. "Hand over the gun."

Tears rolled down his face. He picked up the gun in his lap. "Are you going to tell them?"

"If I survive, yes." She steadied her gun, supporting her left hand with the back of her injured right. "Drop it. I will shoot you, Liam. I will."

He laughed. "No. You won't."

Bile flooded her mouth. He was wrong. So wrong. She tightened her grip.

"You won't." Liam swung the barrel of his weapon under his chin.

She lowered her gun. "Liam?"

"I'm sorry, Fee." Tears slicked tracks through the blood on his cheeks. "I really am." He closed his eyes. "Tell them he raped me."

The gunshot exploded in a flash of red. Blood and brain struck her face, coated her lashes. She wiped it away frantically, blinking until she could see again. See Liam still sitting upright, as if resting, his splintered head fallen forward, chin on his chest.

Another person dead. All that hate. Was it enough now? Was it? Pushing the gun away from her, she dug her hands into the cold, wet earth and sobbed.

"Fee. Querida. Amor." Brooks was impossibly beside her. On one knee, Rifle across his lap. "You did what you had to do."

She raised her head, met his eyes. "I didn't kill him. He killed himself."

Adrenalin gave way to shock. Trembling gave way to violent shaking. Brooks laid aside his weapon, took her gently under her arms, and eased her away from Liam's corpse.

## CHAPTER SIXTY-ONE

Three days had passed since the attack at the island. It didn't feel over. Fee couldn't get the terrible images out of her head. Images of Liam. Images of the other men that Papí, Carey, and Brooks had fought. Killed.

Gazing down at the bandages on her hand, she attempted to move her little finger. It shook violently. That was something, at least.

The surgeon had done an amazing job. She was hopeful that she'd actually get the use of her hand back. And so would Brooks. They were not only patients in the hospital together, they'd each injured one of their hands. Her right. His left.

There was a knock on the door jam. "Felicity? Can I come in?"

Meeks stood in her doorway. Time was up. She'd been anticipating this conversation ever since she learned the special agent had finally gotten permission from the hospital to visit.

"Sure, come on in."

Meeks moved into the private room. She carried flowers and wore a facemask.

"They insisted," she said, pulling at what looked like an industrial strength facemask. This hospital did not mess around. Meeks' gaze softened. "How are you doing?"

The question brought on a wave of sadness. When would answering something like that feel normal? Great. Good. Fine. My ex-fiancée was part of a group that killed my mom. Nearly killed me. And the love of my life. She lifted her bandaged-wrapped hand. "Happy to be alive."

Meeks unwrapped the flowers from their plastic wrap and presented them to Fee, holding them up for her to smell.

Fee leaned down. "Stargazer Lilies are my favorite."

Smiling, Meeks lifted the flowers closer, accidentally shoving a pollen-laden stigma right up Fee's nose.

"Sorry." Meeks awkwardly placed the flowers down on her bedside table.

"It's all right. They're beautiful. Thanks."

As calm as Meeks appeared, Fee knew she'd read her statement to the Canadian authorities. And was undoubtedly here to tie up loose ends. But that wasn't Fee's agenda. It couldn't be. "Where do things stand with the other women on the list?"

Meeks brows drew in. "Some are safe at home. Others are dealing with the repercussions of all that publicity. There were a lot of them, but it'll die down."

"Specifically, Flor, Jazz, and Ali. Have you found them?"

Meeks exhaled, puffing out her mask. "As we discussed on the phone, I'm *not* looking for them. Whatever Liam unleashed into these women's lives, it no longer has anything to do with him or the case."

This again. She got that Meeks wanted this case gone. She did. But to push aside what Liam had told her? It was infuriating. "You're wrong. As I told the

Canadian authorities, and you on the phone, your case isn't over."

Meeks joined her hands behind her back, spread her feet. A military stance. "I understand that Liam tried to deny responsibility, but everything lines up with him being The Puppeteer. We even have a confession from the two men who survived that night."

They'd confessed that Liam was The Puppeteer? "Maybe, they're lying. Maybe, they're trying to cover for the real Puppeteer. Maybe, there's more men?"

Why was she always arguing with Meeks about the case?

Meeks shifted back on her heels, her version of an eye roll. "We're busy rooting out what remains of the group that attacked you. If there are others, we'll find them."

Fee reached for a tissue, wiped at her suddenly running nose. "Before or after the other women on the list are killed?"

"The Puppeteer is dead. His group scattered. Those women are no longer in danger. Believe me."

"But Liam said—

"And we have proof Liam started the group. Years before dating you. Right after working on the Colson case. We have numerous communications between him and the group. He organized monies from the members—one of which was the owner of Tate Security.

"Tate proved to be an avid follower of The Great One, going back as far as twenty years. He teamed up with Liam, providing funds for the survival training and arranging the ambush on Vancouver Island."

"Yes, but—

"Liam was in Vancouver with the group. Two

men were captured alive from the group. Each said they'd had private contact with Liam and that he was Team_Leader. Liam's computer username showed up as Team_Leader. He attacked and nearly killed you. Yet you still suggest he wasn't responsible?"

"He's responsible for a lot, but he's not... wasn't The Puppeteer. Whoever is wouldn't have been on the island. He's not a hands-on killer. He had his men for that. And though all your evidence seems overwhelming, a lot doesn't make sense."

Pushing the button on the remote looped around her bed rail, she sat up. Her lungs burned. "That night on the island, the men and Liam weren't together. They were making sure Liam didn't chicken out."

"Or they were looking for their leader to prove he wasn't all talk." Meeks pressed the fabric on the bridge of her mask, pulling another tissue from the dispenser. She handed it to Fee. "Uh, your nose."

Fee took the tissue and wiped the mucus from her face. "I have evidence. Evidence I haven't shared with anyone yet."

She'd hoped the authorities would find Liam's BDSM video on his computer, but they hadn't. Even after everything, being the one to expose him didn't make her feel any kind of vengeance. Only sorrow. "Before my mom was killed, she worried that Liam was bad for me."

Meeks snorted. "She wasn't stupid."

"Yeah. Well, she wanted me to be able to see for myself. She set up a way for me to go onto Liam's computer. I'm not sure how she did it, but it must've been pretty high-tech, because he never found it. Anyway, right before he arrived, I decided to use it."

Meeks stared at her. "Illegal. But go on."

"I wanted to see if I could find information that might help the others. What I found was a series of videos made while Liam used his computer. In one, he was watching a homosexual BDSM video. During it he got an email with information that told him where to find me."

Meeks' eyes were a cloud of confusion. "That seems to damn him more. BAU had suspected The Puppeteer was sexually repressed in some way. And you witnessed him get information about where you were? That probably came from one of his cronies. Fact is, he stopped everything and came after you."

"Don't you see?" Fee pressed the tissue to her running nose. "Liam told me he was being blackmailed. And Liam was the man in the BDSM video. He received the video as a threat. And my location as direction."

Meeks let out a gust of air. A long moment passed before she spoke again. "So, you're saying he was being blackmailed because of a video of his sexual exploits. It still doesn't dispute all the other stuff."

How could she get Meeks to go help the other women if she didn't believe her? Her chest grew tighter. Taking two deep breaths, she tried to steady her heart. "That's one video. There were hundreds captured through the program."

"The illegal program. You know none of it is admissible in a court of law, right?"

"But you might find better evidence that he wasn't The Puppeteer. The other women.... Please promise me you'll look into it."

Meeks raised her hands in surrender. "I'll look. But don't pin your hopes on anything." She tugged up the sleeve of her jacket and glanced at her watch. "The hospital only gave me a half hour. Would you mind if I came back tomorrow?"

"Actually, I'd appreciate it. I don't feel well." She rubbed along her neck.

Meeks frowned. "Should I call a nurse?"

She shook her head. "I have my call button if it gets worse. Thanks."

Meeks squeezed Fee's foot on her way out. "Get some rest. You did good. I underestimated you."

What an odd thing to say. Fee closed her eyes.

## CHAPTER SIXTY-TWO

Brooks woke up from his second surgery, this one to insert the pins now holding his wrist together, with one demanding thought in his drug-washed brain.

Fee.

They'd flown together in the helicopter, but once they'd landed, they'd each been whisked into surgery. Him for his gunshot, her for her hand. Yesterday, he'd visited her in her room for the first time. He hadn't wanted to leave. Three days and two nights in this hospital. The fact that they were alive should've outweighed everything else. But while Fee was obsessed with what had happened to her list-sisters, he'd wanted nothing more than to be by her side.

Too bad, Papí stood like a sentry in his room. His father wanted him to rest. And the staff didn't need the headache. But he couldn't let go of this fear for Fee's safety because she was convinced that Liam hadn't been The Puppeteer—and so was he. And that meant she wasn't safe yet.

Brooks put down the side of his bed and sat up. "I'm going to see Fee."

Papí pushed him gently back, smiling. "Bad idea, mijo. I saw Meeks go in there when I came up from downstairs."

He frowned. They'd finally given her permission

to question Fee. All the more reason for him to be there.

Brooks hauled himself up. "I'm going. You can help. Or get out of my way."

Papí shrugged. "Good thing your mother went down to exchange the food I brought her. She would not approve. Wait here."

Papí returned moments later with a wheelchair. He helped Brooks into it, undid his pulse-ox monitor, strung up his fluids on the handle attached to the chair, then wheeled him down the hall. They turned the corner just as Annie Meeks was leaving Fee's room, ripping a heavy-duty mask from her face and shoving it into her pocket.

"Agent Meeks, a minute," Brooks called.

She waved but kept going. Odd. Had Fee pressed her about the other women on the list? Meeks had repeatedly rebuffed Fee's attempts to clear Liam and keep the case open. Again, his nerves tingled with an awareness bordering on panic.

They turned into Fee's room. She was sitting up. Shaking. Pale. A tissue pressed to her nose, she smiled wanly at him. "It's burning."

"What burns?"

She stared, pupils as tiny as pinpricks. "Allergies. The flowers. Meeks—"

Fee toppled to one side.

"Papí!" Brooks leapt out of his wheelchair, falling forward, slamming into her guardrail. "Call a nurse!"

Papí rushed out. An alarm sounded from the medical equipment. Fee's eyes rolled white in her head and convulsions jolted her body.

*Broken P*

Ripping the dangling intravenous from his arm, he held her jaw. "Fee! Look at me."

Two nurses raced into the room and shouldered past him like a pair of linebackers. Brooks fought to stay beside her but fell back when something smashed his legs. The wheelchair. He tried to stand again and met the immovable resistance of his father's grip.

He looked up at his father. "Papí?"

"Get him out of here," a nurse said.

What was happening? "She'd been fine. Hurt and healing, but out of danger."

*Like Weaver.*

"She's coding."

Weaver. Not natural causes. Someone had done something to her. Not Jack. Not Liam—he was a scapegoat. Someone higher. Someone who could use their position. Someone who'd been fighting to control this case since the beginning.

Meeks.

"Papí. It's Meeks." He wrestled a lead ball of panic down his esophagus. "She was in here. I think she... The flowers. The mask. Fee's eyes."

Another person rushed into the room. A doctor. She moved over to Fee's bedside.

Papí stepped closer to the bed. He looked from Brooks to Fee to the flowers. His eyes grew wide. "Mijo, there's something on the flowers. A substance. Fee must have touched them."

Fee began convulsing so hard, one of the nurses had to hold her down.

A nurse at the bedside said, "Please go!"

"She's been poisoned," Brooks said, refusing to budge.

"He's right," Papí said. Grabbing a blue-and-white bed pad, he tossed it over the flowers. "Don't touch the flowers. They're poisoned."

The nurses ignored him, but a young Korean doctor checking Fee's running nose met his gaze with growing horror. She yelled to another nurse who'd just come in, "Nasal irrigation tools. Atropine and pralidoxime. And chemical masks. Stat!"

Brooks' heart trembled. Never had he been this helpless in his life. More people came rushing into the room.

"Protocols for unidentified chemical contaminant. Everyone else out," the doctor said to the others who'd entered and to Brooks and Papí, "Isolate. The room next door is unoccupied. Go there."

The chair jerked as Papí tried to haul Brooks out. Brooks wasn't going anywhere. He gripped the plastic wheels, ignoring the friction. Fuck. He wished he had two hands.

Papí leaned down. "Let go, mijo. She's strong. Let them work so she can fight. Let go so you can be here for her when she wakes."

Heart running a marathon, imagination fighting reason, he let go.

## CHAPTER SIXTY-THREE

Fee's footsteps echoed down the corridor. The prison guard's leather gun belt creaked. The keys in his hand clinked. Those were the only sounds. Neither spoke.

The officer opened the second door with a *click*. They walked through. Up ahead, another officer waited by a heavy-duty door.

This was it. Her heart pounded. Her mouth went dry.

Special Agent Annie Edwina Meeks, AKA The Puppeteer, AKA Ed, was behind that door. She'd been extradited from Canada a week ago. She'd asked to speak to Fee five days ago. Five days.

Four of which had been full of arguments with Brooks.

"Fee, the woman tried to murder you. Whatever she has to say to you, she can say from a safe distance. Video conference in. Don't go in person."

In the end, he'd respected her wishes. Just as she'd respected his need to talk it out. They'd come a long way from the arguments that would send them spinning in opposite directions. They'd found a way to compromise.

Brooks, along with Special Agent Juliana Cordova, would watch the exchange from a nearby room. They'd also be able to talk to Fee via an earpiece in her ear. The thing was so uncomfortable. Like someone had shoved a steel raisin in her ear canal, but she was grateful for the backup.

Honestly, she wouldn't have considered coming in person if it hadn't been for Juliana Cordova, the agent in charge of investigating what had happened to Jazz, Flor, and Ali. Meeks had admitted to having information that could help find the other women, but she'd only give it to Fee.

"Why me?"

"After a decade of hiding her devotion to The Great One's writings, she's dying to talk. She wants everyone to know how clever she is and why she did what she did."

"Again, why me? Why not you?"

"I'm not worthy. I'm in the system. I'm playing by the wrong rules. But you? Who better to tell than the one person she deems worthy because you beat her?"

With the agent's reassurances, Fee had agreed. She'd do anything to help her list-sisters

Her recovering hand began to throb. She practiced the flexing movements her physical therapist had taught her. They didn't help. She was too tense.

The two guards exchanged *Hello*s. The first one moved off without a word to her. The second guard, after a swoop of his gaze down Fee's red sweater and jeans, escorted her into the meeting room.

Usually, this space was reserved for lawyers and their clients, but she'd been granted special permission to visit Meeks here instead of the visitation room. Easier to film and record from this wired area. Obviously, the former agent had to know the entire meeting would be taped.

The officer stepped aside and allowed her to come in. Meeks had aged fifteen years in a few days. She was thinner, with dark circles under her eyes and unkempt hair. She wore an orange-and-white striped prison uniform.

Meeks smiled, a slight, almost congratulatory smile. As if she'd not only accepted Fee's spoiling of her plans but admired her for it. "You came? I didn't think you would."

Fee frowned. Did Meeks think she was afraid to meet her?

Truth was, she was. *Terrified.* But she didn't want the ex-special agent to know that.

The guard stepped out with a warning to Meeks, "I'll be looking through that window the whole time. So behave, Edwina." And to Fee, "Press the red button by the door if you need me."

"Thank you, officer." She moved to the table and sat down.

Meeks smiled, as genuinely as the Cheshire Cat. "You never did bother to read his writings, did you?"

"I didn't come here to discuss your lord and savior's writings. I want to know where Flor, Jazz, and Ali are."

Meeks rolled her shoulders. "I have no idea where they are."

Fee got to her feet. "Well, then, I guess—"

"Sit down, Felicity. You're a terrible poker player. We both know you won't leave without your answers. I'm assuming the feds gave you a list of questions."

Meeks pointed to the chair. Fee swallowed. She had been given a list. She'd had her doubts Meeks would answer any, but Special Agent Cordova insisted she would.

Fee sat and moved onto question two. "Why did you create the list?"

Meeks placed her hands onto the table. Cuffs and chains clinked. "When I was first approached by The Great One, he gave me a list of four names. Dorothy Shields, Olga Ortiz, Dana Rahmoni, and Sandra Decker. He told me to impress him. I got his meaning."

Fee inhaled deeply, trying to catch her breath. She watched Meeks' hands carefully. "He wanted you to kill the mothers of four of the women on the list?"

"Yep."

"Why?"

"No idea. I'd assumed they stood in the way of the necessary gender war he spoke of in his writings."

*Necessary?* "You're a woman. You have a daughter." *Her poor daughter.* "How could you want a gender war?"

Meeks' eyebrows rose. "A minor war to prevent a major, global catastrophe. You'd understand if you'd ever bothered to read his writings."

"I read enough."

"Forget the stuff that's out there as bait for your average sausage and two potatoes. You witnessed what I did to men like that. That's the beauty of what The Great One has started. He controls the masses by playing into their pre-existing beliefs, manipulating them into implementing his brilliant strategy."

Fee's belly rolled. Cordova had been right. Every time she'd ever spoken to Annie Meeks, the woman had been reserved to a fault, bottled up. This... this was what had been hidden. *Edwina.* The shift was greasy and oily and terrifying.

Excitement gleamed in Meeks' eyes. "Without his plan, our world, our systems of government will eventually fail. Chaos will reign. It's already started."

A desperate, panicked need to get out of this room swamped her. She pulled on her collar.

The small earpiece in her ear chirped. "Keep it focused," Agent Cordova said. "Ask her why she went after the daughters and not the mothers."

Fee wiped sweaty hands on her jeans. "If The Great One asked you to kill four particular women, why put their daughters on a list?"

Meeks' raised her eyebrows and slanted her head. "He'd assigned me an impossible task. I couldn't get all the women. One was in a maximum-security asylum for the criminally insane. One was last reported in Iran and hadn't been heard from in six years. One was God-only-knows where."

Fee's anger pushed her fear aside. "Except for my mom."

"Right., Except for Dorothy. Through research, I discovered each of the women had daughters, all within ten years age of each other...." Her eyes lit with a kind of joy, as if reliving a delightful memory. "It all clicked into place after that. If my daughter had been in danger, I'd come running. I bet they would, too. The idea for the list was born."

"And Weaver and the other women... You added them as a what? A distraction?"

Meeks acknowledged that truth with a shrug. "Yeah. The same reason we took out Kelly Smith. Distraction. And confusion."

Smart and callous. And sick as hell. Fee no longer needed Meeks to fill in the blanks. She'd lived this. It all made sick, horrifying sense. "Adding other women gave you a way to mislead the investigation. Putting me on the list, tied it all to me. Which tied it all to Liam."

"Yep."

"Me walking in that day, discovering my mother was just—"

"A stroke of luck. You were always going to be on the list."

Nothing she'd done had created the list or changed anything. It made sense. Except... "So why come after me in Vancouver? Why try to kill me before you had the others?"

Meeks slapped her hands together and her chains jangled. "You act like a dumbass, but you're really not."

Meeks rubbed the metal covering her right wrist. "You're right. You were supposed to be the last. Your death would frame Liam and his group—"

"*Your* group."

Meeks spread out her hands. The chains clinked. "Sure. My group. In the end, it wasn't my choice. The Great One took over. He wanted you dead and Liam framed so he could launch his own game. That's why Ali, Jazz, and Flor were simultaneously targeted in the media."

"Fee." Cordova spoke quickly and resolutely in her ear. "Get her to admit that he's after the other women. See if you can get her to say it."

A spasmodic tightening in her middle told her she was close to vomiting. Bile rose into her mouth. She

*Broken P*

ran her tongue over her teeth and swallowed. *Focus.* She had to focus on getting answers, *not* on how callously this woman spoke about murder and stalking women. "The Great One is targeting the other women on the list?"

Meeks smiled. "No idea."

"Why else would he take over unless he's targeting them?"

"That, I don't know."

"Do you think it has anything to do with the fact that Jazz, Ali, and Flor's moms all knew my mother?"

"Of course."

"But you told me before that that didn't matter."

Meeks rolled her eyes. "Maybe it's not an act."

"You lied."

No answer.

"Did you know Weaver's mom met my mom? Is that why you added her to the list—so that that one bit of evidence wouldn't matter?"

Meeks smiled. "Riddle me this, Fee. A banker, a scientist, a journalist, and a politician meet at a conference in New York fifteen years ago. Why?" Meeks wasn't asking out of curiosity. She didn't know—but she wanted to.

"You have no idea why they met, why he wanted them dead, or why he's now seeking their daughters?"

Meeks smiled with genuine warmth. "You could be so much more. Read his writings. And after you do, come back and see me. Let's chat for real."

Fee stared daggers at her. "Do you know how many lives you ruined? Do you even care about your daughter? Or are you happy that she's now added to the list of daughters with infamous mothers?"

Meeks recoiled. "Dalia understands."

"Does she? Does she understand that you did all of this for a man you've never met who couldn't give a rat's ass about you?"

"Fee," Brooks spoke in her ear. "Don't antagonize her."

Too late. Meeks lurched forward. "He cares. He'll come for me."

"Really?" Fee gave a sarcastic laugh "Your mysterious Great One will come for you on his shining white steed? You don't even know his name!"

Meeks lurched to her feet. "I know it!"

"Ask her who he is," Agent Cordova rushed into her ear.

"Tell me. If you know, then tell me."

Meeks face flushed red. She looked at the door then back at Fee. Swallowing, she sat down. A single tear traced down her cheek. "You won. Again. I hope my death will make you happy. All that hate can eat you up."

"I don't hate you," Fee said, standing. "And you dying wouldn't make me happy. Only bringing my mom back could do that."

Fee walked to the door and buzzed the call button. The door opened. The guard nodded and held the door for her to pass into the hall.

"You know something?" Fee turned back to Meeks. "That makes me realize that, though it's impossible to have my mom back, what I do have left of her is nearly as precious. Her values. So, *Edwina*, I'm putting your daughter on *my* list. I'll make sure she learns about all the good things Dorothy "Never Surrender" Shields did in her life. And I'll tell her she could do a lot worse than following in *those* footsteps. Living a life both bold and ambitious and kind."

Meeks leapt to her feet, her chains clacking violently. "Don't be a bitch. Dalia needs to be introduced to The Great One's writings. Your mother was an idiot. And a criminal. She should've been convicted."

"Funny." Fee dragged her eyes over Meeks' prison uniform. "The only criminal your daughter will know about is you."

With the former special agent screaming curses at her, the door closed between Felicity Shields and Annie Edwina Meeks. Fee walked out of the prison and back into her life, head held high.

# EPILOGUE

Delgado Trading resembled an oversized army barracks—one long floor of steel-roofed, no-frills outdoors equipment. There were multiple sections devoted to diving, hunting, and climbing.

It smelled like the outdoors and steel and rubber. Fee liked it. But she pretty much liked anything that had to do with Brooks Delgado and his amazing family. She thanked her lucky stars every day that Papí and Carey hadn't been injured during the fight.

Not to mention Sappho and Blanco. She'd been giving them extra treats while they'd all been holed up in the cabin with Brooks. She and Brooks were growing closer than they'd ever been.

Right now, they were physically pretty close. His hand on her lower back, Brooks escorted her around the store. He drew her even nearer as they moved past a man pushing a boxy steel cart filled with diving equipment. His focus didn't alter until the man passed, and then some. He was still incredibly protective of her—something they were both learning to deal with.

"I think you're a little paranoid."

He grunted. "I'm a *lot* paranoid. But, in my defense, last week Ex-Special Agent Meeks was killed in a maximum-security prison. No such thing as being too careful."

Her death saddened Fee. Not for herself, but her daughter. Dalia had suffered enough. She was too young yet to understand all of it, but, in ten years... well, it would've been good for her to be able to get answers directly from her mother.

Fee hadn't been lying to Meeks. Dalia was now a list-sister. She was a good kid. They'd really hit it off. They met online once a week. She hoped it helped Dalia deal with the fallout from her mother's actions.

"Special Agent Cordova believes the threat to me has passed. Online activity seems to bear that out."

All media attention and online threats had decreased dramatically. Being in Canada helped: out of sight, out of mind.

"I respect the agent's opinion. Still, the woman I love is now trying to uncover information about a global threat, so, until you get answers and your list-sisters are found safe, I'm going to try to anticipate any danger."

She kissed him on his cheek. This wasn't the same as it was eight years ago. Then, Brooks had gone looking for fights. He'd made things worse by his agitation and anger. Now, he was patient and aware and simply paying attention. And, she had to admit, for good reason.

She'd begun a deep dive into the Dark Web and into her mom's old computer files and records, investigating The Great One. Meeks had dropped a huge clue, that meeting fifteen years ago between her mom and Ali's, Jazz's, and Flor's mothers. It might lead to nothing, but, right now, it was the best way she had to go on.

"That's my mom's section." Brooks pointed. "Behind the climbing equipment."

They neared a section of floor-to-ceiling racks of climbing equipment, including multi-colored ropes, helmets, cams, pulleys, ice-axes, carabiners, and even a climbing wall for trying out shoes and equipment. This store was a playground. "Can't wait until we're all healed up and can go climbing again."

"Definitely," Brooks said. "There are some—"

"Mr. Delgado?"

Fee and Brooks turned. One of the store employees, a young man with an eager smile, approached.

"Rich," Brooks said, gesturing to Fee. "This is Fee."

"Hi," Rich said. "Sorry to bother you, Mr. Delgado. But there's a gentleman with a question about the new tours." The young man's cheeks reddened. "Wasn't sure what to tell him."

He wasn't sure because the tours were a new thing. Turns out, Canada had a real problem with a private security company having a gunfight that resulted in international coverage and multiple deaths. They'd called a halt to the training. It was unlikely Delgado's private security training would ever resume.

Fee's suggestion to switch focus to outdoor training, and tours for groups, families, and kids had been met with universal family approval, especially from Soledad.

Rich rocked on his heels, waiting for Brooks to respond. The customer was looking through a binder with all the offerings—climbing tours, kayaking, survival lessons, group overnights. "I'll talk to him."

He started off, tugging Fee with him. She pulled gently out of his grasp and kissed his cheek.

Understandable protectiveness was one thing, needing to have her in sight at all times was another. "I'm going to go hang out with Soledad."

He raised his hands in surrender. "I'll join you when I'm done."

Blowing him another kiss, she headed behind the wall. Passing the barrier that separated Soledad's rock and mineral section, Fee entered a different place altogether.

Several diffusers misted lavender into the air. Well-lit glass cases lined the right wall and circled the interior in multiple sections. Soledad stood with a customer, looking at some orange-and-brown rocks. Fee wandered around.

Relaxing music played from a speaker set up on one of the glass cases. Although, to be honest, the store tended to echo. Kind of impossible to completely block out what happened beyond the climbing wall.

The cases were filled with gorgeous gems and stones, shiny and bright, rough and unfinished, all of them marked with the name of the stone, their uses, and prices. Some of them were pretty pricey. Forty-nine Canadian dollars for a black rock? She read the tag. *Hematite. Enhances memory and focus.* It'd better for that price.

She kept walking, then leaned close to one case that had gemstone jewelry. A black ring sat atop a plush red cushion. A sharp pain of recognition rooted her in place.

She stared in disbelief. That ring. *His* ring. The one she'd had made from a meteorite she'd found while hiking in New Mexico with Brooks. The interior was tungsten. It was—

"Felicity?" Soledad joined her by the case. She flinched. "What's wrong?"

Fee pointed to the ring. "That's the ring I'd planned to give Brooks on our wedding day. How is it here? The last person who had that ring was my mother."

Soledad moved around to the inside of the case, her expression softening. She pulled a set of keys from the pocket of her skirt. Sliding open the door, she brought out the ring on its cushion, placing it on top of the glass case.

Hands shaking, Fee reached for the ring that simultaneously delighted her and broke her heart. She traced a finger along the edge.

Would it be there?

Of course, it would.

She'd never seen the inscription. Mom's assistant had picked the ring up from the jeweler the same day she'd asked Brooks to postpone the wedding. She'd forgotten the ring in all that had happened. Forgotten… or let it fade from her mind. It'd been two years before her mother had asked her about what she'd wanted to do with it. She'd told her, "Throw it away."

"I'll put it in a safe place," Mom had said. "In case you ever need it."

Because it was a pain she'd learned to live with and found best to ignore, Fee had never asked about it again. Lifting the ring to the light, she angled it to read the inside inscription. It read, "To my love. Forever. I promise."

It hit her like a ton of bricks. It hit her with all the hurt and anguish she'd experienced that day. But that sharp pain faded into a knowing joy. This ring had somehow found its way to her. To almost the exact place it belonged.

Wiping the tears from her cheeks, she gazed up at Soledad. "Why here? Why you?"

Soledad wiped her own tears. "After you announced your engagement to…"

Fee's eyes closed tight. She didn't want to hear his name.

"After *that* engagement," Soledad continued, "Dorothy called me. She asked if she could come visit. Of course I said yes. Before I could even open my calendar to check dates, she appeared."

"She called from outside?"

Soledad nodded. "I was as stunned as you are now. We hugged and both shed some tears."

Her mother and Soledad had always gotten along so well. "Did she say why she'd come?"

"Yes. She'd come for advice."

Oh.

Soledad reached down and brought up a box of tissues. She handed a tissue to Fee and kept one for herself. "We always seem to need tissues in this jewelry section."

Tucking the ring into the palm of her recovering hand, directly over the long pink scar in its center, Fee willed her fingers to close. With a great, shaking effort and much pain, they slowly closed down and held the ring safe. She took the tissue and wiped her eyes and nose.

"*Brava*," Soledad said, wiping her own eyes.

The two of them. What a pair. If anyone walked in and found them here crying… She smiled at Soledad. Maybe stones really could heal. Because having this ring in her palm brought a sense of calm and hope and connection to her mom that filled her every pore. "What advice did Mom want from you?"

"She wanted to know how I'd handled the breakup between you and *mi hijo*. She asked me..." Soledad swallowed. "She asked me how did I do it, knowing the two of you bring out the best in each other? How could I let it go?"

Fee tightened her fingers around the band in her hand. *Oh, Mom.* "What did you tell her?"

"I told her that I hold a space open for hope, for true love, for possibility. I don't allow the bad to crush that space or breach it. I hold it open and wait for it to fill with joy."

Soledad reached out and put her hand over top the hand holding Brooks' ring. "Your mother took out this ring. She handed it to me and said, "Then hold this. Create an opening for hope with this. And, one day, if you are right, it will be filled with joy."

"Fee?"

Tears streaming down her face, she found Brooks staring at her with concern. Putting a box he'd been carrying on the counter, he placed his good hand against her face. "¿Mi amor? ¿Querida? ¿Qué te duele?"

She pulled her hand out from under Soledad's. "Joy hurts. I'm so full. I think I could burst."

Brooks used his good hand to wipe her cheeks. He kissed her lightly on her lips. "I know this joy, too."

Opening her palm—a feat that earned her an impressed smile from Brooks—she held the ring out to him.

His eyebrows rose.

She took a steady breath. "Mi amor, will you return home to my heart, take the place that has been waiting for you, that never left you, that never broke its promise to you? Will you marry me?"

Brooks' eyes misted. Very gently, with fingers that shook, he picked the ring from her scar-lined palm.

"Read the inscription," she said.

A look of confusion crossed his face. No doubt he'd seen this ring here before. Turning the ring, he read the inscription. He tried but failed to hold it together. No use. The tears fell down his face.

He kissed her, fierce and intense and triumphant. He pulled back only enough to press his nose to hers. "Yes, querida. My heart never broke its promise either. It has always loved you."

Soledad reached into the case, pulled out the notecard that had been next to the ring. She showed it to them. It read, "For all the ways, for always, we cling to hope, we open for joy. Not for sale."

THE END

# Acknowledgements

I'd like to thank my editor and one of my dearest friends, Terri-Lynne DeFino. Your incredible talent and insights helped transform this manuscript, making it so much more than it would have been without you.

A huge thank you to my copy editor and production editor, Judi Fennell. I sincerely appreciate all of your hard work and advice as I've navigated this self-publishing process.

To my incredible cover designer, Kris Keller, who created a cover that captured the tension of this thriller and also its heart.

I'm so grateful to all of my LatinxRom hermanas for their support, friendship, and their joy. You have enriched my life beyond measure.

Thanks to my Isn't It Romantic Book Club family for hours of reading fun. And for giving me the opportunity to find and meet new and experienced authors.

I'd like to thank all the women doing the hard work of standing up for what is right. Your dedication brings balance and strength to our world.

And thanks, as always, to my agent Michelle Grajkowski for her encouragement, help, and support.

## Want more of Brooks and Felicity?

Click below to read how they broke up:
https://BookHip.com/RSNHHKZ

Click below to download a FREE novel by
Diana Muñoz Stewart
https://dl.bookfunnel.com/500b7xbydx

Made in the USA
Columbia, SC
12 July 2021